The Warrior Woman

The Worlds Apart Series: Book Three

Evelyn Lederman

ISBN-13: 978-0692387344
ISBN-10: 069238734X

All characters and events in this book are fictitious. Any resemblance to actual persons living or dead is strictly coincidental.

Cover Design by Fiona Jayde Media
Editing by Tina's Editing Services

Dedicated to my high school physical education instructor JoAnn Heindel. She graded based on attitude and drive, rather than just physical ability. JoAnn was my Candy. The idea of working with someone to bring out the best of their skills and let them enjoy the sport, what a concept!

Acknowledgements:

~

To my beta-readers. Katherine and Karen were my captives in Mexico, reading the book and acting as my grammar police. My sister, Alice, read the manuscript recovering from bronchitis. What a trooper!

To my editor Tina, for her honesty.

To cover artist, Fiona Jayde Media. Holy Cow! What a cover.

Titles by Evelyn Lederman

    The Worlds Apart Series:

        'The Chameleon Soul Mate' Book One

        'The Crystal Telepath' Book Two

        'The Warrior Woman' Book Three

            Coming Soon

        'The Mind Control Telepath' Book Four

    Nightshade Saga:

        'Nightshade' (Published 7/2015)

Chapter 1

Gingko Terra/Earth

Candy Phillips was going to kill her two best friends. She wasn't sure how, but proficient in self-defense, she could inflict serious damage to the human body. Whatever method, it was going to have to be slow and deliberate. They were going to suffer as she had suffered the last two weeks. Her friends had vanished and she had been frantic. The Sedona police department was clueless related to what had happened.

She had just purchased her third box of facial tissue since arriving in Sedona, when Shirl called. Shirley Tomlinson, Shirl, disappeared while searching for their mutual friend Alexandra Mann.

All three women had grown up together in a Phoenix orphanage and were closer than most biological sisters Candy knew. It hurt that Shirl had not even informed her of Alex's disappearance. Candy had returned home from taking her high school volleyball team to a tournament, to find they were both missing. Candy had been crying non-stop since she arrived.

She never cried.

A feeling of abandonment she had not experienced since she was a little girl, overwhelmed her. Last night she tossed and turned, unable to sleep. Her mind kept running horrible scenarios over and over again about what could have happened to her friends. Now, out of nowhere, Shirl called to request she meet her at a nearby restaurant. And that she not contact the local authorities. What kind of trouble had they gotten into?

Candy pulled into the restaurant's parking lot. At three o'clock in the afternoon, plenty of spots were open. She stopped in a space on the far side of the building. Candy needed to cool down before she saw Shirl.

Tears were once again flowing. She reached for the next box of tissues, pulled off the cardboard cover, and grabbed a couple to blow her nose. She wasn't sure if she was crying because she was furious or so relieved that she could fall apart now. Either way, the fountain of tears kept flowing.

Candy had purchased a chocolate bar at the drug store as well. She tore off the wrapper and broke off a couple squares. If chocolate couldn't make her feel better, nothing would. She popped a few pieces of the creamy, dark goodness into her mouth. Leaning her head against the headrest, she closed her eyes for a moment. After collecting herself, she was ready to confront her friend.

There was not a doubt in her mind, she looked a mess. Her eyes were probably swollen and her nose red from continual blowing. She needed to clean herself up before she met up with Shirl.

She pulled the elastic from what was left of her ragged ponytail. Her hair was her one vanity. With all the sports she played, it would have been so much easier if she had cut it short. Instead, she let it grow past the small of her back. Maneuvering around the steering wheel, she quickly braided it, then was as ready as she ever would be to re-unite with her friend.

Slamming the car door had released some of her pent-up aggravation. It shouldn't have felt so good to abuse her poor car. As she made her way to the entrance, she took several deep, cleansing breaths. The wooden door was heavier than it looked. She put more of her weight's strength into opening it, one of the few advantages of being a big girl. The extra energy she expended further reduced her annoyance with Shirl.

As she entered, her eyes were immediately drawn to a middle-aged man. He was very attractive with his sable-colored hair and light brown eyes. The gray wisps around his temples gave him a look of sophistication. She wasn't normally attracted to older men, but this man was noteworthy.

Her eyes basked in the sight of him; unfortunately her body did not respond in kind. In her twenty-two years, she had never reacted physically to another person. The man held her gaze for an instant and then directed his attention back to his drink. Candy felt a loss, once the man looked away. It was a very weird reaction she had to a complete stranger.

She needed to focus on the task at hand. Candy continued further into the restaurant looking for Shirl. She saw her at the rear of the room. A man she had never seen before was seated next to her. He had strawberry-blond curly hair and his body reflected someone who worked out regularly. The man fit with her friend, as no one had before. She'd had one outrageous thought after another, since entering this establishment. What was wrong with her? Once again, she chided herself. She needed to focus!

Shirl looked up as Candy approached their table. A huge smile crossed her face. Shirl looked absolutely stunning. Her blond hair was pulled back from her face and her light brown eyes sparkled. Candy couldn't remember a time her friend looked happier. Shirl stood and the two friends embraced. Candy felt an overwhelming sense of relief, knowing Shirl was all right. She hadn't realized how lost she was not knowing where Shirl and Alex were.

"Where the hell have you been?" Candy asked. Obviously, she wasn't ready to let go of all her anger. She felt Shirl loosening her hold before returning to her seat and grabbing the hand of the man next to her.

"There is so much I need to tell you," Shirl replied. "This is Starc. He is my soul mate." Candy would have laughed if anyone else had uttered those words. Shirl was not a starry-eyed princess who believed in fairy tales. She had said those words with a certainty Candy had never heard in Shirl's voice. For the time being, she would go along with whatever Shirl said. When they were alone, she would cross-examine her friend.

"It is nice to meet you, Candy. Shirl has told me all about you." Starc had a baritone timbre to his tone. He had no discernible accent to place where he was from. But the man was gorgeous, that was for sure.

"We should be going," Shirl said as she stood. She came around the table ready to take Candy to God only knew where. Shirl wore a tunic with leggings and a copper bracelet Candy had never seen. At first glance, it appeared to have multiple etchings on it.

"What in the world are you wearing?" Candy blurted out. A number of responses played in Candy's mind. None of them were good. She examined her friend's face and body, trying to identify any camouflaged bruises. Shirl was always self-conscious about her looks, unlike Alex, who never worried about physical attributes.

She had been so focused on Shirl, she had momentarily forgotten about her other missing friend. "Where is Alex?"

"Do you trust me, Candy?" Shirl asked. Her friend was dancing around answering her question. It only fueled the suspicions growing in Candy's mind. An uneasiness once again started to consume her.

"Of course, I trust you," Candy said in frustration. By some miracle, she was able to hold back her temper. "But you are beginning to scare me. I want to know where Alex is!"

Shirl paled before her eyes. "I am sure Alex is fine. I need to show you something that will explain everything. Please trust me for the time being."

A pleading look shone in Shirl's eyes. Shirl had never knowingly harmed a soul, as far as Candy knew. When they were children, Shirl played the mother hen where she and Alex were concerned. Never in a million years would Shirl do anything to harm either of them. She'd put her faith in her friend.

"This better be good," she said under her breath. Candy did not like playing mental games. As with sports, she liked to see what was coming at her. *Never take your eye off the ball*, was her mantra. Reluctantly she followed Shirl and Starc.

Candy was steps away from the exit when she heard "*good luck.*" The words had not been uttered, she was sure of that. They came from within her mind, as if telepathically transmitted. She turned and the man she had seen when she first entered the restaurant was staring at her. He raised his glass, downed the contents, picked up his paper, and started to read. Before she had a chance to question what had just occurred, she was being herded into the back seat of an SUV. Two more strangers were in the front seat. Had she just been kidnapped by some kind of cult?

Candy didn't know if she should call for help or just play along. Shirl reached for her hand and held it for reassurance. That gesture calmed her nerves a bit. No one in the vehicle said a word. There was some nodding and a chuckle, almost as if the occupants were engaged in a conversation. Candy needed to relax and prepare herself for any eventuality. Shirl tightened her grip on her hand.

The men in the front were wearing the same type of outfits Shirl and Starc wore, based on what little she could see. The blond driver had the same type of cuff bracelet Shirl wore. Candy glanced at Starc's wrist. He too had on the same copper jewelry. Everyone wearing identical clothes and bracelets only confirmed Candy's worst fears.

If they were a cult, she decided to wait to make a move until she was with Alex. Alexandra was level headed, although she had once thought the same thing about Shirl. She and Alex would find a way to escape and head straight for the authorities. The fact Alex was not with them, told Candy that Alex had not fallen for any of the malarkey Shirl had obviously swallowed.

She felt the SUV slow just before it turned into one of the Boynton Canyon's parking lots leading to the hiking trails. The same spot where Alex had disappeared, according to the police report she had read. Candy barely swallowed past the lump in her throat. Blood rushed through her veins as her pulse rate skyrocketed.

Shirl bounded out of the SUV. She waved for her to follow. Fear momentarily paralyzed Candy. *"Let's go,"* she thought she heard Shirl say, although her lips had not moved.

She was in the middle of a nightmare. That was why she was hearing things not being spoken. Candy would wake up shortly and find herself in her hotel room. This was just another scenario juggling in her mind.

"We mean you no harm, Candy," the man with short black hair and lovely greenish-brown eyes said. He stood just outside the vehicle door, Starc had exited. "Some things have to be witnessed to be believed. If I told you who we are and where we are from, you would not believe me. Have you ever seen Shirl look so healthy?" Candy was not sure how to take his reassuring words.

Candy shifted in the back seat and looked at Shirl with a critical eye. Her friend had been suffering debilitating headaches and looked terrible the last time she had seen her. Today Shirl was the poster child for health.

She slid across the seat and exited the SUV. Candy stood next to her friend to get a better look. There were no circles under her eyes or stress lines across her forehead. Her eyes were clear and bright. "How are you feeling, Shirl?" Candy asked suspiciously.

"I have not had a headache since I left," Shirl said. She had not clarified where she had been since she had vanished off the face of the Earth. Once again, she decided to take her friend at her word and follow them to wherever they were holding Alex.

The tall, slender man with sun-bleached hair who had been driving the car approached. "My name is Darden. It is a pleasure to finally meet you. The man who addressed you earlier is Tarsea. Walk alongside me, as we make our way up the trail."

He stepped to the side and extended his arm, indicating for her to join him. Taking one last look around, she realized no other hikers were visible. Candy reluctantly edged closer to Darden. Starc and Shirl led the way, while Tarsea brought up the rear. There was nothing threatening in how they moved or behaved. But Candy pulled on her self-defense training and mentally prepared herself for any aggressive move on their part.

The canyon was absolutely beautiful, but she was too uptight to enjoy her surroundings. Sedona was one of the loveliest places on Earth and it was all lost on her.

They had walked for twenty minutes when Shirl and Starc stopped. Her friend turned and Candy noticed Shirl's amethyst was glowing. Candy reached out and touched the crystal, bringing a huge smile to Shirl's face. Then Candy noted that Darden and Starc had gems around their necks, also glowing.

"I am a crystal telepath, Candy," Shirl explained. She took Candy's hand and walked with her to a spot on the trail where the air shimmered. "Our late parents came from another universe, parallel to the one that exists in our reality. My mother was the crystal telepath who navigated the portal to bring our parents here. Unfortunately the pollution caused by burning fossil fuels destroyed their telepathic brains before they could escape this world. The headaches I was experiencing would have eventually killed me. I have no headaches in the Troyk universe. Let me take you to your true home, Candy."

At first Candy did not know what to make of the incredible story Shirl had spun. The words rang true, but how that was possible was beyond her comprehension.

Candy stood before the portal, dumbstruck. Shirl's healthy demeanor and the air displacement in front of her were not figments of her imagination. Her friend had read everything she could on string theory and alternate universes, but Candy never believed that crap. Now, the evidence was right in front of her and she had problems wrapping her brain around the fact it was all true. Or maybe she was right all along and she was dreaming. This could not be reality.

"What about Alex?" Candy inquired. Even with the overwhelming evidence before her eyes about the existence of multiple dimensions, Candy could not let go of her concern for their absent friend. Could Alex have been pulled into one of these event horizons and ended up God knows where? Had she literally vanished off the face of the Earth?

"I am sure Alex is fine where she is," Shirl answered. Candy did not like the vagueness of her friend's reply. "Your headaches will start soon, if they have not already. You are two years younger than I am and my headaches started about the age you are now. This world is a death sentence for us if we stay. Our life expectancy here is twenty-five years, if we are lucky." Shirl took Candy's hand and squeezed it. The little girl she once was, knew she needed to follow Shirl wherever she led. "We can walk through the portal together."

Candy was still absorbing the existence of the portal and parallel universes. It was true, she was starting to get headaches. If in fact she was dreaming, what harm would it do to go through the portal? She tightened her grasp on her friend's hand indicating her consent.

The men entered the portal first. Candy took a deep breath, closed her eyes, and stepped in alongside her friend.

Chapter 2

The Troyk Universe

Candy stepped onto solid ground. It felt like she had walked through a revolving door. There had been a small gust of wind, before she opened her eyes. They were on a mountainside trail looking down on a city built of mauve-colored stone. What distinguished this from any trail on Earth, was the purple sky.

Loud male voices broke through her near-obsessed brain checking out this new universe. The three men she had traveled with were arguing with two men farther down the trail. Candy noticed Shirl was alongside the men contributing to the words exchanged. Shirl had always been such an agreeable girl; if Shirl had ever raised her voice, the time did not come readily to Candy's memory. Whatever they were arguing about must have been very personal to her friend.

"I told Jeryl Jarlyn I would bring Candy to him as soon as she assimilated to her new home," Shirl said as she stabbed her finger into the chest of a good-looking brown haired man. Candy had never seen Shirl take such an aggressive stance. "She needs to build her telepathic abilities before she is exposed to any type of mind control. I do not want her to experience the bleeding I went through the first time I had an audience with the Prime Ruler."

The topic of blood shook Candy. Why had Shirl bled? As far as she could see, her friend looked great. She took a couple of steps closer to where the discussion was taking place.

"My orders were quite clear, Shirl," the man replied. "We followed you up the trail, shortly after you left. We have been waiting for your return ever since. Our Prime Ruler is anxious to meet the woman who could possibly be his granddaughter."

"Raine Narmouth, I would not let you within two feet of my friend after what you did to Alexia." Shirl was in the man's face as she yelled. Although she had no idea what was going on, Candy could not help but to be impressed with this new side of Shirl's personality.

Despite the fact that Shirl had three capable-looking men backing her up, Candy aligned herself next to her friend in case Raine Narmouth became violent. She had no idea who Alexia was, but she did not like the man's history with women. The immediate attraction she felt to the man turned into loathing.

The second man who had been standing back watching the confrontation came forward. "Shirl, Jeryl Jarlyn's orders were plain. He wants to meet the girl immediately. If Narmouth's presence is disturbing you, we will head back to The Palace and you can follow on your own." The man took an additional step and extended his hand to Candy. "Welcome to the Troyk Universe. My name is Kelog Potts. I carried your friend off this mountain when she first arrived. She had entered the portal with no knowledge concerning how to navigate and had a pretty rough ride. She was unconscious when we found her."

Alarmed, Candy turned to Shirl. Her friend merely shrugged. "I did not know what I was doing the first time I stepped into the portal. My first experience was a nightmare. Literally, I was a bloody mess when I arrived."

Kelog smiled at Shirl. "I had to throw away the tunic I wore that day. It was saturated with your blood. Do we have a deal, Shirl?" Candy thought Kelog was charming and seemed reasonable. She figured her friend would acquiesce to his plan.

Shirl seemed to be considering her next steps. "Get Narmouth out of here. We will follow after I talk with Candy a while. She knows nothing about the Troyk Universe or how to use her telepathic abilities." That had been the second time telepathy had been mentioned. Maybe the voices she had heard in her head were not her imagination after all.

"Do not be too long," Kelog replied. "I am trusting your word that you will present Candy to Jeryl Jarlyn within the hour. You know firsthand that he has no desire to hurt her or any children of Benko's followers." At this point in time, Candy was so lost trying to understand the situation, she only half listened to the conversation.

It appeared Shirl was going to argue, then Starc put his hand on Shirl's shoulder. "We will be there," he said. Although Starc addressed Kelog Potts, his gaze hammered Raine Narmouth. Obviously there was no love lost between these two men. Starc's expression reflected true hatred.

Kelog Potts and Raine Narmouth started their trek back to the city. Everyone in her group seemed to relax, with the exception of herself. She waited for the explanation Shirl had promised.

"The Troyk universe is full of telepathic beings," Shirl said. "One ability some possess is to control the minds of others. If there is any doubt in an individual's mind, the mind control telepath can make the decision for them. You do not even know the decision was not your own. Free will only exists where the mind control government has no desire to sway the general public."

"That is terrible," Candy replied. What type of world had she entered?

"Our parents thought the same way. Jeryl Jarlyn is the Prime Ruler. He had a son, Benko, who tried to overthrow the government and outlaw mind control. Benko failed in his attempt and our parents left this world with him in order to save their lives. My mother was the crystal telepath who navigated the portal for them. I use her amethyst now."

Candy reached out and pulled Shirl's amethyst from all the other crystals. As long as Candy could remember, Shirl had worn the purple gem. It was the only thing Shirl had from her mother. That was one item more than Candy had from either of her parents. The only thing they gave Candy was a fear of abandonment.

She turned and looked at the city below. Purple plants and trees of every imaginable shade covered it. Even the stone was a shade of purple. "The sky is violet," she said to no one in particular. Talk about stating the obvious. That was all her mind was able to process at this point.

Tarsea placed his hand on her shoulder. "There was an ordinance passed in the Aster Province a century ago that only purple horticultural species could be planted within city limits. I believe those were the exact words. It is believed the Prime Ruler at the time had an obsession with the color. The pollen is so dense, the sky appears purple."

Candy glanced at Tarsea and looked into his beautiful hazel eyes. If they were a shade greener, they would be perfect.

"We should be heading off to talk to this Jeryl Jarlyn. Before we do, tell me about him and more about the Troyk people's ability to use telepathy." Candy was never one to procrastinate. If she had to meet with the Prime Ruler, she wanted to get it over with.

"Most Troyk citizens communicate through a multitude of communal pathways," Shirl responded. "Do you feel any pressure in your brain?"

Candy closed her eyes and concentrated. She had noticed a type of static that had been building since she arrived. She originally thought it was just a side effect of portal travel. It must be what Shirl was referring to. "There is a little buzzing I just noticed. It's really nothing."

"That is the multitude of communal pathways trying to connect with your mind," Tarsea informed her. "As we get closer to the city the noise in your head will grow louder. My brother Tolfer will teach you how to manage the different channels. He is really quite good at it. Tolfer is in great demand to work with children as their telepathic abilities start to manifest." Candy could see from his expression Tarsea was proud of his brother, and it was obvious there was great love between them. She was actually looking forward to meeting Tolfer.

"You will meet Tarsea's brother tonight," Shirl said. "You will be staying with Tarsea's parents for the time being. I lived there when I first arrived, but will be moving in with Starc and Darden. Alexia is still there with Tarsea, so you will have female companionship. We have become fast friends in the little time I have known her in the Troyk Universe. Zane and Leenea Childers are wonderful people."

Candy did not know how she felt about staying with complete strangers. She liked Tarsea, but it was still awkward imposing on people she did not know. It also bothered her that Shirl did not give their friend Alex a second thought. Candy was still worried sick about her.

"Things will be all right," Shirl communicated to Candy. She noticed Shirl's lips had not moved. Transmitted telepathically. Such an odd sensation. Candy knew it had come from Shirl, but it did not sound like her. Her mind had reproduced Shirl's voice since the sound was not coming through her ears.

"How do I communicate mentally back to you?" Candy asked. She was so excited, she put her meeting with Jeryl Jarlyn in the back of her mind. Candy imagined that Kelog Potts would give them some leeway, understanding there was a lot to discuss before they headed to town.

"When you and I grew up at the orphanage, we opened a telepathic channel. Unfortunately, we did not know it existed. We were born telepathic, but were unaware of our talent. Your words were leaking through that channel and I just leveraged it when I responded. You need to concentrate on what you want to say and then project it in my direction. Currently, the channel is just between the two of us. Eventually others will be able to enter since it is a type of communal pathway."

Candy concentrated on Shirl and internally screamed the words to her friend. She was not sure what projecting involved. When Shirl smiled, she knew she had been successful.

"From the look on your face," Shirl laughed, "I bet you were screaming in your mind. You don't have to use all that energy to communicate with me. Remember, our ears are not involved in telepathic communication. Only the number of people within the telepathic channels will increase the volume in your head. That is why you may get some nose bleeds in the beginning, until you learn to manage the pathways. Leenea has an herbal beverage that will also help."

Candy's head was spinning from all the information Shirl provided. They shared a special channel between the two of them that had existed most of their lives and they did not know it. Ironically, Candy had always sensed what Shirl was thinking. She may have inadvertently used the pathway without realizing it. Oddly, she had always had that same reaction with Alex.

"We should start heading down," the tall Malibu Ken said. Candy believed he had said his name was Darden. "You should know that when we meet with Jeryl Jarlyn, he is going to use his mind control powers to determine if you are lying to him. It will feel like a minor tension headache. It does no lasting damage."

Candy could not believe how calm everyone was. How could they possibly know if the mind control usage would do no permanent damage? Growing up on Earth could have changed the chemical make-up of her and Shirl's brain. Maybe that was the real reason why Shirl bled.

"Only answer what he asks," Shirl advised. "Do not volunteer any information. If I can help answer a question, I will communicate through our closed channel. Just don't give away we are conversing telepathically to Jeryl. He does not know about our private channel."

To say Candy was overwhelmed would be an understatement. The whole telepathic multiple channel business was confusing. She could also not figure out why the Prime Ruler would want to meet with her or why he would be concerned she would lie to him.

Then she suddenly remembered Raine Narmouth said she could be the Prime Ruler's granddaughter. If that was the case, what would that mean?

Candy enjoyed walking the streets of the largest city in the Troyk universe, Aster Province. There were no cars. Everyone walked. It was quite peaceful. The static in her head increased as they hit the populated area. Candy started to wonder how much louder the humming would get. She started to pick up snippets of conversations. Sometimes strings of voices were layered on top of each other. It was as if she was in a football stadium with everyone talking and not being able to differentiate who was saying what. How could something be deafening, if the ears were not involved? Tolfer helping her deal with all the noise in her head was gravely needed at this point. Candy was starting to get a raging headache.

If the people they passed took notice of her, it was not obvious. She wore jeans, while the residents were in the tunics and leggings Shirl had on. The outfits looked comfortable. Suddenly, Shirl grabbed her arm and pointed to a large building before them.

The Palace was appropriately named. It was a four-story marble architectural masterpiece. She knew little about different building styles, but she guessed it had a Greek influence to its design. Although that could not be right, since she was in a parallel world.

The sun shining on the marble made the structure sparkle. Candy pinched herself to make sure she wasn't dreaming. Ever since she left the restaurant in Sedona, she'd had one surreal experience after another. Her pounding head should have been evidence enough she was wide awake. Now she also had an aching arm. Why did she pinch herself so hard?

They entered through a side entrance and were told to proceed to the fourth floor where Jeryl Jarlyn had his living quarters. It took little effort on Candy's part to climb four flights of stairs. She worked out twice a day, before and after her classes. Organized sports over the years had given Candy a sense of belonging. Her athletic ability made her popular wherever she went. Everyone automatically wanted her to play on their team. She was a generous player and always helped her less skilled teammates.

When they reached the fourth floor landing, Kelog Potts was there to meet them. There was no sign of Raine Narmouth, which Candy figured was an intentional act by Kelog. This was not the place to have confrontations.

The guys stayed behind as two uniformed men who she assumed were palace guards escorted her and Shirl. The hallway was full of artwork which caught her friend's eye, not hers. Candy never appreciated paintings, sculptures, and other items. She didn't have a creative bone in her body. Any art assignment she constructed in school, was met with more laughter than praise.

They were directed into a room full of large beautiful crystals. She noticed Shirl almost went into a trance, brought on by her surroundings. Crystals had always captivated Shirl. While her friend was absorbed by the rocks, Candy paid attention to its logistics. One of them had to be practical. Were there any exits, other than the one they entered? What about improvised weapons? She nudged Shirl to bring her back to reality. Odds were good they wouldn't be alone for long.

The door to the left of Candy opened and a man in his mid-sixties walked in. He extended his hand to Candy. "Welcome home, my girl." At the last minute the man withdrew his hand and took Candy into his arms. She stood still as her body absorbed the man's warmth. Candy had never been held like this by a man. She closed her eyes and stored the feeling in her memory. Was this man her grandfather? Had Benko Jarlyn been her father?

"Candy," Shirl said, "this is Jeryl Jarlyn. The woman standing behind him is Solfa Teflar. She runs Troyk intelligence." Candy felt Shirl's hand on her shoulder. It was almost as if Shirl wanted to separate her from Jeryl Jarlyn. She wanted to enjoy this stranger's embrace another moment. Candy never realized how much she missed not receiving hugs from a parent over the years. The people who worked at the orphanage made sure they were fed and clothed, but there had been no affection or other displays of caring as she grew up.

The Prime Ruler released his hold on Candy, but took possession of her hand. "Solfa's niece, Alexia, will be staying with you at the Childers's household. She is new to Aster Province as well, although she is not from a parallel world." Jeryl Jarlyn appeared to have a playful side. The man oozed charm. Mind control or not, she could see how the population would swallow anything this man said.

"It is nice to meet you, Candy," Solfa said. "Shirl has told Alexia and me all about you. My cousin is looking forward to spending time with you."

Solfa was a beautiful woman. She had gorgeous chestnut hair, a little darker than Candy's medium golden brown. The woman in charge of intelligence had probing blue eyes. In a world of telepathic people, Solfa stare seemed to go even further than what people were thinking.

Candy would not be surprised if Solfa was able to detect people's deepest, darkest secrets. It spoke volumes about this world that a woman would be put in such a responsible position. For the first time since arriving, Candy wondered how she was going to make a living here. Did they have physical education in their schools? She imagined if they had organized sports, they would be different from the ones she was used to. There was so much she needed to learn. It was all a little overwhelming.

"Candy, please join me on the couch." Jeryl Jarlyn's words pulled Candy out of thoughts, which had side tracked her from what was happening in the room. "Tell me what you remember about your parents and any friends they may have had."

Candy never liked talking about her parents. It was not their fault they had died shortly after her birth. What she could not forgive was that they had made no arrangements for her if something happened to them. It had been irresponsible. Candy had sworn to herself at an early age, she would never be unprepared for anything life threw at her. Boy, she had not expected this.

"They died shortly after my birth. I never bothered to find out what happened. My earliest memories revolve around Shirl. She looked after me. If anyone is a parent to me, it would be Shirl. I know how ridiculous that sounds, considering she is only two years older than I am."

Candy could feel the pull on her brain Darden had warned her about. That pressure on top of the headache she already had was more than she could handle. She placed her head in her hands. "Does anyone have an aspirin? My head is about to explode." There was no sensation to make her believe her nose was bleeding. That was a relief. Whether she had the mental fortitude at this point to continue answering his questions was doubtful.

"Jeryl," Solfa implored, "release her before she starts bleeding. The girl does not know anything about Benko. Candy, drink this herbal beverage, it will help with the static."

Candy could feel the pressure lessen as Jarlyn released his hold on her brain. He looked at her as if she was some specimen in a scientific experiment. She certainly hoped this man was not her grandfather. Her head still throbbed, but it was manageable. She took the mug from Solfa and started to sip. It had a nice flavor and almost immediately the static was reduced.

"Jeryl," Shirl said, "before we head to the Childers's residence, I would like Candy to be assigned to me as a CT Guard." That request was certainly a surprise to Candy. She did not even know what a CT Guard was. She could not imagine working inside all day and escorting people around like the two men who had led them to the room earlier.

"Women are not Crystal Telepath Guards. It is far too dangerous. I am sure there are a multitude of jobs Candy is qualified to do in our world." Candy was disappointed by Jeryl's response. She never liked women not being considered for any position solely due to their gender.

"Candy teaches self-defense and is extremely intelligent," Shirl countered. Her friend was like a dog with a bone. She was not going to let this go. "I am the only female crystal telepath, twice I was separated from my guards because I was a woman. Had a female CT Guard been along, I would not have been unprotected. It is time we include women in the guard."

Jeryl studied Shirl and then focused his gaze on Candy. He appeared to be angry at first, but quickly masked his reaction. Her friend appeared to have some power over the Prime Ruler. "I have women in all areas of my government. Maybe it is time to have our first female CT Guard. Have Candy report tomorrow for initial training. I want you to return to Terra Nova for the crystals you did not return with last time. You, Candy, and I will have dinner upon your return."

Candy looked at Shirl who appeared to pale. Jeryl Jarlyn rose and left the room. As soon as the door closed, Shirl collapsed in her chair.

Chapter 3

"What happened on Terra Nova?" Candy inquired. Her friend's reaction to Jeryl Jarlyn's words concerned Candy. It was the first time she had seen Shirl literally deflate. Candy had developed a lot of self-confidence over the years. Shirl and Alex always seemed to lack it. Alex blended into the background, while Shirl always felt she was judged strictly on how she looked. The mental fortitude Shirl had shown earlier today thrilled Candy. She hoped that whatever happened on Terra Nova was just a temporary setback to Shirl's new self-assurance Candy witnessed.

"Let's talk about it when we get to the house. Enjoy the tranquility of walking these streets. I never realized how stressful walking was with cars all around." Shirl increased her pace, coming alongside Starc. Her friend had developed a talent for skirting issues she did not want to discuss. Candy would just have to wait for her answers. Tarsea stopped and joined Candy as they made their way to his parents' home.

"Do not look so glum, Candy," Tarsea told her. "There is a surprise for you at the house. What is waiting for you changed my life. You and I just met, but I owe you more than I can ever repay. Whatever you need, all you have to do is ask." Candy had no idea what Tarsea was referring to. Before she had a chance to cross-examine him, they appeared to be at their destination.

They came to one of a myriad of stone structures that populated the Aster Province and the door opened. Who needed doorbells when you could telepathically announce your arrival? A middle-aged woman stood there and immediately sought out Candy. "I am Leenea Childers. You are so welcome to my home and family." Before Candy could reply, Leenea embraced her. Where

Jarlyn's hug brought warmth, Leenea's felt like home. It was the oddest feeling Candy ever experienced. She had never considered anywhere home, yet this woman personified it.

Candy let Leenea guide her into the house. They entered a foyer and then a large room. The area had a massive table and chairs that took up half the enormous space. The other part of the huge room had a sitting area with numerous couches and chairs. She recognized Solfa Theffar on one of the couches. Solfa was talking to a small woman who had her back turned to Candy. The woman turned around and Candy stopped in her tracks. Alex was right in front of her.

Her friend got up and ran the short distance that separated them. "Thank God!" Alex said. "I was so worried when I found out they were taking you to The Palace, instead of straight here." Alex embraced her. Candy was lost for words. Shirl had not said a word about Alex being in the Troyk universe.

"Alex had been dragged through the portal following Darden," Shirl explained. "Darden knew who we were since he had met Benko Jarlyn several years ago. Benko has been keeping an eye on us our whole lives. Benko feared gatherers from this universe would arrest him and bring him back to the Troyk universe, so he hid us away together in the orphanage. Tarsea was with Darden when she came through and immediately knew Alex was his soul mate. They brought her here and she has been presenting herself as Alexia Montiff from the Starling Province."

Candy released Alex and took a step back. "You are Alexia Montiff? The same Alexia who is supposedly Solfa's cousin and was attacked by Raine Narmouth?"

"Solfa is truly my cousin," Alex explained. "I can't wait for you to meet my aunt Norri and Solfa's mother Pattrice. Norri was my mother's twin sister. She held on to my mother's clan bracelet for me all these years." Alex pulled back her tunic sleeve and showed Candy the copper cuff. It was the same type of bracelet as Shirl's. "Regarding Raine Narmouth, that bastard has attacked me twice. For some reason that psycho has fixated on me. I keep telling Darden and Shirl, we should push him through the portal to some godforsaken parallel world."

Candy could understand the animosity toward Raine Narmouth she had witnessed on the mountain. The next time she ran into the man, she wondered if she was going to display the same self-control she observed today from Starc and Tarsea. Both men had reason to hate Narmouth, although Candy imagined there were more issues between Starc and Narmouth, than what had happened to Alex. She also understood Shirl's aggressive behavior toward the man. Had she been in Shirl's shoes today, she would have done more than drill her finger into the bastard's chest.

Tarsea came up and embraced both women. "When Narmouth first attacked Alex, the self-defense moves you had taught her gave Tolfer and Koel enough time to come to her rescue. When they got there, Narmouth was in worse shape than Alex. I owe you for teaching Alex. You protected her, where I could not." It was obvious that Tarsea cared deeply for her friend.

With those words, Alex broke into tears. "I love you both so much," Alex cried. Alex was always so stoic. Candy became alarmed by Alex's breakdown. Seeing Candy's distress, Alex said, "Don't worry about me, Candy. My emotions are all messed up because of the baby."

"The baby?" Candy took several steps back and took a serious perusal of her friend's slight body frame. "How did that happen?"

Alex's tears were now a result of laughter, rather than crying. "The usual way, Candy. Turns out my soul mate is insatiable. I never believed in love at first sight or soul mates until I met Tarsea. Well, it was more like lust at first sight. The whole soul mate thing took a little more convincing. We can get into all of that later. For now, I am just relieved you are here."

There was a knock on the door. Candy figured there must be some kind of protocol regarding when you announced yourself telepathically versus the old fashion way. Another tall, good looking man entered the room. This one had dark blond hair and resembled Starc and Darden. He made eye contact with Candy and walked directly to her.

"This is my cousin Koel," Starc was able to say before Koel grabbed her arm. He pulled back the material of her shirt and grabbed her forearm with this hand. It was the most outrageous thing that ever happened to her, outside of going through a portal to a parallel universe.

"She is not my soul mate," Koel declared and dropped into the chair behind him. Candy turned to Alex for an explanation.

"Soul mates can identify each other from their first touch, skin on skin. It feels like you are electrocuted," Alex explained. Her friend sat next to the man who just discovered Candy was not his soul mate. "You will find her one day. I am convinced of it, Koel. Actually, the way you are touching every woman you see, it should not take long at all." Koel must have been bad off. Alex's comment did not have any impact on him.

"Is there anything else I should know about soul mates?" Candy inquired. She kept her eyes fixed on Koel. He looked so defeated. Candy hoped he would recover soon. Finally, she returned her gaze to her two friends.

Alex and Shirl looked at each other. It appeared to Candy that they were having a stare-off and whoever broke contact first would have to answer Candy's question. It was typical of the two of them. She could not wait to hear the answer.

Shirl lost the war between the two friends. "Fine," Shirl sighed, "I'll explain it. When soul mates have sexual relations for the first time, their brain excretes a hormone that brings about the next evolutionary phase of their telepathic abilities."

Candy just stared at Shirl. "Is that all?" Candy started laughing hysterically. Although she had pinched herself and her headache was getting worse, Candy had to be dreaming. Only in dreams or very bad B-movies could anything so preposterous be true. She was laughing so hard, she was afraid she was going to wet her pants. Candy needed to get control of herself.

Tolfer Childers entered his parents' house and heard laughter coming from the common room. He had never heard laughter so musical before in his life. As if following the sound of a siren, he walked to the source of the enchantment.

There having an attack on the couch, was the most beautiful woman he had ever seen. She took his breath away. It was at that moment, he realized he was looking upon his soul mate. Tarsea had described his first response to Alex when he saw her. He said he had felt like he had been punched in the stomach.

For Tolfer, it was as if he had never really seen with his eyes before. Darden brought back books from Ginkgo Terra, where Alex and Shirl were from. He felt like he finally understood what Shakespeare was writing about. The vision before his eyes could only be their friend Candy.

The woman's laughter turned into hiccups. His mother got up and ran out of the common room, no doubt going to retrieve some water and sugar.

Alex looked up and saw him. "Tolfer, this is Candy. I am glad you are finally here. The baby and I are starving." His parents were the worst cooks in the world, including any parallel universes. In order to survive his childhood, he had learned to cook. He became quite accomplished and could have gotten a job in any top-tier restaurant. His cooking was never appreciated to the heights it now reached with Alex. He had never encountered anyone with more of an appetite or more pure joy in eating than his brother's soul mate.

Candy looked up at Alex's words, as she wiped tears from her sapphire eyes. They were a rich blue, only found in the most valuable stones. Her face was set around golden-brown hair. Tresses had escaped the confines of whatever she used to tie back her hair. He longed to set the rest of it free. He wanted to run his hands through it while he looked into her beautiful eyes. She was a gem. His jewel.

"Your eyes are perfect," Candy said. Her face turned beet red, when she realized she said those words out loud.

Rather than letting her suffer over what to say next, Tolfer approached and sat in the chair directly across from Candy. "Alex and Shirl have told us all about you. I am glad they successfully brought you to the Troyk universe." It was rather a dull thing to say. Tolfer did not want to let on that she was his soul mate. He wanted to get to know her, before any pressure presented itself that pushed them to have sex to bring about the next telepathic evolutionary change. Alex and Shirl were both rushed into having relations with their soul mates before they got to know each other. Tolfer wanted Candy to have choices. If they were destined to be together, they would.

He did not know whether it was the shock of seeing him or her embarrassment at the words she uttered, but her hiccups stopped. His mother came in with both a glass of water and a mug of the herbal drink. Tolfer imagined she was having issues managing the communal pathways, resulting in a headache.

Candy took the mug and started to sip its contents. Tolfer could see the stress lessen in her face as the herbs curbed her headache. "I understand," Candy said, "you can help me manage the telepathic channels that are dueling in my head."

He liked the way she had stated she had a headache. "It would be my pleasure. We can start after dinner. Alex will faint from hunger soon, if I do not start cooking."

Tolfer left the common room and entered the kitchen. He needed some time alone to come to grips with having just met his soul mate. Their first touch would alert her to the fact there was a unique telepathic link between them. Tolfer knew he could not have any physical contact with her. The big question was how he was going to do that when all he wanted to do was get his hands all over her?

Candy could not believe she made that comment about his eyes. They were exactly like the eyes she had imagined when she first met Tarsea. They were primarily green with the slightest brown, darkening them uniformly. Tolfer was taller than his brother, probably pushing six feet. It was a perfect height compared to her five feet, eleven and a half inches. He had the cutest curly black hair. She was glad he did not wear it short like his brother.

Leenea came and saved her from further embarrassment when she placed a mug of the herbal tea before her. Candy could concentrate on sipping the soothing beverage, rather than staring at the magnificent male specimen before her. She had appreciated good-looking men before, but with Tolfer it was different.

Not only were her eyes absorbing him, but her body as well. She could imagine her hands touching his biceps or caressing his back. There was no part of his anatomy she was not interested in exploring. The problem was, he seemed indifferent to her. Candy had noticed his eyes taking her in, but he sat so far away from her. He had barely been in the room when he got up and fled.

Alex was going on about something called keen and Tolfer being a wonderful cook. Candy could barely keep up with the subject at hand. She wished she could cook. It would have been so easy to excuse herself and go to help Tolfer in the kitchen. Fantasies about what they could do there played in her mind.

"Candy," Shirl yelled, pulling her out of her daydream. She had been thinking about making something to eat with Tolfer, then sharing the end result with him in bed. "We need to head off to the Crystal Telepath Headquarters early tomorrow so we can get you initiated as a CT Guard. I will be heading back with Starc after dinner and you will be staying here in Tolfer's old room."

She had just swallowed some of the herbal beverage when Shirl said where she would be sleeping tonight. She choked and spewed out the beverage in her throat. Yet again, she had reason to be embarrassed. Generally she had better control of herself. First the laughing fit, followed by her runaway mouth, and now spitting out the tea. What was next?

Leenea handed her the water she had brought in earlier and Candy started to sip it. She needed to move, to get her circulation going.

"Can I have a tour of the house, Leenea?" Candy asked. Since she was going to be staying here, it seemed like a reasonable request. It would also shift the focus of attention away from her. The tour would also take them into the kitchen where Tolfer currently cloistered himself.

The house was actually quite charming. It had what was referred to as a common room, where all socializing took place and meals were consumed. All the other rooms except the kitchen were small and intimate spaces. Leenea's favorite color was green, and there were splashes of that color throughout the house. When they reached the bedroom she would be staying in, she tried to ignore that Tolfer had once slept there. They finally made it to the kitchen where Tolfer was busy preparing their dinner.

Shirl touched her shoulder. "Candy," she said, "let's head back to where you are going to be sleeping. I want to show you the clothing Leenea picked up for you." Candy was happy for the distraction from the man cutting vegetables in the kitchen. She followed Shirl to the back of the house. Alex and Tarsea had momentarily disappeared, which Shirl had told Candy was not unusual. Her friend compared those two to rabbits in a poorly delivered joke.

They stood before a closet full of tunics and leggings. "When I described you to Leenea, she came back with primarily black and dark blue outfits," Shirl explained. Obviously the color selection was too limited for Shirl's tastes. Candy stared at them in wonder. Tolfer's mother had picked out exactly what Candy would have selected for herself. She noted all the colors women wore as they walked the streets of Aster Province. Somehow, Leenea knew her before they even met. Shirl would have gotten all sorts of colors she felt would have gone with Candy's coloring, but did not reflect her personality.

Candy rummaged through the clothing in the closet. Most of them were made with a Lycra-like material that had a lot of give. She already knew she was going to love wearing the material that would contour to her figure, as well as give her the ability to move freely. Her fingers skimmed along the tunics until she came upon a pure black sheer tunic. She pulled it out of the closet and looked at it in amazement. It was so delicate. Candy was afraid she was going to tear it by just holding it. Small black pearls were sewn into the fabric. Candy had never seen a garment so lovely. She would never dare wear something so revealing.

"Women wear very elaborate tunics at night," Shirl explained. "They tend to be more revealing than this one. When Leenea showed it to me, I knew she found something you would be comfortable wearing, and still knock every man out cold." Her friend took the tunic from her and placed it back in the closet. "I want you to be happy here, Candy."

"How can I not, with you and Alex both being here?" Candy replied. "You two are my family."

"It is a little different now," Shirl said. Candy could see her friend was uncomfortable with the subject. For once Shirl was not looking her in the eye when they talked. "We both have soul mates. Starc and Tarsea are part of our lives. I don't want you to feel left out, but I don't know how we are going to prevent it."

"Are you kidding?" Candy responded. "I am in a parallel world. You are responsible for me being the only female CT Guard, whatever that means. Plus, you've got a support structure of friends we did not come close to having before. I also imagine there are a number of secrets that will come to light, that will keep me preoccupied. Besides, if I get desperate, I can always follow Koel around as he assaults every female in the Troyk universe."

It comforted her that Shirl was concerned she would feel left out. They had already started living their own lives back home. She was so overwhelmed with everything that had been thrown at her, she hoped humor would reduce Shirl's anxiety over her well-being.

Shirl laughed, "You are going to be fine. Let's go eat. Tolfer is a great cook, and wait until you see how much food Alex consumes. She has changed so much in this world, you will barely recognize her."

"What happened on Terra Nova, Shirl?" Candy wanted answers. She was going to keep pushing until she got them. Especially now that she was partially responsible for Shirl's safety from a professional standpoint.

"Later, you are right," Shirl said. "There certainly is a lot of secrets to be shared and kept. I just don't want to talk about them right now. Before we head to Terra Nova, I promise, I will tell you everything that has happened to me since coming here. Alex can share her story with you tonight."

Shirl had whetted her appetite for information. She desperately wanted to know the secrets Shirl was keeping. Although she looked great, no longer suffering from migraines, Shirl looked haunted.

Chapter 4

~

"Oh, my God!" Candy exclaimed as they entered Crystal Telepath Headquarters. "I have died and gone to heaven." She had never seen so many good-looking men in her life. Candy knew Shirl was the only female crystal telepath and now Candy was the only female CT Guard, but she was not prepared for the smorgasbord of men assaulting her senses when she entered the building.

The room had been silent as they entered, a result of the men communicating through different communal channels. The quiet was replaced with the hum of private conversations as she and Shirl started to be noticed. Candy did not doubt she was the topic being discussed. The inner sanctum of this totally male-dominated group had been violated. Candy was the one responsible.

"Chin up, beautiful," Starc said as he placed his hand on her shoulder. "You will win them over. They just need to get to know you." Starc gently propelled Candy forward as he took Shirl's hand. Had it not been for Starc, Candy did not believe she would have been able to move. Her feet felt like they were cast into cement. Self-confidence was not normally an issue with her. For the first time in her life she felt like an outcast. Hopefully the men would warm up to her as Starc had said. From his lips to God's ear, Candy thought, as she walked further into the hall.

Shirl was not a threat to these men. She was the lone female crystal telepath, something they almost worshiped. When it was decreed that Shirl needed a larger force to travel through the portal, it was not surprising, almost every CT Guard volunteered for the duty. Shirl was also painfully beautiful. It was obvious that Starc already staked his claim in their eyes. They approached her with reverence, not lust.

The men before Candy did not know that Shirl and Starc were soul mates. It was important to keep that relationship a secret. Unfortunately, both Shirl's brother and the Prime Ruler knew. Jeryl Jarlyn wanted to take advantage of any power Shirl would eventually wield.

The Prime Ruler would keep quiet for his own power-hungry reasons. It was unclear if Cianan had ulterior motives or if he would stay silent to protect his sister. People tended to fear what they did not know and there was little known about soul mate powers outside of legends.

Candy had learned the previous evening that Zane and Leenea Childers were soul mates who had hid their special relationship, even from their children. There were so many secrets to keep in this world.

Alex had shared with Candy last night that soul mates were immune to mind control. Alex also had the power to read other people's thoughts. Those abilities for the time being were temporarily suspended while Alex's body was preparing for carrying the baby. They all knew that if the truth about soul mates and their gift to combat mind control ever got out, their lives would be in mortal danger.

Candy had to concentrate on the here and now. She could not afford to let her mind wander. Various men approached them. They slapped Starc on the back, greeted Shirl, and were introduced to Candy. They all seemed relatively friendly. Starc must have rallied his friends to orchestrate this welcome. He had made possible the beginning of solid relationships, she had to make sure she took proper advantage of keeping them. Candy always had an excellent memory for names. She registered each man in her mind as she met them. She noted physical characteristics, aspects of their personalities evident with their first meeting, and other observations. With this technique Candy, would recall each man's name as she encountered them in the future.

A tall man who could be Shirl's twin approached. "You must be Candace," he said.

Shirl frowned as she addressed the man who Candy assumed was her brother. "Hello to you, Cianan. Candy, this gentleman devoid of social graces is my brother. She prefers to be called Candy."

"She is a CT Guard now," Cianan responded. "A position that requires dedication and warrants respect. Candy is a girl you party with, while Candace is someone in whose hands you place your life."

Candy could not argue with his sentiment. As the men became comfortable with her, maybe they would lapse into a more relaxed relationship and call her Candy. "Candace it is then."

Cianan seemed surprised that she did not offer an argument. Candy figured she had won the first battle with Cianan. The question was how long the battle was going to rage. It was clear brother and sister were still working out the dynamics of their own relationship. In that light, Candy was already in the enemy camp.

"Let us head to sparring room number three. I want to see what Candace is capable of," Cianan said. He turned and started on his way. The man had the power now and was displaying his dominance over her. Candy knew she had to pick her battles against Shirl's brother carefully.

"Unbelievable," Shirl muttered under her breath. "I guess we should follow the bastard. He goes hot and cold. I never know what kind of mood we are going to find my brother in. He is in rare form today." Shirl rubbed the clan bracelet her brother had recently given her. She had told Candy her brother had held onto their mother's bracelet all these years.

Candy did not respond to Shirl's comment. She followed Cianan as he made his way through the hall packed with men. As she passed, she made eye contact with as many as she could. There was no immediate connection with them as she had felt with Tolfer. She tried to ignore the angry and nasty looks she received from a number of them.

Her mind kept going back to the gorgeous man at the Childers's. Alex had dominated her evening, so Candy had little time to spend with him. He helped her manage the communal pathways after dinner. Candy had not had the brain trauma Alex and Shirl had experienced when they first entered the Troyk Universe. Candy was a quick study and Tolfer declared her a natural after spending less than an hour with her. If she had pretended not to understand what he was saying, maybe they would have spent more time together. She was disappointed when he left. Soon she was occupied with Alex and her adventures since entering the Troyk universe.

Cianan stopped in front of the entrance to their sparring room. He opened the door and they entered a small gymnasium. Candy immediately felt at home in the gym. This was her turf.

"You do not have to stay," Cianan addressed his sister. Based on his tone, he was really telling Shirl to get lost.

"Not in this or any other reality, am I leaving you alone with Candy," Shirl replied. She folded her arms across her chest and leaned against the wall. An equally stoic Starc stood next to his soul mate. If Cianan was impacted by Shirl's refusal to leave, he certainly didn't show it.

"Fine," Cianan replied. He walked to the center of the room. Rather than wood, the floor was covered with mats. Cianan picked up the staff that lay at his feet. "Disarm me."

Candy examined his stance and started to circle him. "Can't she just shoot you?" Shirl yelled over her shoulder. Candy heard Starc chuckle at Shirl's recommendation. Ignoring the distraction, Candy continued to study her adversary.

"Good," Cianan addressed Candy. He moved as Candy continued to rotate around him. "Attacking without thought is the quickest way to get hurt. Look for an opening and then act. Do not hesitate. A moment's distraction on the part of your adversary can give you an advantage." Although Cianan was a crystal telepath, Shirl told her he frequently traveled alone. He had to know how to protect himself. Cianan was also in charge of all the missions his sister was sent on. When she was assigned to Shirl, her brother was Candy's superior.

The staff moved so quickly, Candy did not move fast enough to dodge the piece of wood before it made contact with her shoulder. That was definitely going to leave a bruise, she thought, as the impact wound continued to burn. Her shoulder was fine; the only thing really hurt was her pride. Above all, she wanted to make a good impression.

Candy continued to concentrate on Cianan. She was not under any time constraint. As far as she was concerned, she had all day. Candy made several more passes around her subject. There was no way she was going to let him tag her again with the staff. When she had her back to Starc and Shirl, she heard a thump and Cianan's eyes were diverted. It was then that Candy made her move.

Candy proceeded to kick Cianan in the stomach. Aiming for his groin seemed too severe, although she had a feeling that was where Shirl would have wanted her to attack. Candy had momentarily surprised Cianan, who was leaning down. She grabbed his arm and pulled it against his back, while she reached her other arm and wrapped it around his neck. Candy stepped back before Cianan was able to flip her over his head. She finally kicked behind his knees, bringing him down and he dropped the staff. Candy released her hold on Cianan, stepped away and raised her hands in the air. The skirmish was over as far as she was concerned. She wanted it ended before Cianan could counter. All he had instructed her to do was disarm him.

It was only then that she looked over to see what had distracted Cianan. Shirl was on top of Starc, kissing him passionately. No wonder her opponent had momentarily drifted his attention away from Candy. Those two were putting on quite a show. She had noticed in the restaurant how these two fit. Seeing them this way, Candy knew that Shirl and Starc were meant for each other. Soul mates.

She was the one now not paying attention, as Cianan tackled her around her knees. She came down hard on the mat. Candy had the wind knocked out of her, as Cianan placed the staff against her neck. He did not put any pressure against her throat. She could tell by the look in his eye that he had no intention of hurting her. He had made his point.

"Not bad, Candace," Cianan whispered in her ear. "Do not lower your guard until your opponent has been neutralized." He stood up and offered her his hand. A round of applause occurred as she was once again on her feet. Candy turned around to see half a dozen men coming toward her and Cianan. She was surprised when two of them came up to her instead.

"Well done," Kelog Potts offered his congratulatory praise. "We got here about the time Shirl took down Starc and you disarmed Cianan. You brought that son of a bitch to his knees." He patted her on the back, as numerous men had done over the years. She had always been a buddy, never a girl they would ask out on a date.

The other men were loudly sharing with Cianan how they enjoyed watching him take down the upstart female. If she could have snapped her fingers and disappeared, Candy would have done so.

"Idiots," Kelog muttered. "You fought well, do not let anyone tell you otherwise. They will accept you in time. Take my word for it."

"Enough," Cianan yelled. "Starc, take her to the range and teach Candace how to fire a crystal weapon. It would not be a bad idea to give my sister some instruction too. Shirlyn needs to be able to destroy more than a chair the next time she is threatened."

Candy laughed as she saw the frown across her friend's face when her brother called her by her Troyk birth name. She suddenly sobered as Cianan's other words soaked in. Shirl had been in a life and death situation and had not been able to properly defend herself. Once again, Candy wondered what had happened on Terra Nova.

～🌀

The firing center was in the basement. Kelog walked beside her as they made their way down the stairs. Having another CT Guard next to her was reassuring. Rome was not built in a day, Candy kept reminding herself. She was going to build relationships one man at a time. Throughout school she had studied many pioneers and the defeats they had to suffer before they brought about social change. Now Candy was the crusader. Those who came before her would serve as her role models. The thought caused her chin to rise a little higher.

A group of men stood before the entry. They did not seem too eager to move aside. Starc was about to say something, when Candy placed her hand on his arm. "I'll handle this," she said. She moved forward, purposely entering their space. "It is possible that one day I will be fighting beside one or more of you. I would imagine you would appreciate if I hit what I am firing at. Would one of you big, brawny men like to show me how it is done?"

Her question was met with silence. Suddenly laughter could be heard from the back of the group. A muscular man of average height moved through the small crowd until he stood before Candy. "I will be happy to teach you, little girl. You showed some promise when you took Cianan down." Candy had not seen him after the fight. It also did not escape her notice that she was probably three inches taller than he was.

"Are you any good?" she asked. Candy needed to show no weakness. She had to prove she was a CT Guard, just like they were. Playing as one of the guys was always the role she felt most comfortable with.

"I can show you a thing or two," the man smiled at her. "My name is Nance. We can start with shooting and see where that leads." Candy did not miss his eyes traveling up and down her body. It normally happened to Shirl, not to her. Candy was not going to let him rattle her.

"You still didn't answer my question whether you could hit the side of a barn," Candy was having so much fun she was almost purring. There were a couple of confused looks until it dawned on them what she was saying.

"He is one of the best shots around," Starc answered. It spoke volumes that Starc had held back and let her handle things on her own, and it was doubly reassuring he was there in case things went south.

"Well, then," Candy said, "I guess I will let you show me how it's done, Nance."

Half the group left, muttering to themselves how Nance had sold out to a woman. The others stayed to see what she was made of. She was holding her own as far as she could see.

They entered the armory and Nance drew one of the smaller weapons. "It is small and compact, but it will shoot quite a blast. It is powered by a rare red agate from Terra Flora. There are only two crystals in the chamber, so it is only good for two shots."

"Your weapons are powered by crystals?" Candy asked. Between Shirl navigating portals and now weaponry, Candy had a whole new appreciation for the stones.

Nance chuckled again. "You have a lot to learn, but I am willing to teach you." Candy hoped he was referring to fighting, shooting, and whatever else CT Guards were required to do.

"Let's do it," she said as she patted Nance on the back. "By this time next week I plan to be out-shooting you."

"You have yourself a wager, little girl," Nance replied. "We can talk about terms after I see you shoot."

One man at a time, she thought to herself as she followed Nance into the firing range. Her next thought was to hope she did not shoot her foot off, trying to fire the crystal weapon.

Chapter 5

~

Tolfer stood back and glared at the men who surrounded Candy. She had been home for less than an hour, when Kelog Potts and three other CT Guards came to his parents' house for a social visit.

Kelog had gone to school with Tolfer. At one point, he supposed you could have called them friends, although Tolfer never created deep friendships like Tarsea had developed with Darden and members of his family. Tolfer figured he was too much of a homebody. Rather than spending time with his friends outside of school, Tolfer came home and started cooking.

When they graduated, Kelog trained to be a CT Guard. Tolfer felt his calling was to teach children how to control their telepathic gifts. Nothing was more rewarding than seeing suffering children master the pathways. It warmed his heart when they ended up smiling, because their heads no longer hurt.

Now his former friend was here trying to charm Tolfer's soul mate. He battled with himself regarding whether to join the fun or continue to hang out in the shadows. Alex gave him a reprieve from making a decision when she asked him to join her in the kitchen.

"Boy, it's like old times out there," Alex communicated through the Childers's familial link. She obviously did not want to be overheard, since Alexia Montiff would not have known Candy prior to yesterday. *"The guys were always coming by the orphanage and then later Candy's apartment."*

"She must have had a lot of boyfriends." Tolfer figured he must have really wanted to suffer after making that comment. Now Alex was going to give him a blow by blow description of Candy's love life. He felt like he was going to be sick.

"Not really," Alex replied. *"She was always one of the guys. They liked to pal around with her. A couple of them asked Shirl out, but never Candy. I doubt any of the men in the common room are going to ask her out."* Alex got close to him and whispered, "You shouldn't have any competition."

Tolfer paled at her last words. Thank goodness she had not communicated them through the familiar channel. He would never hear the end of it from both his mother and Tarsea. "I do not know what you are talking about!"

"Please," Alex replied. "I have eyes. You look at her the same way Tarsea looks at me. There is a soul mate possession written all over your face. What I don't understand is why you haven't done anything about it."

"Maybe I am giving her time. The time Shirl and you did not have." Tolfer did not communicate that he was not ready for the responsibility of having a soul mate yet. He was twenty-two years old. His motives were not as selfless as he wanted Alex to believe.

Alex smiled and kissed him on the cheek. "I am proud to call you brother soon." Alex grabbed an apple and bit into it. After a couple more bites, she continued. "Don't wait too long to share the wonders of having a soul mate. Why don't I start dinner and you join the group in the other room. Aunt Norri will be here shortly and will help me. I imagine the gang will clear out when Pattrice arrives and starts crying."

Solfa's mother, Pattrice, was an endless fountain of tears, since reuniting with her favorite cousin's daughter. Alex looked so much like her mother, Pattrice was continually reminded of how devastated she was when Alex's mom left the Troyk universe with Benko Jarlyn.

Growing up with Pattrice's bitterness had had a serious impact on her daughter Solfa. Although Solfa was in charge of Jeryl Jarlyn's intelligence, she secretly worked to help dissidents escape. She had turned a blind eye on a number of Tarsea's group operations, as they ferried people to the portal. Solfa hated mind control and felt it was better to fight from inside the government to make lasting change. She helped to keep Alex's true identity secret.

As Tolfer left the kitchen, there was a knock on the door. Figuring it was Norri and Pattrice, he opened the door. To his surprise, he saw three more CT Guards, including Raine Narmouth. Tolfer had been present both times Alex had been rescued after Narmouth had assaulted her. He had quite a lot of nerve showing up with the others.

"Raine Narmouth is here," he communicated through the familial path, alerting both Tarsea and Alex. Simultaneously, he also communicated through the warrior channel. It was a closed telepathic pathway between his brother, their friends, and others that linked in over time. The warrior channel, until recently, was yet another legendary pathway that had existed only in the stories he grew up listening to. Only those loyal to the true ruler of the Troyk universe could enter the channel. It originally opened between Darden and Benko Jarlyn. He knew that by leveraging this channel, he was letting Starc and Shirl know, as well, of Raine Narmouth's presence.

"I will stay with Candy and Shirl," Starc joined the telepathic communication. *"Tarsea is on his way into the kitchen to protect Alex. Remember, Alex cannot communicate through this channel due to the pregnancy. Tarsea will have to communicate through his familial channel any further directions."*

Tolfer saw Candy's face change from enjoying the conversation to concern as soon as her eyes fell on Raine Narmouth. Shirl grabbed Candy's wrist as she started to stand. He saw Raine Narmouth surveying the common room, no doubt looking for Alex. Shirl had released Candy's arm and Tolfer's soul mate was on her way to confront Raine Narmouth. Tolfer knew he had to do something to stop Candy. There were too many people in the room who would question Candy's protectiveness related to Alex.

Tolfer met Candy half-way and grabbed her hand. He knew there would be a reaction the first time he made skin to skin contact with his soul mate. Tolfer just did not expect the magnitude of the soul mate channel opening. It felt like every cell in his body had been electrocuted. Tolfer had to think fast to explain to Candy what she felt. He also had to make sure no communication came through the soul mate telepathic link that had just opened.

Candy felt as if she had been struck by lightning. Every blood vessel in her body felt like they were boiling. The shock to her body was over almost before it started.

Tolfer tightened his grip on her. "Wow! That was some blast of static electricity. Were you rubbing your ass up and down the couch?"

Was he for real? That was more than just an electrical shock that traveled between people. That bolt could have brought down a power line. Candy became aware of people staring at her. She felt normal again, no residual impact. Could she have possibly over-reacted to a little spark of energy between Tolfer and herself? She was attracted to Tolfer to a degree, she had never felt before. Maybe her mind was just playing tricks on her, making something out of an insignificant contact.

"Maybe I got up too fast." It was a weak reply, but everyone must have fallen for it. The group seemed busy welcoming the newcomers. That brought Raine Narmouth back to her attention. She tried to move on, but Tolfer still held her hand. It felt like her hand was caught in a vise.

"Is Alexia here?" Raine Narmouth asked. By this point Shirl and Starc had made their way to Narmouth. He seemed clueless to the hostility that surrounded him. "You cannot keep her away from me." The man was making a scene. It was imperative that Alex go unnoticed as much as possible to protect her cover. Narmouth was now drawing the attention of the other CT Guards in the room.

Still holding her hand, Tolfer addressed the group. "I hate to break up the party, but my parents are expecting company. A number of you are also heading out to Terra Nova tomorrow. It would be a good idea to make it an early night anyway." Tolfer had diffused the situation.

Everyone made their way to the door as two middle-aged women and Solfa arrived. Candy figured the ladies were Norri and Pattrice, as each woman embraced Shirl. Alex did not appear until Raine Narmouth was gone. Candy imagined Solfa's presence eliminated the desire for any of the men to loiter after Tolfer politely asked them to leave.

After introductions were made, Tolfer, Alex, and Norri headed to the kitchen. Everyone else returned to the common room. Candy would have liked to have joined the group in the kitchen, avoiding Pattrice's continual crying. Candy knew she was a deplorable cook, so stating she was going to help with dinner was not going to fly.

"This is part of your initiation into the Troyk universe," Shirl informed her through their closed link. *"Pattrice will settle down once she is less emotional. You are now part of*

her extended family. Darden still hasn't shared anything about your Troyk family, so in the meantime, soak in the love. This woman will adore you until her last breath. Our parents left behind a lot of collateral damage."

As if conjured by magic, Darden and Koel arrived. Darden was going to join them on their trip to Terra Nova tomorrow. In case they got separated, Cianan wanted another crystal telepath along. They had a brief conversation about the logistics of tomorrow's trip. Koel made a couple of recommendations regarding the tactical aspects of the operation. The group went back to socializing after a couple of additional questions about Terra Nova were answered. It felt like they were preparing to go to another country, not a parallel universe. It took some getting used to.

"What can you tell me about my Troyk relatives?" Candy asked Darden.

"How about us discussing that over dinner so everyone can hear and ask questions? Alex will want to know everything that is said and Norri may have actually known them." Candy knew that Darden was right. She did not like how he used the past tense when referring to her family. Candy had been alone her whole life, except for Alex and Shirl. It appeared nothing had changed.

Tolfer set the last of the dishes they had cooked on the massive common room table. His friends and family were all seated at the table, but he could not take his eyes off his unclaimed soul mate. Raine Narmouth had been a convenient excuse to get all the men out of the house, away from Candy.

"Have some of Tolfer's chicken and keen dish," Alex said as she spooned some of the contents of the bowl onto Candy's plate. "It is a grain that is only grown on this planet. I know it's purple, but it is really quite delicious."

He watched as Candy took a bite of the dish. She closed her eyes and inhaled deeply after she swallowed. "That is so good. Don't be stingy, Alex. I'll take some more."

Alex did as her friend instructed and then passed the dish to Solfa. "It is so annoying that Shirl and Candy can still use contractions and I have to continue to elongate my speech." Tolfer had never known there was another way to say certain words by collapsing two words into one. Alex particularly suffered with saying "let us", versus "let's." She always complained that it sounded funny.

"It is too late to change our story about your past, my little pixie," Tarsea commented. At first Alex complained about him calling her a name that described her size. Alex was a bit vertically challenged, compared to her two friends. The first time Tarsea had used those words to describe her short stature, Tolfer laughed. Candy was pushing six feet tall and Shirl was probably less than two inches shorter than Candy.

"I *don't* know," Shirl commented. "I remember when I was in Texas for a seminar. I was saying y'all within two days of my arrival. Maybe after spending time with Candy and me in this universe, Alex can start picking up some of our poor speech habits."

Koel shook his head before he joined the conversation. "There are times you still want to blend into the shadows, Alex. If you start speaking differently than most Troyk citizens, it will draw attention to yourself." Alex had started to work as an intelligence officer for Solfa. Her ability to blend into her surroundings made her a valuable asset. It also did not hurt that she could read people's thoughts.

"Crap, you are right, Koel. I did not think about my new vocation. It is time I start talking like a Troyk citizen, even in private discussions." Alex took another bite and proceeded to attack the rest of the food on her plate. He loved that Alex had a healthy appetite. So did Candy, it appeared. Only Shirl picked at the food on her plate. Tolfer imagined she was nervous about returning to Terra Nova.

"What can you tell me about my Troyk family, Darden?" Candy asked. "I just know their names from my birth certificate. Based on what Alex and Shirl have told me recently about their parents, I assume the names listed were made up."

"Brad and Laura Phillips were really Bradsk and Shelaura Phildrum," Darden informed Candy.

There was a loud gasp further down the table. Everyone's eyes went in the direction of the sound. Soon all attention was directed at Pattrice Theffar.

"I knew your grandmother, Candy," Pattrice said. "Alaura Ketore and I use to play cards together. We both fell apart when my cousin Starta, Alex's mother, and Shelaura left with Benko. I withdrew within my family, while Alaura went looking for trouble."

"What sort of trouble?" Candy asked. His soul mate had lost some of the color his food had placed on her lovely cheeks. Tolfer knew the story and tensed, preparing to hear Pattrice tell Candy the horrific fate of her family.

At this point Pattrice broke into tears. Solfa took her mother's hand and continued the story. "Alaura joined an anti-government group. They wanted a quick revolutionary change to unseat the mind control members of our government. Various explosive devices were planted within The Palace. When they exploded more than a dozen people were killed. Among the people that had been rounded up were Alaura and her son. Your uncle was sentenced to death and Alaura was condemned to spend the rest of her life in the penal colony."

Tolfer looked at Shirl. It was her right to tell her friend what happened to prisoners who were sentenced to death. He imagined if she did not have the strength to tell Candy, Starc would do it.

Shirl rose and walked over to pour herself a stiff drink. Tolfer imagined she needed the alcohol to help numb her nerves. "Candy, your uncle was sentenced to die in the Nightshade universe. It is a world populated by vampires. Our Prime Ruler traded their blood for the crystals that are mined there."

You could have heard a pin drop in the room. Tolfer wanted to go to his soul mate and take her in his arms. Unfortunately, he knew he could not do that without outing the truth about their relationship.

"You are telling me vampires exist and my uncle was murdered by them?" Candy's voice was shaky, filled with contained rage. "I want to know what exactly happened to him."

"No, you don't, Candy," Shirl answered. "I have to live with what I witnessed in that universe. I'll be damned if I am going to sentence you to the same nightmares. If you are truly my friend, don't ask me."

Candy sat quietly for a moment. No one offered any oral comments, although there was a little discussion in the warrior and Tolfer's familial channel. He concentrated on Candy, not the telepathic conversations. Different expressions crossed her face, as she continued to digest all she learned.

"Where is this penal colony?" Candy asked. "Can I visit my grandmother if she is still living?"

"It is off-world," Darden answered her. "Only convicted felons enter that universe. The crystal telepath sets the frequencies. The prisoners are forced into the portal alone. Once someone enters the colony, they never come back."

"This just gets better and better," Candy said under her breath. "Every prisoner sent to this colony spends the rest of their lives there? How long has this charming practice been going on?"

"Twenty years or so," Darden said. "Supplies are sent monthly."

"I assume they include diapers?" Candy asked. Tolfer saw her look at the faces around her and the realization that the people around her had not thought about the prisoners' behaviors after they left the Troyk universe. "If they have women there as well as men, babies are the normal outcome. Your people have sentenced future generations to a life in exile."

"I cannot believe I did not think about that," Alex said. "My brain just concentrated on a sentence without parole. I guess it is not dissimilar to how Georgia and Florida were first settled, as well as Australia."

"Great, my uncle was someone's lunch and my grandmother is living with a bunch of murderers and rapists," Candy concluded. "Shirl, can I have one of those drinks? You can tell me about Terra Nova tomorrow. I have heard all I can take for one day."

Tolfer sat back as his mother and Alex cleared the table. His soul mate was nursing her drink. He longed to communicate with her within their own private channel, but he could not. She took the news about the Nightshade universe and the penal colony better than he had expected.

Candy had not fallen apart, but he doubted at this point she ever did. Wracking his brain trying to find an excuse to travel to Terra Nova with her tomorrow, he came up with nothing. How would Candy react to what Shirl would tell her about what she had unleashed in that universe? Everyone had their limits and he suspected Shirl's confession would be the catalyst for Candy's eventual breakdown.

Chapter 6

Terra Nova

Leaves crunched under Candy's feet as they made their way to Ervin Allaway's village. She had been briefed that Allaway was the Terra Nova chieftain the Troyk Universe had their alliance with. The wind cut through the lightweight jacket Candy wore. Shirl tried to convince her to dress with warmer layers, but Candy did not want to be weighed down with the material. She needed to be able to defend herself and Shirl physically if the three blasts the crystal weapon she carried were used in defense. There was a tremendous amount for her to prove on her first time out protecting Shirl.

Terra Nova was an iron-age world with fighting clans. A battle had raged the last time Shirl was here and she left without the crystals. Something bad had happened here, but Shirl would not talk about it. Candy did know that for a time, Shirl had been separated from the men during their mission. Shirl would still not discuss with her what had occurred that had shaken her so badly. Candy had her suspicions.

This time they had come with a small army of CT Guards. Candy did not know if their numbers were so large to protect Shirl or guarantee they returned with the crystals. What did the Prime Ruler do with the crystals, each crystal telepath gatherer returned with?

Those thoughts would have to wait. A group of men were approaching. Candy did not know if they were friend or foe. Whoever they were, they dressed in animal skins, carried large swords, and were built. They could be on the covers of the romance novels Shirl read.

Cianan stopped the procession and greeted the man who led the party. "Aifric Clacher, it is good to meet you well." Candy assumed that was an expression used in this world. "We have come to trade with you."

Aifric surveyed the group. His eyes first came to her, and he devoured her with his stare. Candy was not used to men looking at her in that fashion. As if they had a mind of their own, her legs shifted out of discomfort. Shirl had told her Terra Nova was short of women and they would have to do some additional trading for both of them to be able to leave the universe. After Aifric's gaze went up and down her body several times, it continued on to Shirl. Aifric came forward and fell to his knees in front of her friend.

"We are once again blessed with your presence, goddess," Aifric addressed Shirl. Candy saw his eyes focus back on her. "I also see you bring another woman with you. Perhaps you will gift her to Allaway. She will produce strong sons." Cianan grabbed Candy's arm before she had a chance to walk forward and set the man straight. She was not anyone's gift!

"The woman is valuable to me, Aifric," Shirl replied. "I learned the last time I could not travel alone to different worlds without a female accompanying me. You must see the worth in that. Please, take us to see Allaway." Candy was proud how well her friend handled the situation. She had kept her cool and answered the man in a way he could understand.

Shirl had changed in the short time she had been in the Troyk universe and traveled to other parallel worlds. There was a new confidence in the way Shirl presented herself. Candy was impressed with how her friend had matured.

Aifric led them through the woods to a clearing where a small village was situated. *"We are going to be separated from the men. It is their way. Don't fight it, Candy,"* Shirl informed her using their closed telepathic channel.

"The goddess and her female will stay here, while we do business," Aifric informed the group. "They will join us in celebration after we have finished bartering."

Candy did as Shirl instructed; she did not object to being separated from the rest of their party. It was the perfect opportunity to find out the whole truth behind what had happened to Shirl. They entered a small stone structure. Thankfully, there was a fire blazing in the small building. Candy and Shirl immediately gravitated to the fireplace to warm themselves.

"All right, Goddess," Candy said, using the same name Aifric had called her twice. She could not help putting a little sarcasm in her voice. "What happened here that causes you to lose color every time Terra Nova is mentioned?"

Before Shirl had time to reply, an old woman entered with a tray. "I bring you food, as I have done before, my lady." Candy noticed the woman's hand was crippled from old age and arthritis. How she wished she had some Glucosamine Sulfate she could give this suffering creature. That was assuming the woman was not allergic to shellfish, the medicine's base ingredient. It hurt just looking at her poor hands.

Shirl walked to the old woman and took her burden from her. "It smells wonderful, Peigi. You honor me with your cooking. Thank you." Old Peigi curtsied and then left the building. "Candy, come here and have some mutton stew."

"What exactly is mutton?" Candy asked. It smelled wonderful. Her mouth watered as she picked up the relic, they called a spoon in this world.

"Older sheep. You've had lamb before. This is just an older lamb, it's a bit gamier than what you are accustomed to."

Candy actually liked lamb as prepared in Greek restaurants. She took a spoonful of the stew and was surprised how much she liked it. "It could use some salt, but other than that, it's wonderful."

"I brought salt to barter with. Starc will place some in Ervin Allaway's stew and prove to him the seasoning is worth a number of the crystals we are tasked to bring back with us." It was obvious the Troyk contingent was prepared for this visit.

Candy almost asked what Jeryl Jarlyn did with all the crystals. However, there was still one outstanding question she wanted an answer to. "All right, Princess. What happened in this world you have been skating around telling me about? I cannot properly protect you without knowing what is going on."

Shirl grabbed the crystals that hung from gold chains around her neck. It was an old habit of Shirl's whenever she was stressed. Her reaction only reinforced the fact that Candy needed to know what Shirl was keeping from her.

Shirl singled out one crystal from the ones she held in her hand. Candy had seen the black crystal a million times. Back home, she had a necklace made from the common stone. "Hematite, so?"

Shirl shook her head, "It is not hematite. You see the orange flecks in it? I am not sure what it is, but it is an extremely powerful crystal." Shirl took her eyes off the stone and looked directly at Candy. "This crystal allows me to harness the energy of the portal as a weapon. Anything standing in front of the energy blast I generate gets incinerated." With those words, Shirl lowered her eyes.

"Is that what happened here?" Candy asked. She was afraid to ask any more specific questions. The look of guilt all over Shirl's face was heartbreaking.

"I did not know what I was about to unleash," her friend cried. "There are legends about the power a mated female crystal telepath can produce. I knew nothing about these stories, but Jeryl Jarlyn certainly did. He sent me on one dangerous mission after another, waiting for me to open a portal and test my true power. Cianan knew, but not about the magnitude of the blast I generated. Dozens from a rival clan were coming at us when I unleashed my power. Candy, I promise you, I did not know." Tears ran down Shirl's face.

Candy took Shirl into her arms. "Of course you didn't know," she said as she comforted her friend. "I have known you my whole life. You would not hurt a fly, unless it was necessary. Can you control the severity of future blasts?"

"I will never open another portal to generate a blast again," Shirl replied.

"You are wearing the crystal, Shirl," Candy said. "Of course you will generate another blast if you, your soul mate, or any of your friends are in mortal danger. The only question that remains is how powerful of a blast you will create. If you can learn to stun, rather than kill, that crystal you wear could come in very handy on a regular basis. This crystal weapon I carry is only good for three blasts. I assume we are talking about the same power source."

Shirl looked at her in wonder. "Alex said almost the same thing about a semi-automatic gun. I had not thought about the crystal generated weapon and my ability being similar."

Candy laughed. "Well, if Alex had already brought up a similar point, we must be right. Who else was there when you generated the blast? Does Jeryl Jarlyn know what you did?"

"Starc, Cianan, and a number of the clan members witnessed the blast," Shirl answered. "The villagers grew up hearing stories about the power of female mated crystal telepaths. They view me as a legend come true that came to save their village."

"In a way you are, Shirl," Candy commented back. "What about Cianan and Jarlyn?"

"Cianan reported I opened a portal and a burst of light was emitted," Shirl said. "My brother promised to keep my secret. I just don't know if I can trust him. He was so bitter when we were re-united. Our mother left this world, primarily because of Jarlyn's obsession with me when I was a baby. Cianan blames me for our parents leaving him behind."

"You were a baby at the time," Candy responded. "By lying to Jarlyn, your brother has tied his destiny to you. He has been good to me since my arrival in this dimension. Maybe that is just another way for him to deal with his earlier abandonment. You cannot expect him to forgive and forget overnight."

"I suppose," Shirl said. She came over and hugged Candy. "Leave it to you to be the voice of reason. I really missed you."

They were still in each other's arms as Starc entered with another man.

It was a good thing Shirl was still holding her when the man entered the structure. He actually made Candy's knees weak, not an everyday occurrence. She did not burn the way she did when she was in Tolfer's presence, but this man was certainly gorgeous!

"Ervin wanted to meet Candy," Starc shared with them. "I thought Shirl and I could get a little crystal practice in while our men continue to barter. Allaway's guard will protect us while we are gone." Candy knew exactly what Starc was referring to after her short conversation with Shirl. They were going to experiment with the severity of the blasts Shirl would be able to produce. That was the primary reason she wore the crystal today. She had not planned to use it as a weapon.

Shirl stepped out of her embrace, wiping the remaining tears from her eyes. "I told Candy what happened. You will be safe with Ervin while Starc and I disappear for a little while." Candy did not have a chance to reply before Starc swept Shirl away.

"Starc has told me you do not have a soul mate," Ervin said. Candy was captivated by his dark green eyes. They were beautiful, but not perfect like Tolfer's. It was strange that she would think about Tolfer at this moment.

"No, I do not have a soul mate," Candy replied. She noted Ervin had not used contractions in his speech, so she followed suit. "My parents were from the Troyk universe. I was born and lived my whole life on Earth. I believe it is called Ginkgo Terra."

"Did you have a man there?" Ervin asked as he walked closer to Candy. He placed his hands around her upper arms and merely held her. Although he grasped her, she felt very little pressure on her skin. This could very well be part of their custom, so Candy did not want to make an issue of his proximity or handling of her body.

Candy had to look up when she addressed Ervin, with Tolfer she could look him straight in the eye. "I have no one. No family, except for Shirl and our friend Alexandra."

"I can offer you, a family and a clan. You would never be alone. Shirl has her soul mate. I know nothing about Alexandra, but she too may have found someone to be with. Our world is short on women. We have little, but I would treat you well."

Candy was overwhelmed. This gorgeous man with dark auburn hair and lovely green eyes wanted her. Shirl had already warned her she and Alex had found their special mates. Candy truly had no one. What had she to lose? Once again Tolfer, came back into her mind.

"I barely know you, Ervin," Candy told him. "I can make no promises to you today, other than I would not mind getting to know you better." She really did not know what to say beyond that.

Ervin released her arms, took her into his embrace, and kissed her. As kisses went, it was pretty damn good! She could feel her legs giving out as Ervin chuckled.

"You are a passionate woman. I believe that we could have a good life. Stay and we will see if we truly belong together."

He kissed her again, this time with more passion. She placed both of her arms around his neck and allowed him to deepen the kiss. She had never been kissed in this manner before. What would Tolfer's kisses be like? Candy clung to him as Ervin steered them to the small bed in the corner. The bed gave way as both Ervin and she came down upon it. His weight bore down on her as his hand started to pull down her leggings. She knew she needed to stop him before it was too late.

Candy broke the kiss, "We need to stop." Her words fell on deaf ears as Ervin continued to force himself on her. She was in a world where men dominated women. How did she let things go so far? She started to pound on his back. "No, Ervin!" Somehow, in this world she got the impression that 'no' did not necessarily mean 'no.'

The weight on her was lifted, as Ervin got off her. Candy looked up as she adjusted her clothing to see Kelog Pitts and Cianan holding back Ervin Allaway.

"Are you all right, Candace?" Cianan asked. "Where are Starc and my sister? They should never have left you alone with this man. They think differently than we do."

Candy got up, embarrassed to have been found in such a compromising position. "Starc and Shirl went on an errand. I do not think they thought Ervin was going to get so amorous." She could barely make eye contact with Cianan as she finished adjusting her clothing. This was not the impression she wanted to make.

"Please forgive my behavior," Ervin Allaway said. "I will join the rest of my men." He left the room with Kelog following.

Candy was now alone with Cianan. She needed to explain to him what had happened. It was imperative Cianan did not think she could not take care of herself or Shirl. "I did not want to hurt him physically. There was the alliance to consider. I was giving him a chance to stop before I inflicted harm." Everything she said was true, but she had gotten herself into the unfortunate position to begin with.

Cianan stared at her and a small grin crossed his face. "That was very honorable of you to consider the greater good of the Troyk universe. This was all my fault. I should have briefed you better about the customs of this world. A kiss is as good as a marriage proposal."

"Are you kidding me?" Candy replied. It had been quite a kiss, but that was all it was to her.

"No, I am not," Cianan said with an edge to his voice this time. "Where are Starc and Shirl?"

"They are working on controlling a portal blast generated by Shirl," Candy answered.

Cianan lost the color in his face. "She told you what happened?"

"Yes," Candy replied, "as well as your role. You should have told her, Cianan. It was unlikely you knew the magnitude of what she was going to produce, but you knew she had the ability to generate energy from the portal as a weapon. The guilt surrounding what she did has almost consumed her. If it was not for Starc and her friends, she may have gone to a dark place, she could not have been able to have left."

"Do you think I have not been haunted myself from what I did? She is my sister, after all. I gave her our mother's clan bracelet." How easy it would all be if inappropriate behavior could be forgiven with a bribe. Not one to think stereotypically, but how like a man such a reaction was.

"Good Lord! You actually think you can bribe your way into her good graces?"

"She said there was only one way I could prove myself, although she would not say how," Cianan said. "I figure if I trained and befriended you, Shirl would forgive me. The first time we touched, I had hoped a soul mate channel would have opened."

"What does that mean, a soul mate channel?" Candy asked.

"The first time soul mates touch, there is a violent reaction. Starc had described it as if his whole body had been electrocuted."

Cianan's words brought Candy back to the first time she had skin on skin contact with Tolfer. Her reaction was exactly like Cianan had described the opening of the soul mate channel. It would make sense that he was her soul mate, based on how she had been lusting after him. Even after Ervin's first touch, her mind went back to Tolfer.

So much had happened to her since she had arrived in the Troyk universe. Information overload consumed her. It dawned on her Alex had told her about a similar reaction she had when Tarsea first touched her. How could Candy forget what she had been told and not realized what Tolfer's touch meant when it happened?

"Let's find Starc and Shirl," Candy said. "We should be heading back to the Troyk Universe. I assume you have the crystals we came for." Cianan nodded. "Good, time to leave." She wanted to get back and confront her soul mate!

Chapter 7

~

The Troyk Universe

Confronting Tolfer about why he had disguised the opening of their soul mate channel as static electricity had to wait. The team had been called to be debriefed at The Palace. She did not know why she had fallen for Tolfer's lame explanation. Candy had known it had been a life-altering event. He just had her so off-kilter she couldn't think straight.

Candy and Shirl were led to a conference room located on the third floor of The Palace where the municipal offices were located. She was not sure how the Troyk government and crystal telepath operations were related. There was so much about this world she did not have a clue about. If Jeryl Jarlyn was involved, Candy reasoned, they would have been brought to the fourth floor.

Solfa Thefflar entered the conference room. Not bothering to greet them, she sat across from Candy and Shirl. This meeting was certainly not going to be a cakewalk. "What were you thinking, leaving Candy alone with Ervin Allaway?" Solfa asked Shirl. Candy could feel Shirl tensing next to her. If possible, Solfa's glare became more intimidating than Solfa's hostile tone. Candy was happy she was not on the receiving end of either. The woman was out for blood. Candy supposed she should be happy Solfa was concerned about her safety.

"It is all right, Solfa," Candy said. "I was never in any danger. Ervin is the leader of the clan and I knew the importance of our alliance. The last thing I wanted to do was demean him in the eyes of his people, by besting him. It was my hope he would back off before I had to inflict injury."

"Well," Solfa said, "at least one of you was thinking. When Jeryl found out, he was furious. The man still believes Candy could be his granddaughter. The whole idea of having the first female CT Guard was to protect you, Shirl. On the first mission out, you leave Candy alone. There was a small army available to protect you both. I just do not understand your reasoning, if you thought at all."

Solfa leaned back in her chair, her eyes still on Shirl. Candy was almost tempted to use their closed telepathic channel to help Shirl answer Solfa's accusations. She imagined there was more to Solfa's tirade then just the mission. Candy and Shirl had become part of Pattrice's extended family. If anything happened to either woman, Solfa's mother would fall apart.

"I hadn't expected him to react that way to Candy," Shirl finally replied. "Ervin knew she was special to me. I thought he'd treat her with the respect he showed me. Besides, men always want to just be Candy's pal."

Candy's surprise by Shirl's response was mirrored in Solfa's face. "Take a look at your friend, Shirl," Solfa raised her voice to a higher decibel. "She is a beautiful, desirable woman. The men of Ginkgo Terra must be idiots. Candy is worth her weight in crystals, to the men who live in the Terra Nova universe. In the future, you will meet with Koel before every mission and walk through various tactical scenarios. I have put him on retainer to work with my organization. There is not going to be a repeat of what happened today."

"Yes, Solfa," Shirl responded. Candy noticed Shirl would not make eye contact with either of them. She was not sure if it was because of what she said or her actions on Terra Nova. There had never been an awkwardness between them before. Candy did not know if she should talk to Shirl or let things blow over.

"The rest of the team is being interviewed to determine if there was anyone in the village who seemed out of place. Jeryl wants to expand missions to different worlds to look for escaped dissidents. The assassination attempt has made him more paranoid about other plots both inside the Troyk universe and from outside. You both need to report back to Crystal Telepath Headquarters for further orders."

Solfa rose and left the room without another word.

Both women just sat, letting Solfa's words soak in. Shirl was the first to break the silence. "I am so sorry, Candy. If I thought for one minute you were in danger, I never would have left you alone with him. Starc and I would have found another opportunity to practice gauging the strength of the portals I produce."

"Like I told Solfa," Candy replied, "I was never in any danger from Ervin." She could not voice how Shirl's words had hurt and belittled her. Candy had become popular once she started playing sports, just attracting men in a different way.

Shirl was always fighting off the type of attraction she got, while Candy enjoyed a camaraderie with men. She figured one day she would find the right guy and she would finally have the intimate relationship that generally developed between men and women. Never in a million years did she think Shirl thought less of her, because of the type of relationships she had with men. Neither had she imagined it would take traveling to a parallel universe to find the man who was literally her soul mate.

"We should be heading out," Shirl said as she rose to leave. Her friend gave Candy a long guilt-ridden look. Shirl turned and started to walk to the room's exit when she hesitated. "It didn't come out right."

"What?" Candy inquired.

"The crack I made about you and men. I didn't mean to discount you or your feelings. You never seemed to want more from men than the chummy relationships you developed with them." Shirl seemed to be struggling to come up with the right words. Candy did not feel obliged to change the topic of the conversation to relieve her friend from the burden of finishing. "You never wanted to become dependent on another human being, including me. Alex was your safety net when you needed help."

There was not a single untruth in what Shirl had said. Candy just did not want to discuss it with Shirl. She often wondered if Alex had not been there, would Candy and Shirl have become as close as they were now. She had not been lying to Jeryl Jarlyn about her relationship with Shirl. Candy had just left out Alex's role in their family dynamics. Alex seemed the glue that held their friendship together. It still bothered her Shirl had not called her when Alex disappeared.

"If we loiter any longer, Solfa is going to come back and investigate why we haven't left," Candy stated. "I do not want to get on that woman's bad side. She scares the shit out of me."

Shirl started laughing. The tension between the women was relieved for now. "It is hard to believe our chameleon friend is cousins with Solfa. Those two are like night and day." Alex did not even need to be present for their friendship to start bonding again. She just always seemed to be the common denominator between the two of them.

ᘯᕇ

This time when Candy entered Crystal Telepath Headquarters, the room was almost deafening with the number of oral conversations taking place. The crackdown on escaped dissidents generated conversations too sensitive for communal pathway usage. The tide of gossip had steered away from her. To say she was relieved would be a gross understatement. Living your life under a microscope was not easy.

"Let's see if we can find Starc or Darden," Shirl said through their closed channel. With the roar of conversations taking place, it was easier to hear each other through their own pathway. *"I was able to connect with them both through the warrior channel. They are getting a conference room where we can meet privately."*

Walking through the crowd of men, this time Candy did not try to make a connection with any specific man. She knew Tolfer was not among the crystal telepathic men and the CT Guards that populated the hall. Candy was still struggling over why he had not revealed the true nature of their relationship when the soul mate channel opened. It frustrated her that she was stuck at headquarters, preparing to go after people not unlike her parents. She was not offered the position of CT Guard. It was inflicted on her. Protecting Shirl was one thing, but going after people who tried to remove the mind control telepathic government from power was quite another. Was she even going to be paid? For someone who planned for every possibility, she was lost.

When they got to the conference room Starc was pacing like a caged tiger. Shirl immediately went into his arms and received a passionate kiss. Alex had mentioned that Shirl and Starc's relationship was strained almost from the beginning. As far as Candy could see, whatever their problem was, it had been worked out.

Darden sat at the table. "Candy," he finally greeted her. A serious look crossed his face. "What happened on Terra Nova? The communal pathways are communicating various tales about the first female CT Guard's maiden voyage through the portal." Originally he was supposed to accompany them to Terra Nova but was pulled off the duty to accompany another crystal telepath to Terra Flora.

"Everyone is making a mountain out of a molehill," Candy replied. She had to laugh at the expression on Darden's face. Obviously, he had not heard that expression before. "Nothing of any consequence happened."

"I would not consider being sexually assaulted as nothing of any consequence," Darden growled, quoting her own words. "Neither does Solfa. Not only she has ordered pre-mission consultations with Koel, I will be joining you for the foreseeable future as you enter the portal."

Candy knew those orders would reduce the amount of time, Darden would be able to spend on Earth with his soul mate Cassie. It would look suspicious if he continued making the number of trips to Earth while accompanying Shirl and her on their missions. She felt guilty, although she knew she did not do anything wrong.

"Why wouldn't they just add CT Guards to accompany us?" Candy asked. "It seems a terrible waste of a crystal telepath's time."

"It is a matter of trust," Darden replied. "Shirl has a tremendous amount of power. She needs to learn to regulate the energy blasts she produces, while not alerting others of her true capabilities." It was all about Shirl and Candy was caught in the crossfire. She once again wondered how she could resign from being a CT Guard.

Her thoughts on that subject were cut short when an alarm sounded. What in the world is happening now, Candy thought.

"CT Guards Narmouth, Potts, and Phillips, report for portal duty" came across one of the communal pathways. A public broadcast of orders seemed a strange way for a quasi-government department to operate.

"What am I supposed to do?" Candy wondered out loud. She knew CT Guards were responsible for guarding the portal. They investigated when an object entered their universe from another dimension. Sensors were set around the portal to sound an alarm. She just did not know the mechanics of what she was supposed to do.

"I will accompany you," Starc said. As a CT Guard, Starc knew all the protocols related to responding to such orders. "I will see you at the apartment later," he informed Shirl.

Starc and Candy left the conference room and made their way to the weapon storage area. This time she was less overwhelmed by all the futuristic pistols and rifles that graced the walls of the armory. The small, lightweight crystal guns she had used earlier were to her right. They seemed the appropriate weapon to use. She had actually done a very good job of hitting the targets when she fired the weapons after Nance had shown her the mechanics of using the weapon.

Starc attached a holster around her waist. Grabbing the weapons in her hands, he placed each into the holster. "We do not have a lot of time. Each crystal weapon has a two shot capacity. The safety is off. They are ready to fire as soon as you release them."

Firing at a target was one thing, but firing at a live target was quite another. "Is there a stun setting?" Candy asked. It was a question she should have asked earlier when she was getting her initial lesson. Candy had no desire to do anyone or anything harm. Back on Earth she had never considered becoming a police officer for this very reason. Self-defense was a different story. She did not mind getting physical if she was protecting herself or someone else.

Starc looked at her as if she was crazy. "We do not know what we are up against. The weapons are set on the highest setting. Once we assess the situation we can reduce the intensity of the blast." Starc must have picked up on her hesitation. "You did great at the range. If there is such a thing as a natural at this type of thing, it is you." He did not seem to understand her reluctance in accompanying them.

It was too late to do anything about her role as a CT Guard. Candy took a deep breath to calm her nerves and followed Starc to one of the side exits. Raine Narmouth and Kelog Potts were already there. They did not seem surprised at Starc's presence. The men were probably relieved they were not going to have to play nursemaid.

"Let us head out," Raine Narmouth ordered. His rank of captain placed him in charge of this mission. For the sake of their safety, Starc and Candy would not let their personal feelings toward Raine Narmouth impact their behavior. He would be dealt with another day.

Once they were outside, their party ran to the mountain trailhead. Candy was in excellent shape and kept up with the men with little effort. Their pace slowed once they started their ascent. There was only one way off the mountain. At this point they could catch their breath. They would be able to recharge their energy to deal with anything that came through the portal.

They continued to climb, making good time. Nothing crossed their path, which allowed Candy to relax a little bit. She was not sure what she would do if anyone challenged them from another universe. She was in the rear, several yards behind the others. She was their safety net, there to make sure nothing got past her and threatened Aster Province. It was also her responsibility to communicate their progress. Based on her reports, headquarters could dispatch additional men to provide back-up. Candy imagined this was the Troyk equivalent of televising police chasing a white Bronco through Los Angeles.

The men in front of her stopped. Something lay on the trail in front of a still-active portal. As Candy got closer she saw it was a human. Narmouth and Kelog were leaning over the body.

"Is he all right?" Candy inquired. She had been informed not to communicate through the communal pathways if a person had come through the portal. "Why is the portal still open?"

"Something is still in the portal," Starc answered. "He is not wearing a crystal. Whoever opened the gateway is inside the void." Starc stared at the portal a little longer. "A crystal telepath can open one portal and then work on opening a second one. Once the second portal is open, the first one closes. He is still going to come through or he ran into some kind of trouble."

"Candy," Raine addressed her, "get off this mountain and get a med-tech up here. I am still not convinced someone else will not come through the portal. Kelog and Starc will stay with me."

Candy had no issue with heading down the mountain alone. She wanted to divorce herself from this case. Without being told, she imagined the person who lay unconscious was a former Troyk freedom fighter. She wondered who he was. What was going to happen to him? Was she going to be forced to deal with the consequences of this assignment? All her questions eroded her confidence.

Chapter 8

Candy had not made it too far down the mountain, when she picked up the communal channels. It was a wonder Alex did not spend time hiking the mountain, away from the telepathic traffic within the communal pathways. The static she had not felt while she was closer to the portal had returned.

Tolfer was within the channels asking her out to lunch. What a strange way to ask a girl out on a date! Using the same pathway, she asked Raine if she could get an hour off after she dispatched the med-tech.

Candy was not surprised Raine gave her the time off. He knew she was living in the same residence as Alex. Better not do anything to alienate Candy. She had the power to ban him from the Childers's household. Considering Raine's obsession with her friend, maybe it would be a good idea not to allow Raine into the house. It would certainly buy her brownie points with Tarsea, her soul mate's brother. There was also the fact Alex was now pregnant.

By the time she made it to the trailhead, the med-tech was checking his equipment before he made his ascent. Living in a telepathic world certainly had its advantages. Troyk medicine was far more advanced compared to Earth's. Alex had told her Tarsea was up and ready to go back to work within minutes of the med-tech tending to his stab wound. Candy could not believe Narmouth had not been imprisoned for his near fatal attack on Tarsea. It all had to do with taking the spotlight off of Alex and maintaining her cover story.

Shirl had shared that the Troyk universe also had a serum that replaced blood loss ten times faster than the body could do by itself. The miracle liquid came from the Nightshade universe. Shirl got a faraway look in her eye when she talked about it. Candy knew there were aspects of Shirl's trip to that world that still haunted her friend. She did not feel comfortable asking Shirl for more details. There was a new strain in their relationship that had not existed previously. Candy had asked Alex, but her other friend told her it was Shirl's story to tell.

Shortly after the med-tech started on his trip to aid the man who came through the portal, Tolfer showed up. She had been surrounded by hordes of good-looking men since coming through the portal, but it was Tolfer who stirred her blood. That was actually a benign way to describe her body's reaction to him. She half expected to blow up in flames when he was near, especially after their first touch.

What she felt was what one soul mate was supposed to feel for another, she figured. Candy could not understand why Tolfer did not acknowledge the connection between them. Her one consolation was he was probably suffering worse than she was. At least that was what she hoped. It would serve him right!

He came up to her and smiled. That simple action almost brought her to her knees. Tolfer brightened her world. Who needed electricity with one's soul mate nearby? Candy needed to get a grip. She was thinking about nonsense.

"How much time have you got for lunch?" Tolfer asked. "I thought it would be a nice change of pace to eat something someone else prepared. Figured you could use a break as well."

Candy held back the giggle that almost escaped from her. She was not that kind of girl. "I don't have to report back to headquarters for two hours," Candy replied. Answering his question and adding nothing more, seemed to control her exterior response to being near Tolfer. Inside, she felt like a teenage girl at a rock concert.

"*Leftovers* is just around the corner. They have very good food and nice ambience."

"Ambience at lunch," Candy responded. "I did not know things between us were so serious," Candy kidded. Once she internalized what she had just said, she wanted to die.

Candy gathered her courage and looked Tolfer in the face after her blunder. Terror was written all over it. Had they not been soul mates, she would have thought the situation was funny. There was nothing humorous about the tension between the two of them.

She was the first to recover. "Lighten up, Tolfer," Candy said. "I was just playing with you. *Leftovers* sounds really nice. Back home, I did not have a lot of money, so eating out was a real luxury. I was a master at the microwave the rest of the time."

Although Candy knew she had to confront Tolfer about being soul mates, now was not the time. She was already stressed out about the fate of the man who came through the portal. Getting to know Tolfer over a lunch date seemed like a nice idea.

They walked in silence to the restaurant. She figured both of them were listening to different conversations within the communal pathways. Neither actively participated in what they were hearing. Tolfer held the door open when they reached their destination.

Candy was immediately captivated by her surroundings. *Leftovers* reminded her of an English tearoom. Small tables were scattered throughout the restaurant. Each table had a bud vase with a single purple rose and was set with china place settings. The color scheme was pink and yellow, a departure from the usual Troyk fashion, namely purple. The aroma of the food smelled absolutely fabulous.

They were immediately seated at a table that had a window overlooking a small garden. Candy was enchanted by the charming view and the silkscreened prints on the wall. Cheerful described the place well. The surroundings made her feel relaxed. After the day she was having, it was exactly what she needed.

"This place is lovely," Candy shared with Tolfer. She could see a lot of the evident tension in him released. His posture had been so stiff when they arrived. He now sat back in a relaxed pose. "I still do not know a lot about Troyk cuisine. Please order for the both of us."

That smile was back on his handsome face. She was thrilled she placed it there. Candy listened as he placed their order, through the communal pathway.

"What do you like to do when you are not cooking for your parents?" Candy felt that was a safe question to ask.

"Actually," Tolfer said, "I am pretty much a homebody. Cooking relaxes me. It started as a means of survival since my parents are horrid cooks. Eventually, it became my passion."

"Why don't you do it professionally?"

Tolfer laughed. "I have asked myself that same question a million times. It finally came down to my fear of losing my passion if it became how I made my livelihood. Besides, I find teaching very rewarding. When I reduce the pain a child suffers before he or she can manage the communal pathways, it makes it all worthwhile."

Candy was mesmerized by Tolfer's voice and the topic. She felt the same way when she worked with a kid who hated sports and improved their skills enough for them to enjoy themselves. There was a sport for everyone. She just had to find it and connect like-skilled kids together.

"I know how you feel. Every year I take some kids under my wing and work with them to find their hidden talents."

"Candy, you are only twenty-two years old. You cannot have been teaching for long."

"Even as a kid," Candy explained, "I took it upon myself to help others. It really bothered me when girls would make fun of the gals who weren't good at sports. I befriended them and worked with them. They would not be getting a college scholarship, but at least they are enjoying themselves. That is the whole idea anyway."

Candy felt Tolfer's gaze on her as she spoke. He seemed to absorb her words. She did not think anyone ever listened to her as Tolfer appeared to be. It was an amazing feeling. They were worlds apart, but had similar experiences and reacted the same way.

Before they could continue their discussion, the server placed three dishes on the table. One looked like tabouli, a favorite of Candy's. A second dish appeared to be sauteed vegetables. Various herbs covered the veggies. Her mouth watered anticipating the burst of flavors she was about to enjoy. The last dish consisted of a marinated mushroom salad.

Tolfer looked at her expectantly. It was obvious he really wanted her to enjoy their lunch together. "Alex said you preferred vegetables rather than protein. These are my favorite vegetarian dishes *Leftovers* serves."

Candy was touched Tolfer ordered with her in mind. She served herself several spoonfuls from each of the three dishes. Not surprisingly, each dish was distinctive and flavorful. She never could understand how people could boil the nutrients out of a vegetable, smother it with fat, and then expect to enjoy it.

"These are incredible, Tolfer," Candy shared with him. "We obviously have similar palates. Have you ever prepared a strictly vegetarian meal for your family?"

Tolfer looked at her in horror. "There would be a mutiny," Tolfer said. "My father and Tarsea tolerate vegetables as a side dish. I think they eat them to pacify my mother. I would never hear the end of it if I tried to make a full meal out of what they refer to as garnish."

Yet again, they both faced the same type of reactions from the people around them. Alex loved burgers and was willing to throw just about anything on them. Shirl ate salads, if she ate at all.

Candy eyed a number of incredible-looking desserts as servers passed her. Alex must not have mentioned to him her number one weakness: chocolate. All she had found in the Childers's kitchen was cocoa. What she would not give for a nice piece of Belgian dark chocolate.

Their waitress came to their table and placed a piece of chocolate cake in front of her. She had not heard Tolfer order it. She gave him a questioning look.

"When we were being seated," Tolfer said. "I whispered our dessert order to the hostess. It is hard to surprise someone if you use the communal pathways all the time."

Candy took a fork full of the sweet, closed her eyes, and moaned loudly. It was so good, she did not care if it sounded like she was having an orgasm in the middle of the restaurant. She heard Tolfer chuckle in response to her enjoyment of his gift. Alex did a great job of letting Tolfer know what Candy liked. What a wonderful job he did executing this perfect lunch.

Too bad she had to go back to work. There was still the fate of the man on the mountain. She hoped her role in his discovery was over. Candy figured that was not going to be the case.

Receiving orders telepathically was an odd experience. Candy was still conditioned to think hearing voices in your head was not a good thing. It led to a lot of therapy sessions and possibly a padded cell.

She had been instructed to report to interrogation room four in The Palace. Tolfer walked her over, stating he was going to listen to the Prime Council discussions occurring on the second floor. Candy liked his company. Being with him felt right. They felt right. She never felt as comfortable with a person, as she had with him at the lunch they just shared. It still plagued her that he had not acknowledged what they were to each other.

Candy headed for the third floor and found where she was assigned to report. Raine Narmouth and Kelog Potts were already standing outside the room. Once she arrived, they entered together. The prisoner had not been delivered. There were three chairs facing the door each of them claimed. No words telepathically or orally were exchanged.

It was a matter of minutes before two Palace Guards escorted the struggling man into the room. He was dressed in a yellow tunic and leggings. The man looked like a giant lemon. Although the med-tech had worked on him, he still was dreadfully pale and the yellow outfit did not help. It made his skin appear jaundiced. The man stopped and stared as soon as he made eye contact with Candy.

"Shelaura!" the man cried. He had called Candy by her mother's name.

Solfa had followed the small party into the room. She had picked up the man's declaration, staring at Candy with a warning to keep her mouth shut.

Kelog seemed momentarily stunned, while the other men seemed unaffected by the name Candy had just been called. A strange expression crossed Kelog's face after he collected himself. Candy was not sure how to read it. Obviously, she was seeing things that did not exist. Kelog had been kind to her from the moment she entered this world. This whole situation had her spooked and her brain was overcompensating, by developing intrigue where none existed.

"I assume you mean Shelaura Phildrum," Solfa said. The man was bound to the chair directly across from her. Solfa pulled a chair to the table's end and sat. "It would appear we know which of Benko's followers your mother was. Unless relationships changed once they arrived on Ginkgo Terra, your father was Bradsk Phildrum."

Solfa's revelation was not news to Candy. Darden had already shared this information with them. However, it was now officially communicated through the communal pathways. Jerlyn Jarlyn no longer had to wonder if she was his granddaughter. She was now partially free from further attention from the Prime Ruler from that respect.

"You speak of her parents as if they were no longer living," the man said. Candy could see sorrow written all over his face. He must have been close to her mother and possibly her father.

"They died shortly after my birth," Candy shared with the unidentified man. She desperately wanted to call the friend of her parents by his first name. "Who are you?"

"I am Symonn," the man answered. "Your parents were good friends of mine. We fought against the hideous practice of mind control together. My brother is a crystal telepath. We have searched for your parents for decades. Something went terribly wrong on our last trip."

Candy thought of the event horizon that remained open, where they had found Symonn unconscious. The portal finally closed thirty minutes after she had left to get the med-tech. It was unclear what happened to the crystal tele-path who opened the gateway.

She could feel Kelog's body tense next to her. Candy shifted her head and glanced at him. There was nothing in his expression that should have alerted her that anything was wrong. Maybe he was just tired after being on duty for so long.

"From your words," Solfa continued, "you are still opposed to our mind control telepathic rule. The fate of rebels against our government is to be sentenced to the penal colony."

Symonn straighted in his chair. "Such a world would be paradise if I am allowed to make my own choices." His voice shook with a tremor. Candy was not sure if it was out of dedication to the cause he fought so many years against or fear to be sentenced to the penal colony. Either way, he sealed his fate with those words.

Kelog looked at the man oddly. Once again, Candy's mind was playing tricks on her. There was something in the way he looked at the man that was not quite right. She just could not figure out why it kept nagging at her. Maybe he was just moved by the man's words and was trying to cover up the sympathy he had for Symonn. Such feelings in this world were not wise.

Solfa rose. "So be it." She turned and addressed Raine Narmouth. "Take him to the portal and execute the sentence of life in the penal colony. We are short-handed due to Cianan taking a small army with him on a mission for the Prime Ruler. Take Starc with you for added security. Shirl will set the coordinates. Potts, you are now off duty. You have worked a double shift and must be dead on your feet."

Candy knew better than to plead for Symonn. He had sealed his own fate with his declaration against mind control. She felt guilty that she could not save her parents' friend. Candy glanced at Solfa. The woman in charge of Troyk intelligence maintained a stoic expression. Candy knew she had secretly been helping those who would overthrow the government. Symonn's capture and confession had been too public to do anything but condemn the man to a life of unknown danger. Candy would have a hand in sending this man to his unknown fate. She swallowed the bile that rose in her throat.

Tolfer heard through the communal pathway that Candy would be accompanying a prisoner to the portal. Since they were undermanned he would volunteer to go along with them. Shirl and Starc's presence would make that desire a reality.

When he arrived at the disembarkation spot in The Palace courtyard, the small group had already assembled. Shirl was the first to notice him. "Good, Tolfer is going with us to provide additional support." She looked at him oddly and then glanced at Candy. It was clear Alex must have told Shirl, she suspected Tolfer was Candy's soul mate. He was not happy she had shared her suspicions. But it made it possible for him to spend more time with Candy. No one would go against Shirl's dictate.

Kelog came beside him. "Glad you are coming along," his old friend said. "Maybe it is time to reconsider your career choice. You could be so much more, Tolfer. When we sparred in school, you use to wipe the floor with me." The other man patted him on the back before he went to stand next to the condemned man.

"I thought you were off duty," Candy commented to Kelog. "This job is tough, I am about to fall flat on my face. It has been a long day."

"We are short-handed as Solfa said," Kelog responded. "It should not take long to deliver the prisoner to the portal. I will head home after the deed is done."

Tolfer noted an odd expression on Candy's face as she stared at Kelog. He knew his soul mate well enough to know that something was bothering her. A mental battle was going on within her mind. Once again, he wished he could reach her through their soul mate telepathic bond. He watched as she shook her head, obviously dismissing any suspicions she had related to his old friend Kelog.

"Let us head out," Raine ordered. Tolfer's attention was once again centered on Narmouth. It was a travesty he retained his rank after what had happened on his first command assignment.

Shirl had shared with him the calamity of that fated mission he led to escort two prisoners to the Nightshade universe for their executions. Raine had stayed behind to be near Alex, instead of properly delivering the prisoners.

The four guards he had sent through the portal were brutally murdered by the vampires of that world. His obsession with Alex had saved his life, but put a stain on his first command decision. "Tolfer, back up Candace," Narmouth yelled over his shoulder. "The prisoner will be sandwiched between the four of us. Starc and Shirl will bring up the rear until we arrive at the mountain."

They walked through streets bare of people. The communal pathways communicated their route. People evacuated the area as they made their way to the mountain trail. Troyk citizens never gawked at the prisoners clad in yellow, as they were led off world. He figured most people were just happy they were not the ones being led away. The prisoner himself walked with his hands bound behind him, presenting no resistance.

Tolfer wished he could communicate with Candy through their private channel. It had been his decision to keep their relationship to himself. He wanted to give Candy the choice to pick him rather than having the uncontrollable draw of the soul mate link prejudice her decision to be with him.

For the first time he wondered if Candy was struggling with feelings for him she did not understand. She was not from this world. He grew up listening to the legendary stories, wondering if he would one day be blessed with a soul mate of his own.

When Alex came into Tarsea's life he saw two people attracted to each other with an intensity all-consuming. He was taken aback when he learned his parents were soul mates. They had successfully kept the true nature of their relationship a secret, even from their own children. He always thought his parents were the perfect couple. Now he knew why.

It was not long before they reached the base of the trail that would take them to the natural portal. Shirl would lead the way since she would set the coordinates for the penal colony. Although she had never set those specific coordinates before, Shirl had trained in the simulator for such an eventuality.

They were getting closer to the portal. Tolfer knew Starc would be right beside Shirl as she set the coordinates. Their joining allowed Starc to navigate the portal alongside his soul mate. Every couple went through a different evolutionary change the first time they made love. What enhanced powers would he and Candy be gifted once they became lovers? He knew it would happen when Candy was both mentally and physically ready for intimacy. Tolfer would have to come clean about the true nature of their relationship to prepare Candy for what would happen after they sexually climaxed as one.

So engrossed in his thoughts, Tolfer had not realized they had reached the portal. It was a good thing he was not a CT Guard after all. Such inattention while he was performing his duties would be inexcusable. Worse, it could cost someone their life.

Natural portals opened as soon as a crystal telepath bearing their gems came within proximity of it. As required by protocol, Shirl partially stepped into the portal and set the coordinates. Not surprising, Starc was at her side. Together they stepped back out of the event horizon's grasp.

"It is ready," Starc reported. Tolfer noted Shirl gazing down at her feet. Her soul mate was taking over her official duty. Shirl must have been consumed with guilt over her role in sending someone to the penal colony. Candy silently made her way over to her, no doubt needing the closeness of a friend as Starc continued in his role as a CT Guard.

"You have the choice of walking through on your own or being dragged and pushed," Raine informed the prisoner. "I have no idea what is on the other side of the portal. It would be prudent to be physically prepared for any eventuality. A forceful arrival would put you at a further disadvantage if you are met with hostile forces."

The prisoner slowly walked toward the portal. Kelog nudged Candy and the two of them followed. Tolfer hoped his soul mate would not be placed in the position where she would have to force the man through. Kelog took a knife and cut the man free of the rope that bound his hands. Rather than sheathing the blade, Kelog kept it in his hand.

Symonn turned and addressed Candy. "I loved your mother" was all he said before before he stepped a foot into the portal.

"Wait, Symonn," Tolfer heard the anguish in Candy's words. He realized this was her one chance to get answers to lifelong questions on parents she never knew. She hurried to the man, not wanting him to go yet.

Tolfer's heart jumped as she moved from his reach. When Kelog sprang after her, Tolfer released his swallowed breath; he thought the guard would keep her safe. But he was wrong.

He watched in horror as Kelog Potts grabbed Candy and plowed into Symonn, dragging all three through the portal.

He looked at Shirl, who was being held back by Starc. It was obvious she was going to follow Candy through the portal. She looked in his direction pleading for him to do something. Tolfer did not hesitate: he ran through the event horizon after his soul mate.

Chapter 9

~

The Troyk Penal Colony World

Candy tried to stop her forward momentum and release herself from Kelog's grasp. She had no idea why he had grabbed her and forced her into the portal. Part of her wanted to beat the crap out of him, but she reasoned it was better to determine what type of greeting party they were about to face. Just as she accomplished freeing herself from Kelog, she was pushed forward yet again by another body exiting the portal. She turned to see Tolfer.

He placed his hands on her shoulders, "Are you all right?" He was addressing her, but his eyes were transfixed on Kelog. They were burning with a fury she had never seen.

"I am fine," Candy replied. He moved forward toward Kelog and Candy grabbed his arm. *"Don't do anything stupid,"* she added, using a connection she felt was their soul mate channel. It was time to end the game they both had been playing. *"We don't know what we are up against. Kelog may end up being needed. Besides, he has a knife."*

Tolfer seemed taken aback by her use of their private channel. He now knew she was aware of what they were to each other. However, there were more pressing matters at hand.

As her eyes swept the area, she saw they were being approached by men with nasty looking spears. Kelog stood next to her, his knife still in his hand. Against half a dozen armed men, the knife did not appear as large as it did when Kelog had used it earlier to cut Symonn's restraints. Why did she not bring along a crystal weapon or two when they delivered their prisoner to the portal? Although they were only good for two to three shots, they would have certainly improved the odds.

"What have we here?" a man walked past the ones with the weapons. He was older than the others, probably their leader. He had an angry-looking scar across his left cheek, stopping just under his eye. Candy took it as a good sign that he was talking at this point. "One prisoner, two CT Guards, and a lovesick fool."

Candy was taken aback by the man's description of Tolfer. Her gaze drifted to her soul mate to see what expression he had on his face to make the man believe he was in love with her. It was a dangerous thing to do, but she had to know.

"I am Symonn Oliverre, a freedom fighter. These children are harmless. An unfortunate impulsive move by my nephew brought them here."

Candy shifted her gaze to Kelog. Why hadn't Solfa's intelligence identified the familial tie between the prisoner and the CT Guard? They must have been communicating through the familial pathway that existed between those who shared the same blood. Deep down Candy must have known. The feelings she had earlier had not been a figment of her imagination after all. In the future, she will need to heed her intuition, assuming there was a future.

"Both of our families are in this world," Kelog Potts replied. "I am tired of pretending to be something I am not, supporting a government I find offensive."

"We will determine your worth," the leader of the gang said. There was an edge to his voice this time. He probably was growing impatient with all the conversation between his prisoners.

"The boy with the curly black hair is not to be hurt," a female voice came out of nowhere. Candy turned in the direction of the voice. A beautiful blond woman walked toward them. She was momentarily jealous of the woman's interest in Tolfer. Candy could never compete with the stunning vision before her.

"Do I have reason to be concerned about your desire for the lovesick puppy, my love?" The man with the scar took the woman into his embrace. He kissed her roughly, staking his claim. If she was not mistaken, the woman was barely tolerating it. Was this something she had to look forward to? Survival had to be her first concern, not what it took to do it.

"He is a friend," the blonde replied, "nothing more. Tolfer is part of a group I owe my life to. It is your bed I share, Franclyn."

"Let us keep it that way, Chartail," the scarred man growled.

Candy gasped at the name. Here was the woman Alex had befriended and then betrayed. The very same individual who masterminded the failed attempt to assassinate the Prime Ruler. The one Shirl saved in the Nightshade universe. Chartail had been recaptured and sentenced to live her life here. Darden had taken her to the portal the day before they came to Earth to bring Candy to the Troyk universe. It did not take Chartail long to ingratiate herself with this powerful man. The woman's self-preservation skills were strong.

Chartail walked and stood before Candy. "Who are you, other than Tolfer's new squeeze?" She appeared to think about her last statement. "Although I certainly do not remember Tolfer being so struck by a woman before."

"My name is Candace, Candy to my friends." It was obvious Chartail recognized her name. Chartail's face lit up with delight. Shirl and Alex had made quite an impression on this woman. Candy had an ally without having to build an alliance.

"Add her to my span of protection, Franclyn. I owe her friend a debt I will never be able to repay. Get your blood-thirsty kicks with the remaining two." Chartail's light tone was contradictory to her dark words.

"As you wish, my love," Franclyn replied. He motioned for the men with spears to deal with Kelog and his uncle.

Candy's own self-preservation mode must have been broken. She stepped next to Kelog, taking a defensive stance. The men hesitated, looking toward Franclyn and Chartail for further instructions. Candy heard Tolfer mutter something under his breath before joining her. He mirrored how she stood. It was questionable whether he would know what to do when the fighting began.

"Looks like we are going to have a show after all!" Franclyn exclaimed. "The two CT Guards will fight against two of my men." It was clear to Candy the man was getting a perverse thrill from all of this.

"Without spears," Chartail yelled. "Kelog, you will have to give up your knife."

"Fine," Franclyn grunted. "If the two CT Guards win, we will negotiate your place in this world. Our victory will result in the immediate death of the freedom fighter and the male CT Guard. The boy will serve my new queen. The female CT Guard can warm the bed of her victor, as Chartail warms mine."

Candy did not like the terms if she lost this battle. It was debatable who had the worse fate if they lost, her or Kelog. She figured her opponent would not do too much damage to her, considering what winning bought him. The largest of the six men stood before her. Just her luck, Candy thought. A second man went to stand before Kelog while the others led Symonn and Tolfer away at the point of their spears. It was obvious Tolfer was not happy with the arrangement. He tried to resist being separated from her and was pierced with the spear. She could see blood seeping through his tunic in several spots.

"You need to let me do this," she communicated to her soul mate. *"If you continue to fight them, you will distract me from what I have to do."* It was clear Tolfer heard her plea and ceased his opposition against the guards. Now she needed to concentrate on winning her contest against Franclyn's man.

She should have kept her eyes on her opponent, rather than watching Tolfer led away. A giant fist came at her, connecting with her jaw. The metallic taste of her blood was mingling with the saliva in her mouth. So much for her first thought that the man was not going to try and do her any harm. She was out-sized, as well as outweighed in this battle. Under different circumstances her best option would have been to run.

The large man charged at her, his forward momentum, bringing them both down before she could react. Candy came down hard. The wind was knocked out of her. She struggled to breathe. The man grabbed her hands and extended them over her head. His weight pressed hard across her torso, making it impossible to move. She had a little movement available in her legs. Candy had no idea how Kelog was doing. Her opponent had taken her out of the battle.

"Wrap your legs around his waist, Candy," Tolfer ordered. *"He has you pinned down pretty well. If you turn it sexual, you may break his concentration. Bite, scratch, do whatever it will take to turn the tables. Fight dirty, Scotty."*

"Who the hell is Scotty?" Candy demanded as she responded to Tolfer. What he was suggesting was insane, but she did not see any other options. There was nothing to lose at this point. She had enough mobility to somewhat straddle her legs against his hips. The strategy paid dividends as her opponent eased up. She still did not have an opening she could take advantage of.

"Tarsea calls Alex "my little pixie." I have been trying to come up with an endearment to call you. With a name like Candy, you can imagine my challenge." Candy did not know who was annoying her more, her challenger or her soul mate. *"Try to shift your legs closer to his waist. A fake moan would be helpful. Make him believe you are hot for him."*

Candy did as Tolfer recommended. She let out the best fake moan she had ever produced. The man on top of her released one of her hands as he started to squeeze her left breast. It hurt like hell, but she let out a groan of encouragement. Candy maneuvered her hand down his side, making her way down to his erect member. She needed to bide her time, making him think it was an act of passion rather than an offensive move to unman him.

"Let me touch you," she groaned, as she came upon the barrier of his thick pants. He would have to release her breast or her other hand, if he was going to free himself. The imbecile did more than free her hand, he temporarily shifted off her. He fit the stereotype of big and dumb to the letter. She could not believe her luck.

Candy sprung to her feet and kicked him in the groin. As her opponent hunched over in pain, Candy went for his knees. He went down, still writhing from her first attack. Payback for the punch in the face was going to be her next move, when she was stopped by someone grabbing her waist. Adrenaline was still pumping through her system, she was not ready to stop fighting.

"Enough," Franclyn called, as he continued to hold a struggling Candy. "Take Melvyn to the stockades where he can lament nearly being castrated by a woman. Drag Fletch to his barracks." Candy was released and looked over to where Kelog had an unconscious man in a chokehold.

Chartail came over to Candy and took her hand. "Well fought," she whispered in Candy's ear. "Franclyn will accept you in the tribe as a warrior. You will not have to barter for your life on your back with a man you detest inside you."

Candy did not know what to say in response to Chartail's comment. Fighting with Tolfer over a stupid pet name seemed so trivial compared to what this woman faced.

"Bring the prisoners to the tribunal chamber for the discussion related to their fate," Franclyn ordered. He walked to Candy and Chartail and extended a hand to both women. Gallantry and barbarity mingled together.

Candy accepted his hand and walked along with the procession, as they made their way to determine her fate.

⌒○

Tolfer did not appreciate being called a boy or a lovesick fool. His options were limited at this point. It had been difficult being held back as his soul mate fought for their standing in the tribe. Thankfully, Chartail was here and helped protect them to the best of her ability. Tolfer never realized how resourceful his brother's former girlfriend was. The failed assassination plot of the Prime Ruler, she instigated, was what got her sentenced here after the scandal of what happened in the Nightshade universe.

Tolfer's eyes bore into the back of Franclyn as he walked with Chartail and his soul mate. More men became visible as they made their way into the village. He noted very few women. Candy presented a commodity to these desperate men. Tolfer noticed Candy's back became ramrod straight as she too must have noticed what he observed. Would she have to continue to fight to protect herself against the men in this village? He had never felt more inadequate in his life.

They stopped in front of a hut. "You will stay here while we convene the tribunal," Franclyn advised. "Chartail you may remain with them. They no doubt have many questions that need to be answered. We will send for you after a decision is made."

Tolfer led the way into the barren hut. There were no chairs, merely animal skins on the floor. He figured it would be a good idea to store vital strength. Tolfer arranged the pelts so he and Candy could sit. It was the least he could offer her after her ordeal.

"I was expecting more people, I must confess," Symonn said. "All those dissidents sentenced to this world over the years. Where did they all go?" There was such a hopeless tone to his words. He could not get caught up in the depressed mood he felt around him. They had to keep up their spirits as long as they could.

"They live across the gorge," Chartail advised them. "We are in the village of the portal guardians. When they first started sending hardened criminals here it was anarchy. The prisoners were pretty much at each other's throats.

They lived like animals. When Franclyn came through he saw the benefit of controlling the portal, especially when supplies started coming through.

"Franclyn banded the group together and built a strong community around the portal. As more people came through you toed his line or you were thrown out. Those people had to deal with this world with no supplies and with mad men, who roamed the area who had survived on their own all these years."

"What about the dissidents?" Symonn asked.

"When freedom fighters started to be sentenced to this world," Chartail said, using Symonn's terminology, "more women started to come across. Franclyn and the others were unwilling to change how things worked around here. Finally, there was an uprising organized by Alaura Keltore. Franclyn expelled them all from the village. They built their own community across the gorge. It gave them a natural defense against the portal guardians."

"Is she still living?" Candy asked. When she first heard that her grand-mother was sent to the penal colony she accepted the fact that she'd never meet her family. Now, she was too afraid to hope.

"Yes, although I have not met her," Chartail responded. "Why do you ask?"

"She is my grandmother," Candy replied. Telling Chartail of her relation-ship with the pioneering woman did not seem an issue. With everything that had happened between Chartail and her friends, she was one person Candy knew she could trust.

"That is something you could use later," Chartail said, "depending on the tribunal decision. Alaura would pay a Prime Ruler's ransom for you."

"Have you heard anything about the Oliverre family?" Kelog inquired. Tolfer was still struggling over why his former friend had forced Candy through the portal. He had known him his whole life and never suspected all he had been hiding. Tolfer and his friends and family had their own secrets. He won-dered if everyone in the Troyk universe lived one big lie.

"I have not left this village since my arrival. Franclyn keeps me on a short leash." Chartail widened her stance, daring anyone to feel sorry or judge her. Tolfer only had respect and admiration for what this woman had been through. They could all learn something from Chartail, she was a survivor.

Tolfer padded the space next to him, indicating for Chartail to sit. For a moment she hesitated and then joined him on the floor. He wrapped his arm around her shoulder and dragged her body closer to his. "It will be all right, Chartail. Somehow we will find a way to free you."

"We merely have to wait and stay alive. Shirl will come for her," Chartail indicated to his soul mate who had also come closer to his body for warmth. "Your brother and the others will come for you. They will not rest until you both are free from this world. Just like they came for Shirl, when she was held captive in the Nightshade universe." Chartail did not have to add that her rescue from that world was only due to their saving Shirl. No one would come to this world for her, but they would for Candy and him.

Tolfer tightened his grip on his soul mate. He could only wish that Chartail's prediction was correct.

Chapter 10

The Troyk Universe

Shirl sat back on the couch as the men discussed various scenarios on how to rescue Tolfer and Candy from the penal colony. No one had questioned Tolfer's decision to follow Candy, once they learned she was his soul mate. Alex sat next to Leenea, comforting her. She had taken them all into her home. It was their turn to look after this wonderful woman. She had been devastated by the news her youngest son had willingly walked through the portal.

"We need an army," Darden said in frustration. "There is no telling what we are going to come across once we enter that world."

Shirl still hesitated in sharing the plan she was hatching in her brain. As she had done so often in the past, she clasped her hand around the crystals that hung around her neck. The amethyst would allow her to enter the penal colony, but would spell ruin if a criminal crystal telepath in that world got a hold of it. Rescuing Candy and Tolfer could not unleash the colony's criminal element on the Troyk or any other universe. She needed to be able to navigate without it.

The black crystal could potentially decimate any force that stood before an energy portal like the one she had opened on Terra Nova. Two dozen men had been incinerated by the blast. She never thought she would ever contemplate unleashing such power again. For Candy she would. Shirl would not hesitate to do anything to save her friend. Things between them had been strained as of late. That did not mean she would not move heaven and earth to rescue her.

For the first time since returning from the Nightshade universe, she wore the blood opal Drake had given her. The vampire who had claimed and protected her had given her the crystal that would give her free passage back to him. To rescue Candy, she would return to the world where vampires ruled. A world she swore she would never revisit. Back to a vampire who generated feelings in her, she did not ever want to explore again.

Multiple male voices cut through the barrier she had placed around her brain as she considered her options. Another telepathic enhancement to her powers.

"We have an army," Shirl said as she cut off something her soul mate Starc was saying. "Actually, we have three armies. I have so much power, it scares and humbles me at the same time. We also have Koel, who is a tactical genius from what I understand. Secondly, Ervin Allaway from Terra Nova owes me a debt I plan to collect in full."

There was a silence as the men considered what she presented. "And the third?" Koel asked.

"The Nightshade vampires," Shirl answered. As expected, that comment was met with angry voices. She let the men vent their opinions regarding the last army she wanted to use. It was critical she had everyone on board. There was not a scenario she considered they could win without the vampires.

"Can they be trusted?" Alex asked. She was as desperate as Shirl was to save Candy.

"Drake can be," Shirl answered her friend. "He gave me this blood opal. No harm would come to me in the Nightshade universe, as long as I present the crystal. They are starving for blood. Just a handful of vampires loyal to Drake would give us an awesome advantage."

"Are they sensitive to light?" Alex asked.

"If they are," Koel said, "we would plan the attack accordingly. These vampires would be an incredible asset if we can control them. No innocents can be attacked." Shirl sighed with relief. Koel was open to discussing the logistics around using the Nightshade forces. If he was not up to discussing working with vampires, Shirl would not have been able to convince the others.

"I cannot believe you are even considering this lunacy," Starc lashed out at his cousin. "You were not there when they literally ate Stephano and four CT Guards."

"But Shirl was," Koel reasoned, "and she spent time with this Drake character. If she feels she can trust him, I am certainly willing to consider taking advantage of the strength they will provide. Our options are extremely limited. I do not like our odds without the Nightshade forces."

Shirl appreciated the trust Koel placed in her. They had spent so little time together, she barely knew her soul mate's cousin. Lately he seemed obsessed with finding his own soul mate. Now, fortunately, his razor focus was on saving her friend and Tolfer.

"I am positive I can trust him and the men he selects," Shirl responded to Koel. Starc glared at her. Disapproval from her soul mate was clear from his silence, not sharing his thoughts even through their soul mate channel. There was no question he was concerned about her past reactions to Drake. Starc could sulk all he wanted, she was going to make this happen. Regardless of what they ultimately did, she knew her soul mate would stand beside her.

Koel rose and started to pace. "Can we enter the penal colony from three separate worlds? Can you navigate without a crystal once we are ready to return? Are the penal colony's sunrises and sunsets the same as in the Troyk universe? How many weapons can we get? Those are just some of the questions we have to address before we can execute this rescue."

Shirl was overwhelmed by the magnitude of what they were taking on. It would take days, possibly weeks to plan. Every nuance had to be identified and planned for. Shirl also knew she was the center point in their plan, if they had any hope of succeeding.

"We also have to determine ahead of time what we plan to do with our allies in that world," Tarsea added. "Namely, Chartail." Shirl knew she and Alex were going to suffer over that decision. She also knew they could not be caught again in this world with Chartail. Jeryl Jarlyn had been understanding regarding why Shirl had rescued Chartail from the Nightshade universe. A second discovered rescue would be disastrous for all involved. This would be a very visible rescue once they returned. The communal pathways were still abuzz about what happened to Candy and Tolfer.

"I want to enter the penal colony through the Nightshade universe," Alex announced. "Checking out Drake is too much of an opportunity to miss."

As expected, Alex's comment brought about another chorus of voices. She was not sure if Alex was serious or yet again testing her soul mate Tarsea.

Shirl leaned back and closed her eyes. She blocked out everything around her. Candy and Tolfer were possibly fighting for their lives. Shirl could only hope they would get to them in time.

Chapter 11

~

The Troyk Penal Colony World

They were led to a large hut in the middle of the village. Candy had been surprised it had taken the tribunal hours to determine their fate. Frankly, she did not know if that was a good or bad sign. It was critical she maintain a calm exterior, even if she was shaking like a leaf on the inside.

The building was so crowded, there was barely room for the five of them. Candy scanned the group and her eyes lit on an older woman. Her face looked like an artist's rendition of the one she looked at in the mirror every morning, aged forty years. Tears formed in her eyes, knowing they were basking on her grandmother.

Franclyn approached her. "The Utopia settlement bartered hard for the four of you. Old man, you will go with them, you are not welcome here. The two warriors are welcome to join our clan. We respect the strong, the smart. You both would find life here an adventure, as you are challenged to fight your way to our elite. Candace, you would have your pick of any man you desire, if the lovesick puppy does not appeal to you. Pup, I assume you will follow the woman warrior. If you go with the old woman, you will be farmers. That life would break the spirit of any warrior. The choice is yours."

"I am honored by your invitation to join your family of warriors," Candy said. There was no reason to insult the man. She was sure they would have to deal with each other in the future. "I am a teacher, not a warrior. My place is within the Utopia community. May I come back and see your queen? Perhaps she can visit me as well."

Franclyn looked between the two women. He appeared to consider his options. An evil smile crossed his face. "You are welcome to come visit Chartail as often as you desire. However, you must fight for the privilege of my queen's presence." The bastard held all the cards where Chartail was concerned.

"I look forward to it," Candy replied. To Chartail she said, *"We will find a way to get you released. If you know what he desires more than you, tell me."* Alex had mentioned Chartail had linked into the pathway that opened when the three of them were in the orphanage. It had surprised the other two, when Chartail joined their telepathic conversations.

"There is a woman that comes and visits him. I know nothing about her. He has not seen her since I have been here."

"I have no idea how far the telepathic channel will reach," Candy shared with her. *"I will stay in touch with you, to the best of my ability. Even if I have to do serious damage to one of these men."* Actually, she looked forward to such an eventuality.

Candy embraced Chartail and joined the contingent from Utopia. Wedged between Tolfer and Kelog, they prepared to leave the portal guardian village. Candy felt the familial relationship between her and Alaura would negate the agreement reached. At no point did Candy look in the direction her grandmother stood.

No words were interchanged as they left the encampment with nothing, just their lives. Candy wondered what these people had to give up to manage their release.

The path they took narrowed, as they entered the forest. Kelog pulled back and walked beside his uncle, leaving her to continue next to Tolfer. There was a momentary reprieve between being hostages to whatever they found in the Utopia village. Candy knew she needed to distract herself from what would happen once they reach the settlement.

"So, Pup," she used their soul mate channel, *"what's the deal with the name Scotty?"* She glanced at Tolfer. A warmth spread over her as she watched him grin at the name Franclyn had given him. Candy knew they were the same age, but he looked younger at that moment.

"Butterscotch is my favorite candy," Tolfer confessed to her. *"Scotty just seemed to fit. Although I have only known you a short period of time, I figured 'baby' or 'darling' would not please you."* He was right about the latter. However, she did not like the name he came up with.

"*Think again, Pup.*" His grin had bloomed into a full smile, when she called him that name again. Candy had never noticed the dimples that graced his face until that moment. How she wanted to kiss each of those adorable indentations.

She was still engrossed in looking at his face when Tolfer grabbed her arm and stopped walking. Her grandmother stood before them.

"I would like to walk a while with my granddaughter, young man," Alaura said. "Get to know my guards, while I do the same with my girl." Jeryl Jarlyn had called her the same name. Perhaps it was a generational expression, used to address younger family members. Drawing any other comparison between the Prime Ruler and her grandmother was not a road she wanted to travel.

Tolfer left her side with no resistance. Alaura came alongside her without missing a beat in her step. Her grandmother was almost as tall as she was. Finally, she knew where her height came from. Considering how women started to shrink when they reached a certain age, Candy figured in her prime Alaura was taller than she was now.

"How did you know I was in the village?" Candy asked her grandmother. It was so odd conversing with a member of her biological family. She had never imagined this day would come. Alex and Shirl had always been her family. Her two friends had found members of their family in the Troyk universe. She had to get dragged into the penal colony to find hers. Whether Kelog did her a favor when he pushed her through the portal, was still debatable.

"Your thoughts were leaking through my familial link," her grandmother answered. "Never thought I would hear another voice in that channel." Her grandmother stared ahead at Tolfer. "You really care for that boy."

Candy now knew what it was like to be cross-examined by a parent over a new beau. When she was in high school, she would listen to acquaintances complain about the interrogations. Secretly, she would have changed places with them in a heartbeat.

"He is caring, nurturing, and has a killer smile." Candy had never thought about Tolfer's qualities. Continually her focus had been on the all-consuming pull of the soul mate connection. She always took care of herself, never wanting to rely on anyone. The characteristics she described were things she thought she would never want. The need to be cared for by Tolfer really shook her.

"Yes, you really have it bad for that young man. What does he do for a living?"

Candy smiled at her grandmother's continued questioning of her relationship with Tolfer. Then it dawned on her that her grandmother did not ask her about her mother or any particulars about herself. Her smile faded.

Her grandmother nodded. "You think I am cold not asking after Shelaura. In this world you have to deal with the here and now in order to survive." Her grandmother patted her on the back. "You must learn to manage the familial pathway. Your young man has been remiss."

"I did not know I had a familial pathway," Candy replied under her breath. She never minded being corrected if there was a reason for it. Candy also did not appreciate her grandmother criticizing her soul mate.

The animosity that was developing between her and her grandmother troubled her. Candy decided to ask a factual question about this world. Something that was not personal, would hopefully curtail the friction.

"Are there other settlements other than yours and the portal guardians?"

"Various people broke off from us over the years. Some did not like the proximity to the guardians. They felt they could live without what meager supplies the Troyk universe sent through that ultimately landed in their laps. Some ventured farther into this world. We never saw them again. There is another settlement half a day's walk. People in that village do not use their telepathic abilities because it was that ability that led them to being exiled here."

"I was born in a world that does not have people with telepathic abilities. Now that I know about and have used it, I cannot imagine only communicating verbally." She decided against mentioning the soul mate channel and the intimacy it provided.

"We will meet tonight, once we are safe in the village. Then you can tell me all about yourself and your adventures." Her grandmother stopped walking for a moment.

Her grandmother pulled back her shirt's sleeve. Two copper familial bracelets became visible. Alaura removed one of the bracelets and handed it to Candy. "This was your mother's."

Candy held back the tears she felt building. Although Shirl and Alex both wore their mother's familial bracelets, Candy figured Shelaura's was lost upon her death. Without a word, Candy placed the cuff around her left wrist. "Thank you," she managed to say. She did not want to start crying in front of her grandmother.

Alaura embraced Candy and whispered in her ear. "Shelaura is dead. I sensed it years ago. Never mention her again." There was such finality in her words. It was as if a door was now permanently closed.

Candy never liked to talk about her parents. Now that it was forbidden, Candy had a consuming need to know about her mother. What was Shelaura like before she took that fateful step into the portal? She stared at her mother's bracelet.

⁓⊙

Tolfer actually enjoyed walking and conversing with Alaura's guards. An immediate camaraderie developed between him and these men. His friends in the Troyk universe were his brother's, not his own. Rather than feeling trapped in this world, he felt like it was a new beginning.

They came to the gorge he had been told about. He figured it was twenty yards wide. Looking down he saw a raging river surrounded by boulders on both sides. Ropes graced the face of the opposite side's cliff. A man was climbing one of the ropes with the fish he must have caught. Several men were still at the bottom trying to catch dinner. It was probably a thirty-foot climb to the top.

A rope bridge connected the two sides. If Tolfer was a betting man, he would wager it was made of hemp. Candy came up alongside him.

"We are going to cross the gorge on that? It looks more like a wall hanging than something that will hold our weight." He had to laugh at Candy's rich description of the bridge that crossed the canyon.

"Scotty, where is your sense of adventure?" She threw him a dirty look. From that expression, he figured he would have to come up with another endearment for her. Tolfer never realized how difficult it was to determine an appropriate pet name for a girl. To be fair to himself, he had never had a relationship get serious enough for him to consider calling a girl anything other than her name.

Tolfer watched as two men he talked with earlier started across the bridge. It looked like it would hold the weight of two people crossing at a time. Each person grasped both sides of the bridge as they moved forward. Reinforcing the bridge with wood would make the bridge steadier. Plans started to germinate in his mind.

"Come on, Sunshine," Tolfer addressed Candy with a new name. Whenever she smiled at him it was like a sunbeam in his heart. The new name was not greeted with any more excitement than the first. "Let us make our way to the other side. Your grandmother just finished her trip. You do not want her to outshine you." Candy grunted at the pun as she walked toward the bridge.

"You first, Pup," Candy said as she extended her hand, inviting him to go before her. Little did she know he was up for the challenge. He had watched the others before them and felt he had the technique down.

Watching from afar was one thing, but actually stepping on the hemp bridge was quite another. It shook with each step he took. He grabbed the makeshift hand railings to steady his nerves, more than his body. The ropes once again gave way as Candy joined him. Tolfer took a deep breath and continued forward.

"Speed it up, Pup," Candy came up behind him. He could feel her breasts crushed against his back. "I want to get off this piece of pre-Colombian art." He had no idea what she was referring to, but he agreed with her sentiment.

"Keep calling me by that name," Tolfer replied, gritting his teeth, "I will have you on your back and show you what kind of animal I am." He had no idea where that comment came from. It created vivid images in his mind, featuring him and Candy. Tolfer got a shot of adrenaline from the interplay in his thoughts.

"Promises, promises," he heard Candy mutter behind him. She matched him step for step as they made their way across and finally off the bridge. He had a momentary desire to fall to his knees and kiss the ground.

Once he recovered from his relief of making it across the gorge, he was surprised to hear children laughing. He followed the sound, as Candy followed. There in the center of the village were a dozen children playing with a number of coconuts. Alaura joined them.

"Children," Tolfer said. He was not sure if he meant it as a statement or a question. It should not surprise him that men and women together in this world would reproduce.

"The Troyk government not only sentenced us to this world, but our offspring. In all the care packages sent over the years, not once did they send diapers or other goods that would aid our babies. Your talents are more needed than you can imagine, young man."

"It would be my pleasure to work with the kids," Tolfer shared with Alaura. "I also have some ideas how that bridge can be reinforced." He was going to make the most out of being here. Back home, he never considered using his hands to create anything. Here, it looked like it was going to become a necessity.

"He can also cook," Candy added as she came up and kissed him on the cheek. It was their first kiss. A kiss between friends. He was going to have to work with her on more intimate kisses. That would fill many enjoyable hours in their new home.

"Any talents that will add value to our collective would be appreciated," Candy's grandmother said. "Tolfer, you and the other men will stay here." The woman gestured to the hut they stood before.

"Where is Candy staying?" Tolfer inquired. He did not like being separated from his soul mate. Living apart from her when she resided with his parents was one thing. This was something totally different.

A knowing grin crossed Alaura's face. "There is a new hut we just constructed closer to the gorge that has not been assigned to anyone as of yet. The two of you can share, if you desire."

"It is desired," Tolfer replied. He grabbed Candy's arm, looking into her eyes, daring her to object. Rather than defiance written on her face, he was met by a neutral glance. Tolfer was not sure how to read that look.

"It is yours then," Alaura stated as she walked away chuckling. Candy followed her grandmother, leaving him behind.

"Brave move, my friend," Kelog replied. Tolfer glanced at the man next to him. He needed his friend to explain why he went through the portal and took his soul mate with him.

"You could not possibly have known what was on the other side of the portal. What possessed you to walk into the event horizon and take Candy with you?"

"I was always envious of your family, Tolfer," Kelog explained. "When you had me over, I was overwhelmed by the love your parents and brother had for you. Even Tarsea's friends would have done anything for you. My parents gave me to distant relatives to care for when they started their anti-government activities. The Potts never wanted me and were staunch pro-government supporters. I never knew what happened to my parents. They could be here."

"But why Candy?"

"Her family is here, Tolfer. When I found out today who she really was, I knew what I had to do. She should be with her family."

Tolfer shook his head. "Shirl and Alex are her family."

"Alexia?" Kelog questioned. It was not long before the realization of Alex's true identity came to his former friend. "But how were you able to hide who she is?"

"She is my brother's soul mate, as Starc is Shirl's," Tolfer shared with his former friend.

"And Candy must be yours. Why else would you follow her into the portal?"

Tolfer did not feel obligated to reply to Kelog's assumption. "Regardless of my relationship with Candy, I still have not determined whether or not I am going to kill you for what you did today. You could have condemned her to a life of prostitution or worse. Just watch your back." He walked away from his former friend. There was not a homicidal bone in his body, but Kelog did not know that. To compensate for his act, he imagined Kelog would do everything in his power to assure Candy was protected. The true question was whether Tolfer was strong enough to protect his soul mate.

Candy walked around the hut her grandmother left her to explore. It was hard to believe her grandmother had agreed with her and Tolfer sharing a lodging. Alaura told her she would be back later with supplies and to accompany them to the evening communal meal. This place was barely large enough for one. How was she going to share these close quarters with Tolfer?

"Cozy, Stretch?" her soul mate said as he entered.

"Enough with the ridiculous names, Tolfer," Candy replied. "I'll strike a deal with you. I won't call you Pup, if you just call me Candy." This tiny place would have the two of them at each other's throats before the day was out.

"But, Blossom," Tolfer had come up behind her and whispered in her ear. "Everyone calls you Candy." He was caressing her neck, driving her crazy. Maybe these stupid names weren't so bad after all.

"Shut up," Candy said, as she turned around and her lips found his. After everything she had been through today, she really needed this.

Candy had kissed boys before, but they never felt like this. Even Ervin's kiss paled in comparison. She almost came undone when Tolfer deepened the kiss. He tasted like something she had never experienced. A touch of citrus from the orange he had eaten this morning, spice she could not place, but most of all he tasted like a man, not a pup after all.

She felt his hands on her, exploring her back and hips. It was the first time they had really touched and he was respecting what he must have felt was her need to take it slow. To hell with slow! She wanted fast and hot.

"Take the damn tunic off me," she communicated through the soul mate link without breaking the all-consuming kiss. She wanted to feel his flesh against hers.

Tolfer followed her instructions, but it meant breaking the kiss as he lifted her shirt over her head. He made short work of removing his tunic as well. For a teacher and a cook, Tolfer was more ripped than she thought he would be. He was absolutely gorgeous. Candy felt his eyes on her, exploring her body as she gazed on his. There was need in his eyes. A need she would make sure was fulfilled.

Candy slid back into Tolfer's arms. She wanted to devour him. They kissed as before. Deep and wet. Their juices intermingling as their hands continued to explore naked flesh. Tolfer finally found one of her breasts. She moaned as he gently massaged the mound. He released her mouth and leaned down to take her breast. Her knees became putty as he continued to suck through her bra. Together they melted to the dirt that constituted the hut's floor.

Tolfer placed his weight on his elbows, not wanting to crush her. She wanted to feel him on her. Her arms encircled Tolfer and brought his mass down to her. Candy wrapped her legs around him, bringing the rest of him to lie against her. Damn, they should have gotten rid of their leggings.

"Your thoughts are leaking through our pathway," Tolfer said. "We are going to have to work on that later." He rose to his knees and started to remove her leggings. Rising to remove his own, Candy took off her bra. She noticed him walk over to grab the animal pelts that lay in the corner. She was relieved, since lying in the dirt was not her idea of the romantic setting she had envisioned would be their first time together.

She watched as he walked over to her, his member erect and ready for action. Candy swallowed with difficulty. He was huge! He must have felt her hesitation. She certainly hoped what she was thinking was not stealing through their private channel. He took her in his arms without dropping the fur pelts.

"We can wait if you are not ready," Tolfer said out loud. "I do not want you to do anything you are not ready for. That is why I hid our true relationship." Now was not a time for confession, but a time for action. She wanted him with a desire that was all consuming.

She felt him release the pelts, all except the one he wrapped her naked body in. The fur felt luxurious against her skin. As much as how wonderful the pelt felt around her, she wanted to be in Tolfer's embrace.

"It's not what you think, Tolfer," she said in a voice barely audible. Candy leveraged the soul mate channel to communicate what she needed to tell him. Somehow it was easier than saying it out loud. *I've never done this before. Well, not all the way. It always felt wrong, so we stopped.* There, she had said it. It had always been so awkward when her girlfriends talked about sex and she silently just nodded in agreement to whatever they said. Only Alex knew the truth. She was the only one she trusted. How could a woman her age still be a virgin?

Tolfer looked disappointed. "I understand," he said.

"No, you don't," Candy cried as she beat his chest with her fisted hands. "I want this. My inexperience will make this awkward between the two of us. Disappointing you would just kill me!" The honesty in what she said was liberating. It was overwhelming how comfortable she was with this man. There would be no more secrets between them.

"You could never disappoint me, silly girl," Tolfer reassured her. He took her back into his arms and licked away her tears. She did not know if it was possible to love anyone as much as she loved him at this point. "Salty. I never want to taste your tears again, unless they are tears of joy." Tolfer kissed her once again.

Candy stepped back, letting the animal skin that sheltered her body fall. Tolfer took a hold of her hips and drew her closer into his body. She wrapped her arms around his neck and opened herself fully to his kiss.

Slowly Tolfer eased her down, arranging the pelts as he did. Tolfer's tongue continued to explore her mouth, as his hands gently squeezed her hips. Candy smoothed her hands up and down his back, not staying at any place too long.

Tolfer caressed her breast. She emitted little sounds from her throat. Her response must have encouraged him, since he squeezed a little harder. Candy moaned, the sound muffled by his kiss. Tolfer released her mouth and inched down her neck, depositing kisses along the way. When he reached her other breast he took possession of it. Candy gasped as his mouth made contact. She nearly bucked him off.

"That feels incredible," she managed to say. She started to knead his hips. Tolfer's response was to suck on her breast's nipple a tad bit harder. "Oh God, don't stop."

She wanted to touch him. She took one of her hands off his hip and made her way to his erection. Tolfer grabbed her hand before she made contact. "You will unman me if you touch me right now, my sweet."

"My sweet," Candy purred. "Now that name I actually like, Pup."

Tolfer chuckled as he brought his mouth back to hers. If it was possible, his kiss was more passionate than any before. She figured he was trying to distract her as one of his fingers entered between her folds. Candy gasped into his mouth.

She was partly surprised at an instant feeling of discomfort. As his finger moved within, her body slickened. An urgency built inside her and she was not quite sure what to do. She had always been able to control every aspect of her body's movements. This was something she was not accustomed to. Against her will, her body started to freeze up.

"It is all right," Tolfer reassured her. He must have felt her reaction to what he was doing. He grabbed her upper leg and lifted it to his own leg. "Wrap your legs around me." Candy complied as a second finger entered her. Tolfer moved both fingers quicker and she responded by tightening her legs around him. She was having problems catching her breath.

Tolfer entered her slowly, letting Candy get used to his size. Candy deepened the kiss this time. She shifted her legs higher, closer to his waist. He continued to enter her inch by lovely inch, Candy's body accommodating him as he drove into her inner core. She shifted her pelvis and Tolfer drove the rest of the way. Her body wrapped around him, as if it was made for him. Candy figured she actually was.

He withdrew and entered her repeatedly, increasing the pace with each round. She met his speed, reveling in the sensations he sent within her. Candy worshiped his body as he did hers. She was not sure how much more she was going to take before she fractured. Candy screamed when she could not hold it back any more.

Their release happened simultaneously. Her second scream was muffled by his kiss. Tolfer collapsed onto her body, taking most of his weight onto his forearms. He lay there for a couple of moments. She figured he was trying to catch his breath. It was not long before he turned onto his side, taking her with him.

She felt her brain sizzle. Alex had described the sensation to her, so it did not alarm her. "The hormone is being excreted. It is a natural process when soul mates make love. There is nothing to be concerned about," Tolfer reassured her.

"Pup, my brain is the least of my worries," Candy told her soul mate. "My whole body is humming after what we just did. I plan on gathering my strength and then we are going to do it again. This time I'm on top!"

Chapter 12

~

Candy woke with a start. She and Tolfer were lying naked on animal pelts in the middle of the hut. Her hair was all over the place. During their second round of lovemaking, Tolfer had released her hair from its binding. The events of today were so overwhelming, she thought she had dreamed them. Candy rose on one elbow, not wanting to disturb Tolfer.

Scanning his body, she noticed the spear wounds were no longer bleeding. She had been so overcome by lust earlier, Candy had not taken notice of his injuries. Fortunately, they did not look deep from her perspective.

At the entrance to the hut there appeared to be a change of clothes and a bucket. She hoped it was filled with warm water so she could clean herself. It was not every day a girl loses her virginity.

Tolfer rose next to her. "Hello, beautiful."

Automatically, she smiled at his words. "Your names for me keep getting better and better," Candy responded. She could not help but kiss his sexy lips. It would be wonderful to lounge in each other's arms. Unfortunately, Candy figured that was not going to happen. "We better get up and prepare for the communal dinner."

Candy jerked her body. Tolfer turned as he rose to find out what was wrong. She waved him off. It was the strangest sensation. Candy thought she saw Tolfer move before he actually did. Obviously she was imagining things.

Her soul mate pulled on a pair of leggings and a tunic. At least the Troyk government had not sent yellow outfits. Tolfer was clad all in black and looked incredible. Too bad they did not have time for a quickie. Tolfer had controlled the urgency she felt simmering under his calm, loving exterior. As his soul mate, she had felt him holding back his overwhelming passion for her.

He brought over the water and the clothes she could change into. "I will wait outside while you change." Candy felt another blush coming on. Tolfer leaned down and kissed her. Leaning on one elbow, she watched him exit their hut.

She slowly rose and placed a couple of fingers into the bucket. The water had been heated. Washing in cold water would have been horrible. Candy was not quite ready to lose the euphoria she felt after being with Tolfer. She quickly washed up. She tied her hair back with a clip she found in the pile of clothes. Her grandmother had left her a dress, rather than the usual tunic and leggings. She rarely wore dresses. It was dyed a light pink and had been an animal hide. The suede felt sinful against her skin. The dress came six inches down her thigh. Her toned legs were very much on display. An image of a pair of high-heeled sandals popped into her brain. She felt her forehead to determine if she was running a fever. She did not wear dresses and heels.

Taking a deep breath, she stepped outside to re-unite with her soul mate. He was talking to a man who had accompanied them to the village. Tolfer had a friendly grin on his face as he conversed. As soon as he saw her, a totally different look crossed his face.

His eyes traveled up and down her body. A man never looked at her the way Tolfer was consuming her with his glance. There was a look of hunger reflected in his eyes. She saw him visibly swallow, as if there was something in his throat. She stood a little taller, proud of the body she had conditioned over the years. Candy had a new appreciation for dresses. She was going to have to wear them more often.

She flew in front of Tolfer, she moved so fast. Candy grabbed a spear, as the man who had been talking to Tolfer turned, and the weapon became visible for the first time. All three stared at Candy's hands gripping the weapon.

"Candace," the warrior said, "I meant Tolfer no harm. My name is Marton. Follow me, I will take you to our evening meal."

"What is going on, Candy?" Tolfer asked through the soul mate channel.

"I don't know," Candy replied. *"Just like before in the hut, I sensed movement. What just happened definitely is not my imagination. I reached for the weapon before I knew it existed."*

"It must be one of the telepathic enhancements the hormone brought about," Tolfer informed her. *"A fable about a soul mated warrior woman who had foresight was one of my favorite stories growing up. She knew what action an opponent would take before he took it."* He looked at her in wonder. *"I became obsessed with the character as a boy."*

Candy held back saying something sappy. She was his warrior woman come to life. Or how about, she was a dream come true. A number of silly comments kept popping into her brain.

Tolfer chuckled next to her. He leaned in and whispered in her ear, "You are my dream come true." Tolfer then nibbled on her ear.

Yet again, she felt her face redden with a blush. *"Lord, we need to work on my not leaking private thoughts through the channel."* She gave his shoulder a little punch. Hopefully it proved she was not some lovesick twit.

"You have it, Canny," Tolfer responded. She gasped at the latest name he had for her.

"This just keeps getting weirder," Candy muttered. "Alex called me Canny when we were little. She could not pronounce the letter D."

Tolfer shook his head as he took in what she just communicated. "We were worlds apart, yet somehow we connected. That was the name I gave my imaginary warrior woman. She had rich, beautiful brown hair and sapphire eyes." He took a strand of her hair and wrapped it around his finger. *"For the time being we keep this between the two of us. Even the part about us being soul mates. I do not know who we can trust in this world. Kelog suspects, but I have not confirmed his suspicions."*

They arrived in the center of town where numerous tables were laden with food. It looked like a Thanksgiving feast. Wood had been carved into platters, bowls, plates, and utensils. There appeared to be fish, fowl, vegetables, and fruit in abundance.

"We do what we can with the few knives we have been able to gather over the years," Marton shared with them. "Kelog's knife would have gained him an invitation to our village, if we had not already accepted you all as a group."

Kelog had regained possession of his weapon. Candy imagined Chartail had a hand in bringing about that miracle. She would have to explore the proximity of the portal guardians' village for other gems Chartail may have been able to liberate for them.

She scanned the crowd looking for her fellow CT Guard. Candy finally found him. He was surrounded by a group of people. An older woman had her arm around his waist. She wondered if the woman was his mother or perhaps an aunt. Candy was glad he had found his family in this world. Symonn was also with the group, grinning like an old fool.

"Candace," her grandmother said as she approached. Her voice was laced with excitement. "There is someone I want you to meet." Her grandmother led Candy to a woman about her age. She was surrounded by a number of older women. "This is my daughter Darah, your aunt."

Candy held her welcoming smile as Darah raised her eyes to gaze at her. There was true evil reflected in those eyes. Madness evident in her gaze.

Tolfer must have sensed the same insanity as she had. He positioned himself closer to her and half a step closer to Candy's aunt.

"You are not welcome here," the girl growled. "Mommy is all mine!" Her eyes came down to the familial bracelet Candy wore. A look of pure hostility crossed Darah's face. She reached out to take the bracelet, scratching Candy in the process. Stepping back out of the girl's reach, Candy looked to her grandmother for some kind of reprimand related to what Darah had just done.

"Now, Darah, you do not mean that," her grandmother hugged her daughter. "You have to play nice with her, like we tell you when you are with the children. Candy is sweet, like her name."

For the first time in her life, Candy knew another human being wanted to do her harm. Her grandmother was blind to the danger her daughter posed.

Tolfer felt the fear emanating from his soul mate. As Tarsea had to have someone guarding Alex from Raine Narmouth, he knew he would do the same for Candy. His soul mate's grandmother seemed oblivious to the danger that existed within her own community. The comment she made about Darah's interaction with the village's children confirmed his decision. He had to reach out to Kelog and Marton for assistance until he met other men and women he could trust.

"Darah takes her meals with her friends," Alaura explained. "She does not like crowds. We will all get together tomorrow as a family. I know the girls will become great friends."

Candy's aunt was led away by the women he assumed were her caregivers. Alaura obviously knew there was something wrong with her daughter.

"The father," Tolfer inquired, "does he reside in this village?" Perhaps the man could be talked into keeping Darah away from his soul mate.

"He took me by force when we were in the portal guardian's village," Alaura responded. "When he slept, I took his knife and left a warning on the side of his face to never touch me again." Her matter of fact tone gave Tolfer a chill. Tolfer wondered what losing both of her older children and living in this world had done to Candy's grandmother's sanity.

"Franclyn," Candy said under her breath. *"We need to get Chartail free of that monster,"* she shared with Tolfer.

"Yes," Candy's grandmother confirmed her assumption. "When I found out I was pregnant, I knew I could not raise a child in such an environment. We mustered together a small group willing to risk their lives to challenge his rule. There were enough of us that Franclyn decided we were more trouble than we were worth. We left with only the clothes on our backs."

Tolfer looked around at all they had built out of nothing. "How did you manage?"

"Sharp rocks, weaving together fern leaves," Alaura answered. "Anything and everything we could to survive. We traveled for days to find our way across the gorge. Over time we formed raiding parties, sneaking into the guardian camp to steal what we could. When Franclyn learned I was with child, he started to give us supplies. Now we barter with him with what we farm and hunt."

"What of Darah?" Candy asked.

"She adores her father," Alaura replied. "We barter for medicine and other supplies we cannot produce ourselves for time with his daughter. If I had not allowed visitations, I feared he would attack and take her."

Tolfer wondered if Darah had been born with the madness or if the situation between her parents led to the girl losing her mind. It did not matter how she got the way she was. The girl was a threat to his soul mate.

Darah must be the woman Chartail had indicated could be Franclyn's Achilles heel. Candy was just not sure how she was going to manipulate her grandmother to use Darah to free Chartail.

Candy watched as Darah was led away. For the first time she wondered if insanity ran in her family. Orphans knew very little about the genetics related to their relatives. It never had been important enough for Candy to care.

A procession was run past them, as they were introduced to people who lived in the village. Even the children were given the opportunity to greet the newcomers. Candy figured ultimately she and Tolfer would be spending the majority of their time with the younger members of the community.

Most of the people they met were sentenced to this world because they were dissidents against mind control. There were a few thieves in their numbers. Candy remembered her grandmother mentioning stealing supplies from the portal guardians in the early days of the settlement. These criminals' skills must have come in handy during their raids. Everyone had been candid about why they had been sentenced to this world. Secrets plagued the Troyk universe, but that did not seem the case here.

There were no violent offenders in Utopia. Such men and women lived in the portal guardian village or were exiled to a lone existence. She and Tolfer had been warned against walking alone outside the community. There had been instances of Utopian citizens being attacked by lone marauders over the years.

Every Utopian member had to train to protect the village and serve guard duty. When Candy had shared she taught self-defense, the community got excited. She was immediately assigned to take over a number of classes starting the next morning.

Rotations were also assigned for cooking duties, farming, and child rearing responsibilities. Children were the responsibility of the whole village, not just the parents.

Tolfer immediately started working with the children, as they ate. They flocked to him with the promise of reducing the pain they experienced managing their telepathic abilities. Candy immediately saw the relief cross a number of the kid's faces, as their headaches were mitigated. Tolfer agreed to take a group out the next day to search for herbs that could be made into a tea to also relieve their suffering. She knew firsthand how the herbs his mother prepared helped her and her friends.

As the fires waned, Candy felt Tolfer stir next to her. *"Let us head back to our lodgings, Canny."* She could not help but smile at the endearment name he had finally settled on. It was perfect. How ironic the name she had been called as a child, was shared with a legendary warrior woman Tolfer grew up hearing stories about.

They walked hand in hand through the village. Occasionally they would stop and talk to a couple they had met that evening. It was amazing how quickly they had been accepted by the people in this village. True, she was the leader's granddaughter, but it felt like their acceptance had to do more with their own personalities and skills.

Candy never fit in anywhere. For the first time, she felt at home. Ironic, it would be on a prison planet in a different dimension. Candy still struggled with the whole string theory concept. Maybe they were traveling between planets, rather than dimensions. She used to love to watch *Stargate*, whether it was the movie, the Showtime series, or when it moved to the Sci-Fi channel. Candy even had the first season on DVD. That was all her meager budget allowed. Now she was living it.

She squealed with delight, when they entered their hut to find a bed. Well, actually it was more a stuffed mat, but it was better than sleeping on the ground.

"The father of one of the kids I interacted with this evening was working on this," Tolfer shared with her. "When his son's pain was reduced, he told me he would deliver his creation for our use."

Candy knelt down and sprawled on the bed. "It feels wonderful! What is it made of?"

"They keep the feathers from the birds they use for food. In addition, they also collect them when the egg-producing fowl are molting." He joined her on their bed. Tolfer scooted closer and took her into his arms. She could feel him sniffing her hair. "You smell great!"

Candy laughed. "I used your mother's lavender-scented shampoo this morning." He brushed the hair off her face in such an intimate manner, it took her breath away. "It seems like a century ago, so much has happened today. It kind of blows my mind."

She saw alarm, then understanding cross his face. Not having grown up on Earth, Tolfer was not aware of some of the expressions she and her friends used on a regular basis. Alex used sayings Tarsea was unfamiliar with, to drive her soul mate insane. Candy just did it without forethought.

He smiled and brought her deeper into his arms. "I am going to have to start writing down some of these expressions. If we make it back to the Troyk universe, Alex and I can double team against Tarsea. It has been entertaining to watch my brother deal with Alex's little games."

Candy enjoyed the relaxed discussion they shared while they lay next to each other. She was not ready to sleep. Her body had been craving his touch all evening and now she wanted more. "Your time to be on top," she whispered into her soul mate's ear.

Chapter 13

Candy stretched on their bed, like a cat waking from a nap in the sun. She was warm and content. They had made love three times last night. Where Alex generally looked exhausted after spending the night with Tarsea, Candy felt energized.

She had a self-defense class to teach, so she couldn't lounge too long in bed. Who would've ever guessed that living in a penal colony would be so wonderful? Candy could not come up with a time she was happier.

She was just about to kneel beside the bed in order to stand, when a premonition hit her. Her hand snapped out over the edge of the mattress and wrapped around the neck of a thick serpent. The snake was helpless in her grip. Candy did not know who was more surprised, she or the snake. Assuming a snake could even be surprised. The realization of what happened and what she had in her hand hit her hard.

"Tolfer," she let out a blood-curdling scream.

Several men ran into their quarters. One of the men came up beside her and took the viper. He obviously knew what he was doing. As they took the snake from the hut, she thought she heard one of the men saying they would be eating well again tonight.

As soon as Tolfer arrived, she ran into his arms. After she was relieved of the snake, Candy had shared with him telepathically what had occurred. Candy figured she must have seen something on television about snakes and had reacted instinctively. She trembled in Tolfer's arms as he tried to soothe her. What would have happened if she did not have the telepathic gift that warned her of the snake's attack?

"Are you all right?" her grandmother asked as she joined them. The communal pathway was buzzing with what had occurred. "How in the world did a snake get in here? They are primarily found on the other side of the gorge. We keep a couple here to create anti-venom medications."

Before she could totally absorb what her grandmother told her, an alarm came across the communal pathway. Darah had disappeared. She was last seen heading toward the portal guardians' encampment.

Candy gave her grandmother an accusing look. "You cannot imagine Darah was responsible for this," Alaura countered in response to her granddaughter's stare.

"That is exactly what I believe. Your homicidal daughter does not want me here. It is very convenient that a snake you had in captivity, ended up in my quarters just as she disappeared. I am also not deaf to the whispers about her in the communal pathways." Candy did not believe in beating around the bush. Her life had been placed in peril and she was not going to dance around the fact her aunt was insane.

"We must go after her," her grandmother said. Irritated because Alaura had discounted everything she just communicated, Candy did not move. "She is not scheduled to see her father until tomorrow. It is not safe for a girl her age all alone out there."

"Fine," Candy mumbled. This was one battle she was not going to win. Besides, if she was wrong and something happened to Darah, she would never forgive herself.

Candy had been paired with Kelog in the search for her aunt. Tolfer had stayed behind to help with the children. There was such a delicate balance within the Utopia community, that any occurrence from the norm upset them. Tolfer's natural affinity with children helped calm them.

It was the first time Candy had been alone with Kelog since arriving in the penal colony world. Although they taught combat and self-defense sessions together, they seldom spoke about anything other than what was required to prepare for the classes. Now they were trudging through the woods together.

Candy was the first to break the awkward silence. "We should head toward the old trail to the portal guardians' encampment. Someone would have noticed if Darah had gone over the bridge."

"Exactly what I was thinking," Kelog answered. "We make a good team." He glanced in her direction, it was obvious he was struggling to find a safe topic for them to discuss. "I am glad to see things are going well between you and Tolfer. He really cares for you. It took a tremendous amount of courage for him to come up to me and ask me to keep an eye on you, when he was not around. Darah is a frightening creature."

Candy could not help but smile. "That is putting it mildly. I cannot believe we are risking our lives with these prehistoric weapons going after Miss Fruit Loops." Homemade spears were not her idea of state of the art weaponry. What she would not give for a crystal power laser pistol.

"Who?" Kelog asked. "Never mind. I have spent enough time with Shirl to know half the things coming out of her mouth are lost on me."

Candy grabbed Kelog's arm and stopped suddenly. Something was not right, although she was not sure what was wrong. Kelog had sparred enough with her lately, to realize she was aware of the moves he was going to make before he made them. He respected her abilities without mentioning them.

It was not long before they heard the cries just north of their position. They cautiously followed the sound of the pleas for help. The forest ended and they entered a small clearing. Grunting sounds came from the left of their position. A small bear was circling a tree Darah had managed to climb.

"Stupid girl," Candy said. "Bears can climb trees. What was she thinking? The bear seems to be playing with her."

"What are we supposed to do? I have only seen bears in the zoo."

"The natural portal is on a mountain pass; you don't have bears in the Aster Province?"

"Not that I know of," Kelog confessed. "So what do we do?"

"Letting the bear eat her, I guess, is out of the question," Candy said. "We can throw rocks at it and make a lot of noise. The bear probably will not want anything to do with us. They are reclusive creatures and generally want nothing to do with humans. We'll approach sidestepping. If the bear decides to attack, stand your ground."

Candy hoped her gift of premonitions included a bear that was going to attack, just as she knew the snake would. The last thing she wanted was to be mauled to death by a common bear, while attempting to save her deranged aunt. Taking a deep breath, she was ready to deal with Yogi.

They left the confines of the forest and found a small wealth of rocks on their way to confront the bear. Candy reached down and grabbed some of the larger specimens. Right behind her, Kelog followed suit. At the top of her lungs, she started to sing *Magilla Gorilla*. She had no idea why she remembered the stupid song. A song about Yogi Bear would have been more appropriate, but she could not remember if he had a theme song.

The bear turned around, made a couple of grunting sounds, and then bounded off. Candy was grateful she was not going to have to deal with the animal. When she went hiking where bears lived, park rangers informed them what to do if one came upon them. Until now, she had never encountered one in the wild.

Darah started to climb down the tree. She rushed into Kelog's arms, not even acknowledging Candy's presence. "You were so brave to come after me, Kelog. I am so glad you decided to follow your uncle into the portal."

Kelog unwrapped Darah's arms from around his neck. It was pretty close to a chokehold, based on what Candy could see. Even showing signs of gratitude, her aunt was unable to judge what she was doing.

"We better get her back," Candy informed Kelog. "My grandmother is worried sick."

"You need to mind your own business," Darah growled. "This is a dangerous world, a person can get hurt showing up places they are not welcome. The woods are full of snakes and other nasty things."

Although Darah did not admit she was responsible for this morning's close encounter with a poisonous viper, it was clear to Candy she was. Her warning was as good as a confession in Candy's opinion. She needed to put some distance between her and her aunt before she did something dumb.

"Head on back with her, Kelog," Candy ordered. "I will take up the rear just in case the bear decides to double back." It was unlikely the bear would, but it sounded good.

Two close encounters with this world's wild life was more than enough for one day. She wanted to get back and collapse into Tolfer's arms. He made all the bad things disappear, if only for as long as it took for them to make love. One thing was clear, though, she was eventually going to have to do something about Darah before her aunt got the best of her.

Two weeks passed without any further attempts on her life. Candy and Tolfer had become an integral part of the community. They became particularly friendly with two couples that were a bit younger than they were. Their new friends were first-generation Utopians, born in this parallel universe. The Troyk government unknowingly condemned these children of criminals to a life with few options. One of the women was pregnant and Candy started to share experiences with her that she had hoped to share with Alex.

She missed her friends dreadfully, when she had a free moment to think. Candy had never worked so hard in her life. What looked to be an ideal life in this community, took a lot of effort. The whole village would take a late afternoon nap before preparing their evening meal, similar to the Mexican siestas. When she and Tolfer were finally free to spend time together later in the evening, they were too exhausted to do more than make love and fall asleep in each other's arms.

Candy had even managed to get Alaura to allow Darah more visitations with her father in exchange for Chartail spending time in Utopia. Every unattached man in the village made a play for her. Chartail had them wrapped around her little finger, including Kelog Potts. Candy also had to admit it was nice not having Darah in close proximity to her.

Tolfer came up from behind. He pushed back the hair that fell over her left shoulder and started to nuzzle her neck. The man could produce sensations within her, she never imagined possible. If they had eternity together, she would never tire of him.

"I have a surprise for you," he communicated through the communal link. *"We have the afternoon off. There is a hot spring I was told we should explore."* They often used the communal link to communicate information that was not sensitive. It also alerted the village they would be leaving its confines.

"I promised Chartail I would teach her self-defense moves," Candy shared. Although the communication was for all, she put a cute little pout on her face just for him.

"Kelog has that covered," Tolfer responded. "He has it bad for her." Although he spoke those words aloud, it was not news to anyone about Kelog's obsession with Chartail. She knew Kelog was going to be devastated when Chartail dropped him.

Candy was not sure who Chartail was going to end up with. She just knew her new friend was destined for greater things. With everything Chartail had gone through since the Nightshade universe, she had developed into a formidable woman.

She took Tolfer's hand and together they left the protected area of the village, each grabbing a spear as they left. Candy stopped by to make sure Chartail was good with Kelog, and then borrowed his knife. Tolfer did not give her a he-man attitude and demand to carry the blade. He knew she was better trained and had the gift of foresight.

They walked along the trail for thirty minutes when they reached a charming grotto nestled within a small opening between the mountains. Candy figured it had been carved over time by wind and rain. The hot springs Tolfer had been referring to were in the middle of the grotto. Tall trees surrounded it with vines forming a natural fence around the small pool. Ivy grew up the sides of the mountain walls providing a breathtaking backdrop.

As she approached the pool, her nose was assaulted by the smell of sulfur. Candy slipped off her shoes and stuck her toe into the water. The temperature was perfect. After two weeks of only cleansing with a towel and a single bucket of tepid water, immersing herself in the pool would be nirvana. Regardless of the horrid smell.

She waited beside the water and watched as Tolfer removed his clothes and made his way in. Candy could not get enough of looking at him. Over the last two weeks his body had become leaner and meaner. The hard work he performed had developed muscles he had rarely used. She had felt the subtle changes in his muscle mass each night, as they made love. If she had any artistic ability and the necessary supplies, Candy would never need another model to inspire her work.

Once upon a time she would have been shy undressing in front of anyone. However, doing it in front of Tolfer was liberating. She felt his eyes on her. She deliberately slowed her progress, hoping to drive him mad with desire.

Candy entered the spring and let loose a moan. It felt so damn good. The water caressed her body as a lover would. Tolfer allowed her time to enjoy the healing properties of the liquid. This was his gift to her. He waited for her to come to him.

The pool was deep enough for her to submerge entirely. What she would not give for a natural sponge. It was not long before her body started to burn for Tolfer's touch.

She swam over to her lover and placed her arms around his shoulders. Her body felt his erection. With a wicked smile on her face Candy stared at him as she positioned herself over his stiff rod. She had once had fantasies of making love to someone in a hot tub. What she was about to do was going to make those wet dreams seem positively mild in comparison.

Slowly she impaled herself on him. Their breathing became erratic as she continued to take more of him into her body. Tolfer bent his head back and Candy leaned forward to lick the salt from his neck.

She finally took all of him into her body as she continued to ride him. Her need was frantic and uncontrollable. He grabbed her hips as she increased the friction generated by their bodies. Water lapped against them as the contents of the pool reacted to the motion they created. Waves of desire transitioned to spasms of an orgasm that took them both.

Tolfer was still inside of Candy, recovering from their latest joining. The intensity of what happened between them increased with each coupling. He wondered how much more he could take. They would eventually have to reach their zenith before they literally burned each other out.

His soul mate's forehead was against his own. She was exhausted from the frantic ride she had just taken. His hands had a life of their own as he leaned her back and placed his hands on her breasts. Candy's legs wrapped around him tighter in order not to float away. Her hair skimmed the top of the water, creating a long crest around her head. If ever a water nymph was personified, it would be Candy at this moment.

Tolfer's mouth watered as he lifted her and brought one of her breasts into his mouth. Moans of encouragement came from his soul mate as his tongue played with her breast. Tolfer pulled on her nipple and Candy screamed aloud. As he released one breast to enjoy the other, Candy muttered something he could not make out. He followed the same wonderful routine and got the same response from her. His mind was in a lustful fog, so making love to her without thinking about the mechanics worked for him.

Candy started to move again, forcing his erect member to become harder within her. She rode him as before. He was so deep inside her, he was half afraid he was hurting her and was too absorbed in his own pleasure to notice.

"Canny, am I hurting you?""

"Don't be ridiculous," Candy answered between gasps. "Shift a little to your left. No, my left, your right." He did as she requested and Tolfer was rewarded with the biggest groan out of her yet. Tolfer loved all the sounds that gushed out of Candy as they made love.

She continued to ride him until neither had any energy left. Their second orgasm came hard and was overpowering. Candy was a lump of clay in his arms as he staggered to get them both out of the water. They collapsed on the softest grass he had ever felt. If he was destined to relive one period of time over and over again, it would be the time he spent with her in this grotto.

They dressed, giggling to be so carefree. Well, Candy did. Men did not giggle. He just never knew it was possible to be so happy. As much as he dreaded leaving this peaceful place, Tolfer was assigned to help prepare the evening meal. It was time to start heading back to Utopia.

He and Candy were not far from the grotto when Candy took a defensive stance. He had not heard anything, but knew enough to trust her gift.

Out of nowhere a crazed man charged Candy. She fended him off, bringing him down with a kick to his knees. Tolfer had never seen anyone move as quickly as Candy did as she secured the man's ankles and wrists with sturdy vines from along the path. The man would not have known what hit him had he been of sound mind. She had not even drawn the knife.

Tolfer called for assistance through the communal pathway. Candy stood next to him, barely winded. She appeared to have actually enjoyed herself. The hormone had transformed Candy into the ultimate fighter. She was truly his legendary warrior woman come to life.

It was not long before reinforcements came from the settlement. The group seemed disappointed there was not more for them to do. Candy and Kelog's work with the population of Utopia made them want to see action. Any type of action.

"What is going to happen to him?" Candy asked Klark. He was in charge of the Utopia army, if you could call them that.

"We will feed him and care for any wounds," Klark answered. "Zak is basically harmless. He has mood swings that make him unstable. From time to time he comes into the village for a meal. Seeing too many people confuses him. He has never done anyone too much harm. I am glad you did not hurt him."

"He charged me like a rhino," Candy said. Everyone looked at Candy with blank stares. "It is an animal from Ginkgo Terra."

"Head on back to the settlement, Candace," Klark said. "Your grandmother must be worried sick. Although we have communicated you are safe, I am sure she will want to see for herself. We will take care of Zak."

They walked back to the village, hand in hand. He had so much to ask her about what he had witnessed. The last thing Tolfer wanted to do was make Candy feel awkward. He still remembered how Shirl had thought people would think of her differently after what happened on Terra Nova. He did not want Candy to go through that.

"You were incredible back there," Tolfer said.

"It was amazing," Candy replied. "In the past, I had to think and then my body would react. Now my limbs respond as quickly as my brain reacts. I am so much faster." She could barely contain her excitement. He was mentally drained by what happened, while his soul mate was charged up.

"Do you think your body is still absorbing new powers from the hormone?" Tolfer asked.

"Yes," Candy answered. "I was not this fast with the snake. When I am working out, I have not noticed any differences. My adrenaline is still flowing. I am frickin' Wonder Woman!"

Candy looked at him critically. He could see she was in the process of germinating another thought. "What about you, Tolfer? Have you noticed any enhancements in your telepathic abilities?"

He did not feel any different. Tarsea had developed the same ability to read thoughts as Alex had. Shirl had developed more powers than Starc. Starc now had the ability to navigate the portal frequencies, when he was with his soul mate. Their time in this dimension had been so physically trying he had not the luxury of time to test his telepathic talents.

"Nothing so far," Tolfer answered. "I am enjoying watching you too much."

Although he gave her a carefree answer, he was anything but. His soul mate was in danger in this world. Tolfer needed to discover what evolutionary change he had gone through and find a way to turn it into a weapon to protect Candy. Although Chartail was convinced Tarsea would come after him, Tolfer could not rely on waiting for something that might never happen.

Chapter 14

~

The Nightshade Universe

Shirl stepped out of the portal into the Nightshade universe. A world to which she swore she would never return to. However, this time she was not defenseless. She could annihilate any vampire that came at her. As before, her eyes had to adjust to the dark environment. Only torches burning in the distance, provided any light.

She grabbed the blood opal and spoke before she was aware of any vampire's presence. "Drake has given me and my companions safe passage in this world." Shirl had Starc, Alex, and Tarsea with her. The most important people to her in any universe were by her side. She was wagering a great deal that Drake's word would be honored by Yorik. The master vampire had honored Drake's dictates before. She could only hope he would once again.

Relentless was a good word to describe Alex's determination to accompany them on their mission to rescue Candy and Tolfer. Pregnancy was a condition, not an illness, she kept ranting. At one point, she was so frantic about not going, Tarsea finally relented. Shirl had never seen her friend so emotional. Even Alex admitted she must be possessed, after throwing the last temper tantrum. To Shirl, it was debatable whether it was the Nightshade universe or saving Candy that drove her friend. Now their fates were sealed together in this bleak world.

They would leave for the penal colony from this world in eight hours. She had no idea if Drake was still present in Yorik's hive. If he was not here, she hoped he would be able to arrive before they had to enter the portal to meet the others. Cianan and Ervin Allaway would leave from Terra Nova. Darden and Koel would leave from Earth. They felt it was too risky to leave directly from the Troyk universe. The portal was used by too many crystal telepaths in their world. Timing was imperative if the mission to rescue Candy and Tolfer was to be a success.

"New blood is always welcome," a voice from behind her claimed. Shirl would know that voice anywhere. Yorik! The same chill as before ran through her body. This creature was evil incarnate, but she knew she had to strike a deal with him.

She turned to address the master vampire. Shirl was shaken by the presence of the girl next to him. Afton, Yorik's daughter, whom they had brought into this hellish world in order to free Shirl.

The girl had long black hair. She was dressed in virginal white and was dreadfully pale. Shirl could not let the guilt she felt about Afton cloud her actions. Candy's life was in danger.

"I have come to see Drake," Shirl informed Yorik. She needed to appear strong, invincible. It was time to play her trump card, something even Yorik could not turn down. "Blood will be awarded to those who assist me. However, Drake must captain the Nightshade contingent on this campaign."

Yorik's eyes grew larger at the mention of blood. He rose from his throne and approached. "Perhaps a down payment is called for." A shiver ran down Shirl's spine as Yorik approached.

Starc and Tarsea stood in front of each of their soul mates. Their actions were futile if Yorik decided to attack. Only Shirl had the ability to protect them. The master vampire did not seem affected by the action of the two men. They were insignificant as a threat in the vampire's eyes.

Yorik hesitated in front of Tarsea. "Your mate is with child," Yorik said. "A true blessing. Please come forward, my little sweetheart." Shirl just hoped Alex would not react to Yorik's words. She was always sensitive about her diminutive size.

Alex placed her hand on Tarsea's back and walked around her soul mate. Her face was awash with fascination at seeing her first vampire. Yorik seemed as captivated with her best friend as she was with him. Alex generally had something to say, but appeared to be dumbstruck by what was before her.

Yorik knelt before Alex. He placed his hands on her abdomen. "A special child you carry," he said. "You must bring her back to this world when she is of age. Nightshade is her destiny."

Alex found her tongue with those words. "I don't think so. Never in a million years would I subject my daughter to the horror you have exposed your child to."

Shirl stiffened. She was petrified the vampire would strike out at her friend. To her amazement Yorik laughed. He snapped his fingers and one of his guards came over to receive his orders. There was a short exchange before the guard left the room.

"You have fire, my girl," Yorik said. "It is too bad you found your soul mate. My little sprite, you would have given me years of entertainment and blood."

Tarsea immediately reacted to those words. He moved to place himself between his soul mate and the vampire, who was infatuated with her. Shirl braced herself for a confrontation when Starc came to stand in front of her. Silly man. She had the ability to deal with Yorik with a simple energy blast.

Yorik seemed amused by the men's posturing. He laughed as if he was reacting to a private joke. "Relax, my Troyk warriors. No one is safer in my realm than this little girl, and Shirl is under Drake's protection. He should be here within the hour. In the meantime, let me introduce you to my daughter Afton."

Shirl could feel the obstruction in her throat grow larger. She could barely swallow. It took all her mental fortitude to look the girl in the eye. Afton was staring back and forth between Starc and Tarsea. The men were part of the group that had taken her from her safe existence on Earth. A human exchange to save Shirl and ultimately Chartail. The girl stepped forward, she offered no welcome. As if having second thoughts about meeting them, the girl sat back in the chair next to Yorik's.

"I will be happy to return Afton home," Shirl offered. "Her friends must be frantic by now. She is a child of light. Her aura is dimming with all this darkness." She had read a lot of new age books but never had seen such an example of someone's life force being drained as she witnessed seeing Afton.

"This is her home now," Yorik informed Shirl. "However, I can make sure she is exposed to sunshine. Her intended is arriving with Drake. Your timing is really quite remarkable."

A Billy Idol video flashed in Shirl's mind. Although the woman in the clip was not wedding a vampire, she was being forced to join in some type of demonic ceremony. Drake had promised to protect her and Yorik was forcing Afton into a union with a vampire. Shirl could feel the bile backing up in her throat.

"I cannot allow this girl to be victimized any more than she already has," Shirl warned Yorik. She had time to rectify this terrible situation before she left this world for the penal colony. Shirl was ready to release a power she swore she would never unleash again. There would be no regrets if her hand was forced.

"A mated female crystal telepath is threatening me," Yorik said, once again seeming amused by this interchange. "How powerful are you?"

"Powerful enough to remedy a kidnapping that should never have occurred," Shirl responded.

Yorik stared at Shirl. He must have been measuring the threat she posed, with what he gained having his daughter in the Nightshade universe. "I am her only family," the vampire said. "She represents the mortality of my bloodline. Do you really believe I would do her harm?" Shirl had no idea what he was talking about, but he seemed genuine in regards to what Afton meant to him.

Shirl looked for Yorik's daughter to offer some type of response. The girl sat there mute. Shirl could tell nothing of how she was feeling from her body language. How could she jeopardize a mission to rescue Candy and Tolfer on a girl who could not communicate what she wanted? Was Afton that terrified?

"She looks no worse than when we brought her here," Starc communicated through the soul mate link. *"Afton was dreadfully pale when I first saw her on Ginkgo Terra."*

Although Shirl could wield unbelievable power, it was Alex who had the courage to stand up to Yorik. "As far as I can see, your daughter appears to be petrified. She is too afraid to even voice her own wishes."

If it were possible, the girl became paler. Her posture in the chair straightened. Alex's words broke through whatever invisible walls Afton built around herself to retain her sanity. "I wish to stay," Afton said in a voice barely audible. There was no emotion in her voice. Shirl could not tell if she meant what she said.

"This may be your last chance to go home," Alex said as she approached the girl. "I found myself in another world. It was terrifying. But I was surrounded by people who cared for and ultimately loved me. I want nothing less for you. My soul mate was one of the men who brought you here. Please, let us make things right."

"I am of his blood. Things were never right on Earth," Afton admitted. "Maybe I will find a place here to belong."

Shirl could understand a little how Afton felt. She had been born in the Troyk universe, but was carried through the portal to Earth when she was a baby. The only people she had been close to were the two offspring of Troyk dissidents, Candy and Alex.

Since Drake was coming with the man that Yorik was forcing his daughter to marry, perhaps he was not the monster her father was. Although Drake was a vampire, he had kept his word to Shirl during her captivity in this world. She could only wait for his arrival and size up the man who accompanied him.

After their audience with Yorik they were led to a part of the fortress Shirl had not seen during her time in this world. They were served a meal by servants who had not been ravaged by the vampires for their blood. Shirl had no appetite. Her anxiety grew with each moment. She glanced at Alex and had noted her friend had barely touched anything on her plate. It spoke volumes about this world when even Alex could not stomach food here.

Restless, Shirl started to pace the room. It was spacious, containing only a table and a number of chairs. The room was as musty as the rest of the building. She wondered if the enclosure that protected the vampires within its proximity was responsible for the poor circulation of air. The table where the others sat was rotting away. If Drake did not arrive soon she was going to have to find a way outside to get fresh air.

It had not taken long for Shirl to reach her limit. Her skin was crawling with anxiety. She asked a servant to lead her outside. Starc stayed behind at her request to help guard Alex. Yorik's interest in Alex's baby was troubling. The fortress was like a maze and she wondered if there would be a chunk of cheese at the next turn. Finally the woman she followed opened a door that led to a small exterior courtyard.

Fresh air cleansed her lungs. Glancing up, she saw the purple canopy that filtered out the sun's harmful rays. Seeing a purple sky was soothing to her soul.

"I told you there was beauty in my world." Drake's words startled her. She had not heard him approach. "But it pales in comparison to your radiance."

Moving closer, Drake started to nuzzle Shirl's neck. His tongue found the scar that covered the bite marks he had made to claim her as his. As his smooth lips started a suction movement that brought her tender flesh into his mouth, she was captivated. Shirl cried out before she could stifle the sound. How could she feel so wonderful in Drake's arms, when she was mated to Starc?

"Whatever you are doing," Shirl dictated, "you need to stop. The soul mate connection is not yours to manipulate." Stepping out of his arms, she stared into his hypnotic eyes. They were so dark they appeared black. Drake's normally brown eyes had darkened with passion. His dark hair rode the top of the midnight blue shirt he wore. Sinful as the most expensive dark chocolate, Drake took her breath away.

"If you expect me to apologize for using every tool at my disposal to possess you again, you will be terribly disappointed." Drake had a non-expressive look on his face as he uttered those words.

"Possession," Shirl uttered, "what an empty word." With the connection between them severed, once again she was able to reason. Her eyes still drank in his beauty, but the enchantment was gone. "I need your help. We should join the others." The less time she spent alone with him the better.

The journey back to where her soul mate and friends waited seemed to take a fraction of the time it had taken to reach the courtyard. Leaning outside the room was a blond vampire who made Drake look like chopped liver. He was the statue of David come to life, only the slingshot was missing.

"This is Lorenz," Drake growled, obviously aware of her reaction to the vision before her. Shirl extended her hand in greeting. Drake grabbed it and guided her into the room where her friends waited.

Alex gasped upon noticing their presence. No doubt she was overcome by the vampires' exterior appearance, as Shirl was. "Let me introduce my friend, Alex, to you both. I believe Drake already met Starc and Tarsea. Alex, this is Drake and his friend Lorenz."

"Ah, the little chameleon, you talked about." Drake walked over to Alex and took her hand and brought it to his lips. Fortunately, Tarsea did not attempt to stop Drake. "I had heard whispers that an unborn child was within the confines. It is truly a blessing to have new life in a place such as this."

Alex retrieved her hand. She had allowed Drake enough time to kiss her hand, before she liberated it from him. Alex was always as cool as a cucumber in stressful situations, making it possible for her to behave in a diplomatic way as not to insult Drake. It was only when her soul mate was in danger that her best friend became a basket case.

"With all the humans in this world," Alex said, "I don't understand why you are so enamored with the fact I am with child. Somehow, I imagined you would have viewed the creation of a new life, in a breeding program frame of mind."

Drake's eyes opened just a little wider in response to Alex's comment. "Yes, well, we do have such arrangements in parts of this world. A vampire cannot breed in most cases. On rare occasions a woman with a specific genetic marker has conceived a half vampire child. It is a very rare occurrence. My brother Lorenz is betrothed to the offspring of such a woman. Please, let me introduce you all to him."

The blond Adonis stepped forward and gave them a short bow. It was a greeting from times long gone on the planet Earth. Shirl found it absolutely charming. Lorenz approached her and took her hand as Drake had earlier taken Alex's. As with Tarsea, Starc held back.

"It is a pleasure to meet you, crystal telepath," the blond vampire said before he kissed her hand. Shirl was partially relieved the reaction she had to Drake's touch was non-existent when Lorenz touched her. It was troubling that she could not explain away her attraction to Drake simply because he was a vampire. Regardless of corrupting the link she shared with Starc, there was a legitimate attraction to the raven-haired vampire. Lorenz gazed into her eyes as he continued to speak. "What is it you wish to ask Drake?"

Shirl waited until Lorenz released her hand before she responded to his question. "I need assistance rescuing a friend from the Troyk penal colony world." She knew she needed to sweeten the reward for assisting her to get the vampires to even talk to her on the subject. "You can take whatever blood you wish from the people who prevent us from taking Candy from that world."

Drake and Lorenz glanced at each other. Lorenz nodded as Drake approached Shirl. "I will take a down payment now," Drake said as he took her into his arms. Shirl braced herself for Drake's fangs to penetrate her neck. In the past his bite had only brought pleasure. She did not want Starc to witness her enjoyment of the act. He would not understand; she was not sure she even did.

"Later," she heard Alex say. Shirl saw Alex's hand was on Drake's arm. "You will weaken her. Candy is our family and I need Shirl at her most powerful when we enter that world."

Drake released Shirl. Alex's hand still grasped Drake's arm. Shirl was shocked Alex had taken such an aggressive step. Her chameleon friend continued to leave the shadows and step into the light. By some miracle Tarsea had not intervened. Alex must have warned him of what she had planned and asked him not to interfere.

Drake looked at Alex in wonder. "I can feel your daughter's heartbeat through your touch," Drake said. "The girl is so small, I did not sense her when I held your hand. She carries the genetic marker that will allow one of my brethren to one day mate with her. I will do whatever you wish, payment will not be required."

Alex had become as pale as a ghost. She released Drake. Her hand had migrated down to her abdomen, where her daughter had just become an embryo. Had their mission to save Candy condemned Alex's unborn daughter? The vampires would never have known about her existence had Alex not accompanied them into the Nightshade universe. Shirl also did not like the way Drake looked at Alex in such a possessive manner. The look frightened Shirl. She needed to shake off the feeling that was consuming her and re-focus on Candy's rescue.

Shirl placed herself between Drake and her recovering friend. "Let's concentrate on the matter at hand. I need you and as many of your kind you can trust not to become overwhelmed with blood lust."

An angry look crossed Drake's handsome face. "My kind, as you so diplomatically stated, cannot bear the rays of the sun. How do I know we will not be incinerated as soon as we enter that world?"

"The Troyk government did an initial survey of the planet before sending prisoners," Starc informed Drake. "Their sunrises and sunsets align with the sun's movement in our universe. We have timed resources entering the penal world from here, Terra Nova, and Ginkgo Terra. The attack is planned within an hour of sunset. That should give us ample time to free Candy and Tolfer, and open a portal for you to return to this lovely place." Starc's voice was laced with sarcasm.

Drake sat in a nearby chair. Shirl was surprised it took his weight, considering how rotted the wood was. She sat next to him. Her uncensored words had upset him. Shirl needed Drake on her side if her plan to rescue Candy was to succeed. Fortunately Alex's child would be the reason Drake and Lorenz would ultimately agree to aid them.

"Will you help us?" Shirl asked.

"There are half a dozen men from our world, I can trust to only take blood from the men we fight," Drake finally answered. "It would be a bonus if we could bring the prisoners back with us. A tribute given to Yorik in your name will help to re-open negotiations between our people again." Shirl knew his words were for her, but his eyes were on Alex.

Lorenz took Drake aside and they talked briefly. Once they completed their conversation the blond vampire stood before Tarsea. "I will join my blood brother to free yours," Lorenz said, "Ties of blood are important among kindred. Two of our elite guards will join us and protect your mate. Nothing is more precious than your daughter."

"Thank you," Tarsea replied. For the first time since leaving the Troyk universe, Tarsea seemed to relax a bit. Shirl glanced at Drake, whose eyes were still locked on Alex.

One problem at a time, Shirl told herself. They were about to enter a world she knew nothing about. Every fiber of her being needed to concentrate on their upcoming battle.

The vampires had been assembled in the time they had available before leaving for the penal colony. Frankly, she had not noticed much of a difference between these creatures and the ones that surrounded Yorik. At least the guards that were assigned to watch over Alex did not have red glowing eyes.

Starc indicated it was time for them to leave. There was no going back now. Shirl opened a portal and stepped into the great unknown.

Chapter 15

~

The Troyk Penal Colony World

Candy woke with a start as Tolfer slept peacefully next to her. They had worn each other out making love after their daily chores. The village outside their hut was quiet. She could have been awoken from a bad dream or some animal crying in the distance. Somehow Candy knew that was not the case. Something was coming and it was not good.

She shook her soul mate. "Tolfer, wake up. We are about to be attacked." Candy got up and started to dress. The people of Utopia had to be warned and prepared for the upcoming battle. Candy had no idea whether it was a solitary madman or the guardians of the portal.

Side by side, Tolfer and Candy ran through the village and sounded the warning bell. She was certain that when the Troyk government had sent the bell with one of the supply shipments all those years ago, the portal guardians had cast it aside. Some forward-thinking Utopian citizen had grabbed it and now the warning would save lives. Since their arrival, they had practiced a myriad of different scenarios to make sure the village was ready to defend itself.

Based on the time of day, the Utopian citizens took the bell seriously rather than just another drill. The late afternoon siesta ritual was never toyed with. They came armed and ready for battle.

"What have we got?" Klark asked. As leader of the guard, Klark would be responsible for staging their defenses. Candy had fought beside him during many of the drills they ran to prepare for today. Through these exercises they had grown to respect each other.

"I am not sure, but we are going to be hit hard," Candy replied. Since coming to the village no one questioned how Candy knew the things she knew. They all took it as a gift from God. "We should get the children in the center hut and set up for whatever is coming at us."

Tolfer called the children to come around him. He had a way with kids beyond just his ability to lessen their pain. The village had decided Tolfer would oversee the safety of the children if they ever came under attack. He would be able to keep them occupied during the early stages of the battle. If they lost their perimeter around the center structure, Tolfer would be the last line of defense, in protecting their most valuable loved ones. The three pregnant women would support Tolfer in caring for the young.

"*Be safe, Canny,*" Tolfer communicated through the soul mate pathway as he led the children into the closure where they would remain until the all clear was called.

Candy turned to see her grandmother and Darah coming their way. Her eyes immediately focused on the blade in her aunt's hand. She got a strange feeling seeing the knife. Candy involuntarily stepped closer to Klark. This was one of the many times Candy wished Darah was with her father. Although, Candy imagined he was the one who was about to attack the village.

"*What is happening?*" her grandmother asked through the communal channel. They had all been instructed not to use the telepathic channel when the war bell was rung. There was no guarantee whoever was attacking them did not have access to any of the telepathic pathways used within the community.

"Speak out loud, Grandmother," Candy scolded Alaura. This was not the time for people to abandon protocols put in place for the safety of the village.

Her grandmother nodded, "I am sorry. That bell would have warned whoever is coming we are aware of their presence anyway."

"You and Darah should join the children and assist Tolfer in keeping them calm," Candy said. She wanted the distraction of Darah's presence gone. Everyone knew her aunt was unstable and presented a risk to the village if she was not contained during the battle. Her grandmother took her daughter and walked toward the center hut.

It was time she made her way to the area, she and Kelog were assigned to cover. They were the perfect combat team. Any doubts Candy originally had related to Kelog had been removed over the weeks they trained the people of

Utopia together. She understood why he did what he did and came to forgive him. Her telepathic gift enhancements also made her aware of how her partner was going to move. How he would react. She could modify her actions based on his movements. He never questioned how she knew, he just took it for granted they were in sync.

Chartail had been able to share with her what weapons the portal guardians possessed. With the items they had been able to steal, as well as produce, they were fortunately evenly matched where weaponry was concerned. The ability to do harm was their opponent's greatest strength. Candy knew if lives were in jeopardy, the citizens of Utopia would do what had to be done. They would deal with the psychological consequences of what was required to safeguard the village afterwards. Over time the villagers would develop the mental toughness it took to truly be a force to be reckoned with. The loss of their innocence would be tragic, but it was necessary for their continued survival.

Candy noticed movement in the tree line to her left. Assuming they were from the portal camp, the enemy had not used the bridge that crossed the gorge but took the long way around. The guardians were going to hit the village where it was most vulnerable. Her eyes surveyed the area to see if there was other activity.

She knew it was a man she had seen, not an animal roaming the exterior line of the forest. The only question was how many men they were up against. Candy's grip on her spear tightened as she mentally prepared to throw the spear when the time came. She worked to slow her heartbeat.

She heard cries from her right. Candy turned momentarily, as men, to the west of the area she had been watching, emerged from the forest. Her worst nightmares had become a reality. It appeared the portal guardians had come to attack their village.

Shirl stepped from the portal onto the soil of the Troyk penal colony. The first thing she saw was a pristine lake. It was twilight and the water almost appeared black. The moon was full and acted like a spotlight on the water. How odd it was to see such a beautiful sight, when she expected to be in some type of battle as soon as she entered this world.

She looked around. Although the sun had set, there were enough fires in the encampment they entered, to recognize the people present to greet them. Cianan was there with Ervin Allaway and members of his Terra Nova clan. She did not recognize the older man who stood near Darden and Koel. Although she had not met him, Shirl knew the man was Benko Jarlyn. Shirl had not expected the future leader of the Troyk universe to be present for this rescue. She approached the man so many laid their hopes on.

"I have so much to say to you," Shirl addressed Benko, "but now is not the time." She turned to her brother Cianan. "Where is everyone?"

"We have no idea. The fires were blazing when we arrived so someone had been here not too long ago. Some of Ervin's men are searching the area to see if they can find anyone." Her brother's gaze drifted to the vampires that stood behind her. "I cannot believe I am saying this, but it is nice to see you, Drake."

"I must say I am disappointed," Drake stated. "We promised our men blood and a battle. They will be hard to control if we cannot find someone for them to eat." Shirl knew Drake was kidding, but did not bother to tell her brother. She thought she'd let him suffer a little before she let him know Drake was playing with him. Who knew a vampire could have such a caustic sense of humor?

Two of the Terra Nova warriors came forward, dragging a woman behind them. It did not take long for Shirl to recognize Chartail. She immediately went to rescue her friend from the well-meaning barbarians.

"Let her go," Shirl commanded. She approached Chartail and helped her to her feet. "Are you all right? Where is everyone? Is Candy here?" There were so many questions she had, she could not stop from asking as many as she could without giving Chartail the ability to answer.

"That is enough, Shirl," Starc came to rectify the situation. Shirl stood back as Alex held the weeping woman in her arms. Chartail's tears of relief were quickly replaced with screams of terror. The vampires were now visible to the hysterical woman.

"You are safe now," Alex stroked Chartail's back. She continued to talk softly to the distressed woman. "Drake is here to help us rescue Candy. You have nothing to fear from him or the others, he brought with him. They will feast on the men who abused you. Tell us where they went and where we can find Candy." Chartail kept weeping in her arms, only jumbled words and gulps of sound came from her. Alex focused on Chartail then visibly paled. "They have gone to attack a village where Candy and Tolfer are living. We need to get going," Alex informed them.

Shocked back into reality, Chartail stopped crying and looked at Alex in wonder. "How did you know that? I could not get the words out."

"I have the ability to read minds. The baby has disrupted many of my abilities, but somehow I was able to get a clear transmission from you. She must know how important that information was. Can you lead us to this village?"

Chartail nodded as she stood. She initially looked at Alex's midsection, but realized now was not the time to talk about the baby. Chartail pulled the hair from her face and got herself further under control. "The first force left early this morning. They were going around the gorge to attack the village from the forest side of their encampment. Franclyn left not long ago. They were going to cross the bridge while the Utopians are fighting off the first wave of invaders from the other side of the village. We have to hurry."

Chartail started running. Tarsea, Darden, Starc, and Koel quickly caught up to her and continued by her side. Those four men were a tight unit, having been the first who entered into the warrior link. Alex walked along with the vampires, her guards were on either side of her. They were promised their share of blood for protecting Alex and would only attack in defense of her friend. Benko Jarlyn conversed with the men from Terra Nova as they made their way to the Utopia settlement.

"You have been keeping a huge secret, little sister," Cianan said as he came up beside her. "Although you did not bother to introduce him, I know that man is Benko Jarlyn. How did you manage to keep that information from our Prime Ruler?"

"I never met the man before today," Shirl snarled back at her brother. "Now is not the time to have this discussion. We need to focus on rescuing Candy and Tolfer. You asked me what it would take for me to trust you, well, getting those two free from this world is going to be a great start."

Shirl could barely tolerate being next to her brother at this point. She would have preferred to be up front with the men who helped plan the rescue. However, the vampires were cushioned in between. She had no desire to get any closer to them than she already was. Alex was conversing with Drake and

Lorenz as if they were longtime friends. The changes in her once-shy friend were truly amazing.

The group started to slow as they ran out of real estate. They had reached the gorge. Benko handed a pair of binoculars to Koel, who started to survey the area. Shirl could hear cries in the distance and see fires lighting the village. She could only pray they were not too late.

It had been easier to see during dusk. Candy kept her eyes peeled to where she had seen the earlier movement. Although the perimeters of the village were well lit with torches, their immediate surroundings were now dark. She and Kelog needed to maintain their position and not react to the cries in other areas of the village.

A man came out of the darkness and ran toward them. Candy picked up her spear and threw it like a javelin. Never in a million years would she have imagined the skills she learned in gym class would now have real life applications. She aimed for his upper thigh. Candy wanted to stop the man, not kill him. If he stayed down, she would accomplish her goal. The spear hit exactly where she had aimed. The man stopped momentarily to pull the weapon from his leg and continued to move forward. This time Candy had no choice. She had to go for the kill. There were children to protect.

She held her breath and threw a spear once again, this time aiming for the man's heart. The velocity of the projectile was greater this time. It hit the mark and the man fell to his knees and then keeled over. One down, but more were coming at them. Candy had an arsenal of spears at her feet. The village had prepared for such an attack. She threw her third spear. This time she went for another kill shot. Candy no longer had the luxury of mercy.

One of the portal guardians had breached the village border. Candy grabbed a staff and went after the man. She had watched *Robin Hood* with Errol Flynn a million times with Shirl. Where her friend wanted to be Maid Marian, Candy wanted to be one of the merry men. Her favorite part of the movie was when Robin Hood and Friar Tuck fought with staffs. Although she was not in Sherwood Forest, Candy was ready for battle.

Candy approached the man, staff in hand. There was only one problem, her opponent had a knife. She needed to disarm him and use his weapon against him. Candy circled her opponent and struck at one of his kidneys. Although he groaned, she had done little harm. He lunged at her with his knife. Candy actually reacted to the move before he made it. His forward momentum caused him to fall off balance. Candy took immediate action by hitting him behind his knees and then gave another blow to his back. She whipped the staff with such power, it surprised her. Her telepathic gift gave her even more strength. Before Candy reached for the knife her opponent dropped, she swung her staff one more time. This time it connected with his head, knocking him unconscious. Candy picked up the knife, stuck it in her leggings, and went to find her next opponent.

Kelog was now in hand-to-hand combat with one of the portal guardians. She came up behind his opponent and swung her staff against his knees. Kelog took advantage of the enemy's momentary incapacitation and jammed a spear into his chest. Candy imagined Kelog had never killed anyone before either. Her comrade seemed momentarily dazed. Candy knew the thoughts that must be going through his mind.

"We will deal with all these emotions later, Kelog," Candy told him. "Right now we have a job to do. The children are counting on us to protect them and keep them safe." Kelog nodded and grabbed more spears to confront another guardian who had breached their village's border.

"*Candy, we need you on the north end,*" Klark communicated through the communal pathway. "*The enemy is coming across the bridge. Everyone else needs to maintain their positions. We are getting attacked from all sides.*"

Candy ran to the far entrance into the village. Klark was battling with one of the attackers who had made it across the gorge. She was ready to confront the next man off the bridge, when the one behind him, threw something that was on fire. Candy watched in horror as a bottle full of alcohol and a lit rag, plummeted onto one of the huts. The structure burst into flames. Several more bottles came flying over her head, making contact with more buildings.

The smoke from the buildings made it hard to see, as well as breathe. Fortunately, her gift allowed her to battle the man that charged toward her.

The rest of the villagers were not as lucky. It had finally sunk in that they were going to lose this battle. Worrying over what would happen to the children in the village momentarily distracted her from an opponent's attack. Candy took a blow to her side and fell to her knees.

Chapter 16

Candy rose from her knees and brought up her staff to react to the next blow her opponent was about to deliver. She was able to deflect the club he wielded against her. It was questionable how long she was going to be able to hold him off. Her eyes continued to water and she tried to suppress the hacking cough caused by inhaling all the smoke.

She was losing the battle her body fought against the fire's by-product; she could no longer hold back the cough that started to shake her body. Out of nowhere, Darah stood in front of her attacker, taking advantage of Candy's incapacitating spasms, and drove a knife into her shoulder.

Once again, she found herself on her knees. She did not know if she should keep the dagger in her shoulder or pull it out. The last thing she wanted was to bleed out. She prepared herself for another attack from her aunt. Only one of them was going to survive this confrontation. The smoke had nullified her telepathic enhancements. Her advantage had been lost.

"You never should have come here," Darah cried. "My mother belongs to me and only me. Her world abandoned her and I am her consolation prize in this world. You are from a daughter she has long forgotten." Despite the darkness, Candy could see the madness in Darah's eyes, as she continued to rave. "My father taught me how to fight. I am going to end this now."

Darah came after her one more time in Candy's mind. Her gift had not left her after all. She was able to react before her opponent actually moved. This time she was prepared for her aunt. Candy shifted, painfully aware of the knife in her shoulder. She lifted the staff and with all her might struck Darah's knee, shattering it. Darah cried out in pain and came down just short of where Candy had fallen.

"We are here, Candy," she heard Alex communicate through the closed telepathic channel she shared with her two friends. *"Don't get freaked out by what is about to happen."*

Candy had no idea what Alex was talking about. She was just relieved her friends had finally arrived. Candy looked up and saw a number of well-built warriors with swords attacking the portal guardians. Candy recognized a number of the men from her short stay on Terra Nova. Her friends had leveraged allies to come and rescue her and Tolfer from this world.

Candy was about to get up when her aunt started to come at her one last time. A blond draped in black appeared from out of the smoke and took Darah into his arms. To her amazement the man bit into her aunt's neck.

Candy watched in fascination, as what she could only assume was a vampire, feasted on the girl who had stabbed her. The guilt associated with her aunt's death was not going to fall on her shoulders. When he was done draining Darah, he dropped her like yesterday's garbage. He looked at her and smiled. Although his mouth was covered in blood, he had to be the most handsome man she had ever seen. How could anything that lovely be so cold and deadly?

The pain in her shoulder was overwhelming. She was light-headed as she stood on shaky legs. *"Tolfer, I need you. I have been stabbed,"* Candy managed to transmit to her soul mate, as she once again came down hard on her knees. Her legs could no longer bear her weight.

Soft hands grabbed her uninjured shoulder and gently helped to lie on her back. Her head was in someone's lap. "Relax, I am here," Alex's soothing voice embraced her. Although they were surrounded by fighting, Candy knew everything was going to be all right. Alex was here. Chartail was right all along. Tarsea had come to rescue them. By some miracle, Alex had talked her soul mate into letting her accompany them on the rescue mission.

Dazed, Candy looked around her. Two men stood guard over them. There was no way to miss what they were: vampires. "How did you manage to get those creatures from Nightshade to join you?"

"We needed every advantage we could get," Alex shared with her. "Shirl felt Drake owed her and was able to talk him into helping. I went to Nightshade with them because I wanted to see what a real vampire looked like. It was unlikely we would have been victorious without the Nightshade fighters."

"Why aren't these two attacking as well?" Candy asked Alex. The two men cloaked in black stood over them. Candy was concerned with the blood exiting her body. Would the vampires be able to control themselves? After everything she had been through, she did not want to be a vampire's snack. Candy was concerned, there was more blood on the ground than in her body. She knew that was not the case, but it certainly felt like it.

"They are guarding me," Alex responded. "Turns out they hold pregnant women with great regard. My unborn daughter may also carry a genetic marker that will allow them to breed with her." Candy could feel Alex's body tremble as she said those words. "Just the idea of one of those monsters with my daughter grosses me out. Tarsea is threatening to lock the poor thing in her room, until she is seventy-five." That seemed like a perfectly reasonable reaction to Candy. If their daughter was half as stubborn as Alex, there were going to be some interesting arguments in their future.

"Where is Shirl?" Candy asked. It astonished her they were calmly conversing as mayhem was all around them. Her reality had become so surreal.

"She is preparing to open a portal to generate an energy blast if we cannot get the upper hand on the enemy," Alex answered. "It is a last resort, naturally. Drake cannot pay his men with dust if Shirl is forced to use the energy blast. I don't look forward to us having to provide the blood we promised, if we cannot get it from the enemy. Drake told us there would be no charge for his assistance, but the other vampires are out for blood." Candy almost laughed. That saying was true both literally and figuratively.

Lifting her head, Candy saw a number of men in the clutches of the vampires. She could not feel any pity for the portal guardians or her aunt. The ground was saturated with the blood of the villagers she had grown to love and respect. As she continued to survey the area, she saw Tolfer approach.

Her soul mate came down on his knees and examined the knife that was still in her shoulder. He placed some kind of cloth around the dagger and then grabbed the handle. "I am going to pull it out on the count of three," Tolfer told her. "One, two," he counted and pulled the knife on the second count. Candy screamed as Tolfer removed the blade. He covered the wound with more cloth, reducing the amount she was bleeding out. "You are going to be all right, Canny. They have a med-tech device. As soon as we take care of some of the more severely injured villagers we will take care of your shoulder."

"I am good with Alex for now," Candy said. "See if you can calm the children. They should not witness what is happening in the village." She did not feel she needed to elaborate. Several of the captured portal guardians were brought forward and Alex's guards were now being rewarded with their blood. This time she turned away, not wanting to watch what was happening to the men.

"It is troubling, I am sitting here with you as the vampires take their bounty," Alex stated. "I should be horrified, but I am mesmerized by it all. Tolfer called you Canny. Wasn't that what I called you before I could properly pronounce your name?" The juxtaposition of the topics Alex brought up momentarily caused Candy to pause.

"Yes," Candy finally answered. "He was coming up with atrocious endearments to call me. It was almost comical." The lightheartedness of their conversation with everything going on around them was startling.

"That is Tolfer," Alex said. "He is always joking and laughing. Once you entered his life he sobered. I am glad you two are finally together. Maybe some of his light heartiness will return. It's almost over, Candy. Hang on a little longer."

Candy continued to lie in Alex's lap as the fires were put out and the prisoners dealt with. The village took stock of who was still standing, who was injured, and who hadn't survived.

Her grandmother had been one of the villagers who died in the attack. Candy did not have to face telling Alaura her daughter had stabbed her and then had been attacked by a vampire. She wished she could feel more in regard to losing her grandmother. Alaura had been a courageous woman. However, although they were related by blood, Alaura was not really her family. Shirl and Alex were.

One of the villagers started to work on Candy's shoulder, using the med-tech device. The piece of equipment was able to heal a wound from the inside out. It was not long before her shoulder was as good as new. She was also given an injection containing a serum that would accelerate the replacement of the blood she had lost. The medicine was courtesy of the Nightshade universe. There had been nothing altruistic concerning the serum's creation.

Shirl and Chartail were by her side when she got back to her feet. Everyone was covered with soot and ash from the fire. The four women walked to the center hut where the survivors of the battle would determine what to do with the remaining prisoners.

Candy walked between Alex and Shirl. She had killed today. There was blood on her hands. Now that the adrenaline was gone, she found herself in a funk. Everything she told herself she would deal with later, was now before her. Candy had to come to terms with everything that had happened. There was no feeling of remorse, only a slight depression in her mood. It troubled her that she had not broken down at this point.

Victory was not always sweet, Tolfer thought as he held a crying child in his arms. The villagers and their liberators came together in the center hut to discuss what needed to be done now that the fighting was over. Every face was blackened from the ash the fires produced. Before he entered the structure, he noted there were some huts still smoldering. His temporary home was in ruins.

He had almost lost his soul mate this evening. If his brother and their reinforcements had been minutes later, Darah might have killed Candy. Tolfer blamed himself, he should have noticed Darah's absence. When Alaura left the building in search of her daughter, Tolfer was inundated with terrified children. There were others who could have comforted the little ones. He knew what that crazed woman was capable of, yet he stayed behind.

Tarsea was consulting with Darden, Koel, and an older man he did not recognize. His soul mate was with Shirl, Alex, and Chartail. He noted the woman who had planned the Prime Ruler's assassination was staring intently at the older man. Candy gazed at the man as well, confusion was written all over his soul mate's face.

His brother approached. "Hand over the child to one of the women," Tarsea ordered. Without thought, Tolfer did exactly what his brother requested. Why had he not done that earlier, when Candy needed him? "We need to settle some things before we head home." As he did when they first came together after the battle, his brother embraced him. He tightened his hold on Tarsea. Tolfer had lost faith they would ever be rescued.

Tolfer followed his brother as they exited the building. Their friends and the women followed. Cianan and Starc were in discussions with Ervin Allaway from Terra Nova. The vampires stood alone in the shadows.

"Ervin," Tarsea addressed the head of the Terra Nova clan. "We appreciate the aid you provided today. I do not know how we are ever going to repay you."

"No thanks are needed," Ervin answered. "We merely repaid a debt we owed Shirl." Tolfer noted the clan leader's eyes on Candy. There was a possessiveness he did not like to the look. Tolfer went to stand next to his soul mate, staking his claim.

Tolfer heard laughter in his brain. "*You finally admitted to Candy you were soul mates,*" Alex said through their familial link. "*I can't believe it took her being literally kidnapped for you to acknowledge your relationship. Candy has always been my family and now we are actually going to be sisters-in-law. How cool is that?*"

If Allaway noticed Tolfer's actions toward Candy he did not visibly show it. "We offer our home to any displaced members of this clan. Although you were originally from a more advanced world, the way you have lived here is quite primitive. Women are scarce. Any woman who joins us will be treated like a queen. I give you my word, you will never be forced to mate against your will."

Three women came forward. Tolfer was preoccupied with checking to see how Candy was while the women conversed with the men from Terra Nova. He heard bits and pieces of discussions. One of the women wanted to know if they could return here if they were not happy on Terra Nova. Shirl had promised to check on them regularly. At no point did anyone ask to return to the Troyk universe. That was one complication they did not have to address currently. Goodbyes were said and the women accompanied the Terra Nova men through the portal Shirl opened.

The vampire, Tolfer heard addressed as Drake, walked forward. "We should be leaving as well. It will not be long before the sun rises." Drake kissed Shirl's cheek and Alex's hand. The vampire's eyes lingered on Alex. He was not sure whether Tarsea saw the look.

Right or wrong, the remaining prisoners would return with the vampires to the Nightshade universe. It was payment for their lives and the only way to assure the safety of the Utopians.

Shirl once again opened the gate. The vampires and their reluctant guests entered the portal. Tolfer felt a sense of relief now that the vampires were gone. He owed these creatures a debt too precious to place a value on.

Klark looked around him in bewilderment. "What now?" It broke Tolfer's heart to see this proud man broken. The Utopians were going to have to heal both physically and mentally.

"We rebuild closer to the portal," Chartail answered. "This village is destroyed, but the portal guardian village is intact. The monthly supplies from the Troyk universe will now be all yours. We need to find a crystal telepath among our numbers to help open portals where we can gather more supplies."

Chartail did not even broach the topic of returning to the Troyk universe. She had found a home here. Tolfer watched Chartail in fascination. His brother's former girlfriend was now a leader.

"We can bring crystals on our next visit and train anyone who can open the portal," Shirl added. "For the time being, you need to stay away from the Troyk universe. There are other worlds you can explore."

A young woman who Tolfer had worked with came forward. "When can we return to the world of our parents?"

"Soon," Darden answered, as he looked at the man who had been by his side throughout the aftermath of the battle. Tolfer still did not know who the man was.

"I remember you now," Candy said, addressing the unknown gentleman.

"You were at the bar where I met Shirl on Earth," Candy stated. It had been driving her crazy trying to place where she had seen him before. He was the man seated at the table when she entered the restaurant in Sedona, where she was re-united with Shirl. She had thought he had wished her luck as they were leaving. Why was he here now?

"We need to be circumspect with the information we share," Darden responded in a telepathic channel, Candy had not accessed before.

"*What is going on?*" Candy asked using the same channel. She heard a number of murmurs around her as others were questioning the same thing. Did a new communal channel open in the aftermath of the war they just fought?

"*Hold up three fingers if you are picking up transmissions in this channel,*" Darden instructed. Candy raised three fingers and was astonished when everyone around her did the same. She gazed over at her soul mate who was not holding up his fingers. Tolfer was too busy surveying who had responded to the request. Darden and Tarsea looked shell shocked.

Shirl walked up to her brother and grasped his three fingers in her hand. "*I need to make sure you can really hear within this channel and are not just copying what everyone else is doing,*" her friend addressed her brother through what Candy could only call the new communal link. "*Sit on your butt if you truly hear me.*"

Candy watched as Cianan sat in front of Shirl. Her friend started to cry and she reached out her hand to help her brother up. "I can truly trust you now," she said as she embraced him.

"I am lost," Cianan said aloud. "What is happening? Why are you overreacting to communication through a new communal pathway? It is understandable when a new group interacts with an existing group."

"But it is not a communal pathway," the man from the bar answered. "It is something altogether different." He directed his attention to her and walked to stand in front of Candy. "My name on Earth is Ben Clark. I have been watching over you, Shirl, and Alexandra your whole lives. My Troyk name is Benko Jarlyn."

Benko had increased the volume of his voice when he announced his true name. There were gasps and cries among the people gathered around. His name had been a rallying call for decades. A name that stood for hope and a promise of a better future without mind control.

"You all linked into the warrior channel," Darden shared with everyone. "A channel that is shared by the true ruler of the Troyk universe and his most loyal followers. You are no longer prisoners, but future liberators. Many of you are here because you called for change." Darden stopped conversing at that point and looked at Benko.

"I guess it is time to start planning my return to the Troyk universe," Benko said. Those words were met with both cheers and tears. "This dimension seems the best place to plan such an event. It is literally the last place my father would ever consider looking for me." Benko gazed at Candy, Alex, and Shirl, the women he indirectly raised. "It is also time to bring JoAnna home. I will no longer be safe on Earth once that happens. Darden and Cassie should also relocate here, once JoAnna is brought over. My father will be too suspicious once a fourth surviving offspring returns to the Troyk universe."

From the corner of her eyes Candy saw Chartail approach Benko. "I am Chartail Adholm and I plotted to kill your father."

"So I have heard," Benko chuckled. "It must have bruised my father's ego to have such a beautiful woman plan his assassination. I will make sure to stay in your good graces." Benko had certainly inherited his father's charm.

Candy could see sparks flying between the two strong-willed people. She started to consider the warrior link and the channel that opened between her two friends and Chartail. Their closed link did not feel like the communal channels she accessed here and in the Troyk universe. Perhaps it had to do more with Chartail than with Candy and her friends.

"Touch her," Candy demanded. She was not going to let Chartail lose one minute with her soul mate, if indeed that was the case.

All eyes fell on her. There was laughter in Benko's eyes. He moved forward and touched Chartail's shoulder. Before Candy could say anything, Chartail made the necessary skin to skin contact, to determine if the two were soul mates. It did not surprise Candy when the two reacted to the touch.

"Son of a bitch!" Benko said as he devoured Chartail with his eyes. Candy, Shirl, and Alex came to stand behind Chartail as she stood in shock.

Realization of what happened finally crossed Chartail's face. That look transitioned to one of apprehension as she looked between her and Shirl. Benko was probably not aware of everything his soul mate had suffered. Chartail was anything but damaged goods. Each obstacle she hurdled made her stronger.

"May I speak with him about what you have been through?" Shirl asked her future primess. Candy was not sure what title was appropriate for the Prime Ruler's consort or wife. Relief was visible on Chartail's lovely face.

Chartail nodded, still in partial shock that she had found her soul mate and he was Benko Jarlyn. "Take Candy with you to complete the story," Chartail suggested. "I will stay with Alexia in the meantime, or should I say Alexandra."

"Alex," her friend responded. "It does not matter the world I am in. Either way, I am Alex. I need to speak with you anyway and come clean." A frown crossed Chartail's lovely face.

Candy knew Alex was going to tell Chartail about how she had read her mind and betrayed her. She did not know which conversation was going to be more difficult. Shirl and Candy were going to tell Benko about what happened to his soul mate in this world and in the Nightshade universe. Alex got to confess about her betrayal in order to clear the way to save her best friend Shirl and get her into the Troyk universe. All roads had led them to where they were today. Benko was finally stepping up to return to the Troyk universe and Chartail had found a soul mate to fight alongside.

Candy and Shirl spent about ten minutes alone with Benko sharing Chartail's story with him, so she would not have to. The man was enraged with what he heard. He had been aware of Shirl being held in the Nightshade universe. He had been ignorant of Chartail being raped, brutalized, and drained of blood by Yorik.

Benko communicated he needed to strengthen his relationship with Drake to one day exact revenge against Yorik. When the time was right, Shirl would aid him in his quest. In the meantime, they needed to return to the others.

Candy was nervous about how Alex's discussion went with Chartail. If Chartail turned against Alex they were all sunk. Candy would stand next to her friend, regardless of what it will mean politically or socially in the future. To her relief, Chartail and Alex were embracing when they returned. Alex was crying and Chartail was comforting her. Her friend was mumbling about hormones and the inability to control her emotions.

It was time to return to the Troyk universe. For the time being, Benko and Chartail would stay behind and help the Utopians move into the portal guardian village. Most of these people were here directly or indirectly because of Benko Jarlyn. He was named the new community leader. Klark retained his position as head of security. Tolfer's friend, Marton, was named his lieutenant. There were promises of more supplies and covert visits.

Candy stepped through the portal ready to continue building her life in the Troyk universe with more secrets to keep and a soul mate. First and foremost was explaining how she was able to escape the penal colony. They could not afford to endanger the lives of the true ruler of the Troyk universe and the people she had come to love in this world.

Chapter 17

~

The Troyk Universe

All eyes were on them as they made their way through the streets of Aster Province on the way to The Palace. It was decided they would go directly to be debriefed before heading home and cleaning up. Candy would have loved to have taken a shower first. She was caked in dried blood from head to foot. It was a wonder she was able to continue to swallow the bile that kept coming up her throat. Her hair was partially tied behind her head while strands kept coming loose. Candy had to continually shove the wild wisps from her face.

Tolfer walked next to her. He had taken her hand as soon as they came off the mountain pass and continued their journey beside each other. They were both physically and mentally exhausted. Staying within the penal colony and helping them settle near the portal, had not been discussed. It had been hard on her soul mate to leave behind the children he had grown so close to.

With Benko Jarlyn now in that community there was no question they would be returning to that world. Tolfer would be able to keep working with the children while Candy prepared the adults for the battle of their lives. No one knew if unseating Jerlyn Jarlyn would be a peaceful revolution or bloody. She decided to hold off on that thought for another day. Candy had seen too much blood today. Oddly, it was not the vampire blood feast that had gotten to her, but the horror they inflicted on each other. It troubled her, she was not an emotional mess reacting to all the lives she had taken. Perhaps she was still in shock and her brain had not internalized all she had done.

The warrior channel was active with conversations regarding the upcoming stories they would all share. They would confess to the involvement of the vampires from the Nightshade universe, but not the men who had fought beside them from Terra Nova. Too many gatherers visited that world to risk bringing visibility to Ervin and his men. The people of Terra Nova shared and kept Shirl's secret.

Naturally, no one would mention the involvement of Benko Jarlyn and his presence now in the penal colony world. Fortunately, Solfa would lead the interrogations. They would be interviewed as a group and would then be separated. The warrior channel would be used to share discussions across rooms in order to guarantee consistency in what they communicated.

Within a block of The Palace they were met by two dozen guards. Although Candy had been warned they would be coming, it did not reduce the anxiety she felt being surrounded by these armed men. The group walked in silence for the remaining steps until they reached their destination.

Nothing was being shared within the warrior path. The communal pathways were abuzz, but none of them contributed to the discussions. Their stories had to be first shared with the Troyk intelligence community. No one had ever returned from the penal colony before. Tarsea and Shirl were going to talk about planning the rescue, while Tolfer and Candy were to inform them about life in the penal colony.

It was the first time she entered the Palace through the front doors. The foyer was filled with people gawking at them. Candy stared at the staircase before her. On any other day she could have taken the stairs two at a time. Today she wondered if she would be able to make it up one flight. The interrogations would take place on the third floor. Tolfer tightened his grip on her hand as they started their climb. He knew without her telling him she was exhausted. Knowing her soul mate was there gave her a second wind.

They were led to a large conference room. Medical personnel did cursory exams to make sure there were no life-threatening injuries before they continued. Candy thought that was odd. If anyone had been gravely injured, they would have telepathically shared that information as soon as they came in range of the communal pathways. She figured it had to be some kind of procedure that was followed after difficult off-world trips. Candy sat in the chair she was told to occupy. It was comforting that Tolfer was right beside her. What little energy she had left, was fueled by his presence.

To her surprise, Jeryl Jarlyn entered the room with Solfa. He came and immediately gave Candy an awkward embrace. Considering how gross she must be, Candy was surprised he even touched her.

"I am so glad you have returned to us safe," Jarlyn told Candy. "Although you are not my granddaughter, for a short period of time I felt you were. The affection I felt for you did not diminish when I learned the truth of our relationship. You are a daughter of the Troyk universe."

His words hit Candy like an eighteen-wheeler. She was struck by what he said and the sincerity behind them. Candy broke down. Tears that had not been shed for her grandmother and all those who had died today came streaming down her cheeks. She shook with sobs and the inability to control her body.

"*Shirl, you need to go to Candy and help control her grief,*" Alex shared in their private pathway. "*They cannot know Tolfer is her soul mate. It would make sense to the Prime Ruler that you are closest to her.*"

Shirl made her way to Candy and brought her into her arms. "Can we do this another time?" Shirl asked no one in particular. "She battled for her life today and has been held captive in the penal world."

"No," Solfa answered. There was a hardness to her voice. Had Candy not known she was on their side, Solfa's tone would have brought on even more violent sobs. She had truly lost control of herself. "I want to know what happened in the penal colony and if a gateway had been opened to any other dimensions where convicts could be loose."

There were three crystal telepaths in the room, but it was Shirl's back that got as straight as a rod. "We went to that world to rescue Candy and that was it," Shirl answered with an edge to her voice. "The criminals taken from that world left for the Nightshade universe. Their blood was payment for the assistance I was able to arrange with their master vampire."

"You entered the Nightshade universe?" Solfa said in disbelief. Candy had to admit, she was a great actress. It was her understanding that Alex's cousin had been involved in the tactical discussions associated with the operation to come after her and Tolfer.

"I needed invincible warriors to get my friend back," Shirl answered. "Those monsters owed me!" Everyone knew what the female crystal telepath had suffered in that world. Evidence of the vampire's bite was still on her neck.

"Unbelievable," Solfa said under her breath. "I noticed that Kelog Potts is not present. Did he die?"

"Kelog survived the battle," Candy shared with the Troyk officials. She had managed to get control of herself once again. "He entered that world because he had family there and wished to stay with them."

"Did you leave Chartail Adholm behind?" Solfa inquired. "This group has a bad habit of rescuing that woman."

Candy knew those words would get Shirl's dander up. "Listen," Shirl almost growled, "I would not leave a soul in the Nightshade universe, not even you."

Solfa approached Shirl and the two women were almost nose to nose. Candy almost expected a fight to break out between them. They were giving quite a performance. Alex jumped to her feet and placed her hand on her cousin's arm.

"Shirl is not the enemy here, Solfa," Alex said. "We went to rescue Tolfer and Candy. Tolfer has become a brother to me during my stay with his parents. We left Chartail in the other universe, where she belongs. She plotted to kill our Prime Ruler."

Jeryl Jarlyn left Candy's side and embraced her friend. "Little Alexia," he said. "I was surprised to hear you joined in the rescue."

"How could I not, sir," Alex replied. "Besides, I wanted to see what a vampire looked like. It was a good thing Shirl had Drake under her thumb. Those vampires were terrifying. They were starving and were willing to assist us. We have Tolfer back and I will try not to think of what it cost."

An older man who had entered the room shortly after Jeryl Jarlyn and Solfa arrived came forward. "You saw my daughter Chartail? How is she?"

Alex had been haunted by betraying Chartail. She had even demanded to be on the mountain to say goodbye to Chartail before her sentence was executed. Candy had been told that Chartail's father had not even appeared at his daughter's trial. Alex walked forward to confront Chartail's father.

"She was brutalized both in the Nightshade and penal colony worlds," Alex said. There was such hatred in her voice toward Chartail's father. Even Candy was surprised. "There had to be a better alternative in dealing with your daughter. You knew what she faced in the Nightshade universe, yet you did nothing."

Chartail's father did not respond to Alex's comment or look her in the eye. Candy did not have any baggage when it came to Chartail's fate. She wanted to reassure this man his daughter was all right.

"Chartail was being held by the leader of the violent portal guardians," Candy shared with Prime Adholm. "She would visit the Utopia village where I lived while Fraclyn's daughter visited him. Chartail is a survivor and does what is necessary to go on living. I do not believe I have ever met a stronger woman in my life. She is now free of that man and has joined the Utopia community. The vampires were given the survivors who had attacked our peaceful village. Your daughter is safe."

"Thank you," Prime Adholm said to Candy. She felt there was more the man wanted to say, but he stopped there. He removed himself from the group and sat in one of the room's corners.

Candy knew she had to bring to the attention of the Troyk government the condition of the penal colony. She lived with these people and pledged to be an advocate for them with the Troyk government. "There are children in that world your monthly supplies must start addressing."

The room was silent after Candy dropped her bomb. How these people had not considered what would happen after they pushed people through the portal into the penal colony world she could not fathom. All criminals, regardless of their crimes, were sentenced there for life. Would they continue to send murderers and rapists to the world she just left?

"Children," Jeryl Jarlyn repeated. "How very short-sighted of us. We will make sure to include more appropriate supplies in the future."

"What about the fate of future criminals?" Candy asked. "Are you going to repopulate that now-peaceful community with people who would harm those children?"

"We have many decisions we have to make about what to do going forward," the Prime Ruler answered. "I want to hear what you experienced and who you met." Jeryl Jarlyn turned to his head of intelligence and said, "It is time for the debriefing, Solfa."

Tolfer kept quiet as his soul mate and her friends addressed Jeryl Jarlyn, Prime Adholm, and Solfa. They did an excellent job of staying with the story, they agreed would be shared and bringing to light the plight of the penal colony's children. Going forward, nothing was more important than the welfare of those kids.

The group was dispersed for the individual interviews to be conducted. He currently sat in a room with Prime Adholm and one of Solfa's female lieutenants. Tolfer had seen the woman around, but did not know her name. He sat patiently waiting for the questioning to start.

Prime Adholm would be the mind control telepath in the interview. One would be in attendance in each interrogation. They would be able in most instances to tell if the subject was lying or not. Since he had made love to his soul mate, he was immune to their telepathic powers.

"Let us get started, Tolfer," the woman said. "My name is Stelalyn. I worked the mission with your brother and Alexia that captured the two remaining plotters in the assassination attempt against our Prime Ruler." She did not mention Chartail by name because Stelalyn was seated next to Chartail's father.

"It is nice to meet you," Tolfer answered. "Can we get this over with so I can go home and take a long, hot shower?" His hands were covered with his soul mate's dried blood. He had a layer of ash from the fires that destroyed most of the Utopia village, coating his entire body.

"Fine," Stelalyn replied. "Why did you enter the portal after Candace and Kelog? That was quite a sacrifice to make for someone you went to school with, but did not maintain a relationship with over the years."

"I did not go after Kelog," Tolfer said. "Candy was staying with my parents and in the short time she lived there, we became friends. At the time I did not know why Kelog did what he did. I could not let Candy face what was before her alone."

"That is admirable," Prime Adholm added, taking over the interview. "Tell me about your dealings with my daughter in that universe." Tolfer knew he was not talking to a mind control telepath, but a father.

"She was present when we first arrived," Tolfer shared with him. "I figured she saved our lives. We were traded to the Utopian village shortly after arriving. Candy's grandmother found out she was in the village. Chartail would visit from time to time, while Alaura's daughter visited her father near the portal.

142

Your daughter held up well, considering. When our rescuers came, Chartail led them to us while we were under attack by the portal guardians. If they had arrived any later, I do not know if anyone would have survived. Your daughter is one of the reasons the villagers are still alive. She lives among them now, free of the sexual servitude she was subjected to."

Tolfer did not feel the need to mince words with Prime Adholm. He was partially responsible for the policies over the years that led to both the creation of the penal colony and what drove his daughter to do what she did. The Prime was also one of the men who could change how they dealt with the penal colony in the future.

He could see his words hit the mark. Prime Adholm looked stricken. Tolfer needed to hit while the target was still in sight. "There are children that need to be cared for in that world now. Perhaps one day even your own grandchild. Necessary supplies need to be sent through the portal immediately. Medicines and more med-tech kits are sorely needed to care for those who were injured in the attack. What resources they had must be used up by now."

"Yes, yes," Adholm muttered. "I will see to it, personally. Do you think Chartail would appreciate some of her things sent with the next shipment?"

It was clear to Tolfer that Prime Adholm was not handling things well. The man could barely hold it together. The guilt associated with his daughter, was consuming him. At no time during the interview, did he feel the pull of mind control telepathic powers on his brain.

Stelalyn finally rejoined the conversation. "Tell me about the Nightshade vampires' involvement."

Tolfer shrugged his shoulders. "We were losing and then the vampires entered the village. I had screaming children in my arms hearing the cries first of their parents and then the enemy. It was my job to protect them. I did not see the vampires attack. Only after the battle was done did I venture out and see the devastation around me. Most of the huts we used for shelter were destroyed. The village was still smoldering and we were all feeling the negative effects on our lungs. I do not know what else to tell you."

The intelligence officer stared at him. Her eyes were glistening with unshed tears. Tolfer figured the interview was over as she got up and left the room.

"Thank you for letting me know my daughter is safe now," Prime Adholm said. "You can join the others in the conference room. I have no more questions for you." The Prime stood and made his way to the door. He hesitated for a brief moment before turning to address him once more. "I will make sure things are set right for the welfare of those children and my daughter. Perhaps one day we can bring them home."

Tolfer was not far behind Prime Adholm upon the completion of the interview. He made his way to the conference room, hoping Candy would be there. She had been very emotional earlier and he was concerned about her interview. To date, Candy held up extremely well under pressure. The question was, how much more could she take before she truly fell apart? Earlier, she had cried with relief. She still had not dealt with the toils of war.

If Candy was asked the same question again for the millionth time she was going to scream. She knew one proper cross-examination technique was asking the same question over and over again. Sometimes the question was phrased different ways. The interviewer's job was to find a hole in her story or an inconsistent answer. On top of her frustration in going over the same items over again and again, the mind control pull on her brain was causing a headache. As her patience wore thin, the headache increased in intensity.

"I don't know what else I can tell you," Candy yelled at the people across the table from her. Rubbing her forehead, did little to relieve her pounding head. She was sick and tired of being treated like a criminal. It was not her fault Kelog shoved her into the portal or that she was rescued. "My grandmother is dead and so is my psychotic aunt. She barely talked to me about my mother and how much she loved her. The actions my mother took were ancient history. Early on she told me not to mention my mother again. Alaura's focus was on the survival of the Utopia community and controlling her insane daughter."

She cried out to Tolfer through the soul mate channel. He was done with his interview and was waiting for her to be finished with hers. Tolfer tried to calm her. His words did little to impact the anger and pain building inside her.

"Did your grandmother mention where Benko Jarlyn and your mother went?" her accuser asked. Candy wanted to reach across the table and punch the woman's larynx. Her own violent reaction scared Candy. Imagining herself doing this unforgivable act, gave her pause. One thing was clear, she needed out of this room.

She took a deep breath and calmly answered the question again. "We did not talk about my mother's activities. Each day was about surviving in that world. She wanted to get to know me, not dredge up a past neither one of us could change."

Candy could feel liquid running down her nose. She did not have to look at her hand, as she wiped the liquid away, to know her hand was covered in fresh blood. Alex had gotten numerous nosebleeds since coming into the Troyk universe, so Candy was not concerned. The woman across from her did react. She stood and raced out of the room. She said something about getting her some tissues. The pull on her brain stopped.

"I am sorry if I caused you any discomfort," the man across from her stated. He had introduced himself when he entered, but she did not remember his name. Her usual talent for remembering names had been eclipsed by the events of the day and their return to this inquisition. Candy did not bother to acknowledge his words. She just continued to wipe away the blood.

The woman returned with a box of tissues. Candy did not bother to reach for one. "Look at me," Candy screamed. "I am covered in blood. Do you think a little nosebleed matters today after everything I have been through? If you cannot deal with it, then leave the room. I have been stabbed today and have killed to protect innocent children. You have the nerve to sit there in judgment of me! This interview is over. I am going to take a hot shower and sleep for a century."

Candy got up and returned to the conference room where she knew Tolfer waited. The two people who had been interviewing her had the good sense not to follow. She could not be held responsible for the damage she would do to their bodies, if they tried to stop her. None of the guards she passed attempted to detain her either. Candy immediately went into Tolfer's arms when she was re-united with him.

"Take me home, Tolfer," Candy cried into his shoulder. "I can't handle any more questions."

Tolfer held her for several minutes before he released her. Alex had entered the conference room as they were preparing to leave. Her friend was mumbling to herself. She looked as annoyed, as Candy was angry.

"Idiots!" Alex announced to everyone in the room. "We are surrounded by banal dolts! Did they ask me about the Nightshade universe? No! Did they ask me about what I saw at while in the penal colony world? No! Once again, I was asked about Benko Jarlyn!" Alex then screamed at the top of her lungs, "I do not know Benko Jarlyn or where he can be found!" She was lying through her teeth, but boy, was she convincing!

The guards who were in the room seemed at a loss about what to do with Alex. Starc came into the room and let out a long whistle. "I could hear you all the way down the hall, Alexia. Although you were quite loud, I cannot disagree with what you were saying. They asked me over and over again if I knew anything about Benko Jarlyn's whereabouts."

Alex approached the guard who stood next to Starc. "I demand you get my cousin Solfa Theffar here immediately or I will start ranting through the communal pathways."

The guard looked petrified and quickly exited the room, hopefully in search of Solfa. Through the warrior's link Candy knew Solfa was currently in the interview room with Shirl. They had been conversing while Alex was blowing her stack. Due to her pregnancy, Alex could not hear all the comments being sent through that pathway. The once quiet Alex, was certainly blowing up a lot of dust in her wake.

Moments later the beleaguered guard re-entered the room with Solfa in tow. Alex approached her cousin. "I know you are a hot shot in this government, Solfa. But these interviews are a waste of everyone's time. You spend most of your free time with us. Do you not think you would know if we were keeping such a huge secret from you? Plus, look at Candy. She is dead on her feet and needs to clean herself up. I cannot believe you allowed her to be questioned in her current condition. My stomach is heaving, just being close to her."

If they were back on Earth, Candy would have embraced Alex and totally grossed her out, since she was caked in blood. However, in this world they were newly-made friends and it would have been totally inappropriate. Candy figured she would have a little fun with Alex at home before she jumped into the shower. After weeks in the penal colony, Candy would never again take indoor plumbing for granted.

"I have called a halt to all the interviews that were still being conducted," Solfa shared with them. "You can all go home and clean up. My apologies for not allowing you to refresh yourselves before the interview."

With those words they were free to go. By the time they made it to the main hall, the rest of the crew was waiting for them. They all headed to their respective homes. It was decided they would reconnect in the morning. Everyone had enough for the day. They just wanted to bathe and make love to their soul mates. Darden and Koel decided to meet up and hit the bars. Darden's soul mate was on Ginkgo Terra and Koel had not found his, so they decided to get drunk.

Candy walked alongside Tolfer as they returned to his parents' home. She had so many decisions to make about her future in the Troyk universe. But first, she wanted to shower and have her soul mate buried deep inside her.

Chapter 18

~

Water pounded on Candy's back. She had never felt anything better. Well, that was not exactly true. Tolfer did amazing things to her that generated sensations within her she had not thought possible. Candy blushed, remembering everything they had done together in the penal colony world. Her mind was captivated with her memories of her time with Tolfer, while her body was being caressed by the pulsating liquid that fell from the showerhead.

Candy had scrubbed her body from head to toe several times. At one point the water at her feet was red from washing off the dried blood that had been caked to her body. She shampooed her hair so many times, she was afraid it was going to fall from her scalp. Candy was naive if she felt cleaning her body would erase the horrors of the day. She was probably facing years of therapy.

She was so deep in thought it startled her when the shower door opened and Tolfer entered. He was as naked as the day he was born. Candy stared at his lust-filled eyes. She had fantasized about showering with a man and all that involved. It appeared her dreams were now becoming reality. As soon as Tolfer stood before her, water rushing over his glistening skin, Candy moved her gaze down his incredible body. His chest was wide and muscular. Water beaded on his pectorals and she longed to lick the liquid from his body. His member was erect and ready for her.

He did not say anything out loud or through their pathway. She stepped into his arms without uttering a word. Candy did not want to break whatever enchantment surrounded them. His lips met hers and she breathed a sigh into his mouth. This was better than any fantasy she had earlier devised.

"*God*," Tolfer finally groaned through the soul mate link. "*You taste so good. I could live to be a hundred and never tire of you.*" She felt the same way but did not want to mirror the sentiment back to him.

"*I waited for you,*" she told him. She communicated telepathically since she did not want to break the kiss. "*Somehow I knew the perfect man was out there for me. I did not want to settle while other girls experimented with sex. I knew it was not right for me.*" They had never discussed the reason she had held onto her virginity. She was not saving herself for marriage, but for a soul mate, she had not even known existed.

Tolfer lifted her and placed her against the tiled wall. Her body welcomed the cold marble against her back. The rest of her was close to the boiling point, being next to Tolfer. She was so hot for him she could barely stand it.

Candy wrapped her legs around his waist and brought him closer into her body. They still had not broken that incredible initial kiss. Her still soapy hands moved from his hips and glided up his flesh, ultimately ending with them entangled in his now wet, curly hair. Candy loved his wavy black locks. Her fingers massaged his head, as they deepened their kiss.

Tolfer adjusted his hold as he drove into her. His mouth absorbed her scream. She wound his hair tighter around her fingers as she held on for the ride of her life. Releasing her mouth, Tolfer craned his head back as he let out his own cry. Her scalp started to burn as her hair was lodged between her and the wall. Tolfer masterfully stepped back, taking her with him. He backed up a few inches until he was now against the far wall of the shower. Her knees and shins now knocked against the tile as they continued to make love.

Candy wanted more of him, but did not know how to manage it. He filled her to the hilt. She moaned into his shoulder. Her teeth gently grabbed flesh and held on as her body continued to rock. A small growl escaped from Tolfer as she continued to mark his shoulder. Careful not to draw blood, Candy nibbled gently on his tender skin. This was a different experience from watching the vampires ravage their victims today. Going forward, this was the image she would carry.

Tolfer's legs became a little unsteady, as they both reached the ultimate orgasm together. Not surprisingly, Candy was a wet noodle in his arms. She was not ready to stand on her own two feet. He must have sensed that because he did not release her. They moved back so Candy was once again pinned to the wall. Pulling her silky strands with one hand, Tolfer swept her wet hair over her shoulder. They continued to stand there, as the water from the shower cooled.

"I think we used up all the hot water," Candy muttered into his shoulder. She licked the teeth marks she had left as a reminder of their latest encounter.

Tolfer released his hold on her. With one hand he turned off the water and with the other he opened the shower door. He grabbed a towel and wrapped it around her. The soft, warm cloth felt wonderful after the cold water. Tolfer led her out of the stall and dried her. He stood soaking wet, as he ministered to her. As soon as he completed toweling off every bead of water from her body, he encased her in a warm plush robe. He lifted her onto the vanity before he dried himself.

"Tarsea and Starc are taking their soul mates out for the second seating at one of the local meeting place restaurants," Tolfer informed her as he continued to rub the towel over his hair. The motion mesmerized her. It was so damn sexy, she could barely stand it. "They want us to go with them. It is important to act as normal as possible. The sooner our stay in the penal colony is no longer a topic in the communal pathways conversations, the better."

Candy had heard about the second seating. It was when Troyk women dressed in the revealing outfits. She had been wanting to wear the lovely black creation that hung in her closet. "I'm game to go," Candy uttered. For some reason, she did not want to sound too anxious. Maybe she was a little nervous about wearing that daring outfit.

"Perfect," Tolfer said as he kissed her nose. "I will quickly dress and give you time to dress and put on make-up."

Tolfer was gone within a blink of an eye. Candy continued to sit where she had been placed. Make-up? Never in her life had she worn cosmetics. Facing a horde of spear-carrying savages was less intimidating than applying make-up. She did not know where to start.

Candy stared at herself in the mirror. There was more flesh showing than material covering her breasts. She knew she was stunning in the outfit. Candy was just too shy to be seen in public in such a revealing piece. Maybe she and Tolfer could have a quiet evening at home. The beautiful outfit should stay hanging in the closet.

Tolfer's parents were going out as well. Leenea had basically been a shut-in while her son was in the penal colony. She was inconsolable while he was gone. Tarsea told them he was afraid she was not going to release him, when he came to say goodbye to them, before he left to rescue his brother. Leenea had hugged her son with a grip Tarsea had never experienced from her before. He had not thought she had such physical strength.

There was a knock on the bedroom door. Alex and her aunt Norri entered, with Shirl close behind. Norri carried several bags. It did not take a brain surgeon to figure out what they contained.

"We have come to do your hair and make-up," Alex said as she made her way to Candy. "Well, actually Norri is going to do it. We are going to watch. She did my make-up the first time I went out with Tarsea. I was a nervous wreck. I would have gouged an eye out with the eyeliner if I had done it alone."

"You look beautiful, Candy," Shirl commented. "Every man in the restaurant who had seen you and not asked you out before, is going to regret it. They had their chance and they blew it. Good thing, too, considering Tolfer is your soul mate." Shirl embraced her and then started to adjust Candy's outfit. It was a habit Shirl easily fell back into. Shirl would always tuck in labels, Candy had not realized were sticking out. She would pull down the back of a shirt when it had ridden up Candy's torso. It had always annoyed Candy. Now it felt like home.

"Let us go into the washroom where the light is better," Norri said. The older woman continued on her way expecting the younger women to follow. Never having had a makeover before, Candy was secretly looking forward to it.

Shirl brought a chair for Candy to sit in, while Alex's aunt worked her magic. Norri started by applying moisturizer and base to Candy's face. With all the sports she played outside, Candy was religious about applying sunscreen. Unfortunately, she was just not good about reapplying it. There was a little sun damage on her face the make-up covered. She opened her eyes wide as a dark purple eye pencil was applied around her eyes. Originally, Candy thought it was a Troyk thing. Shirl explained purple was just one of the colors they were going to use. Shades of blue, brown, and gold eye shadow were masterfully applied.

Black eye shadow was used on the corner of her eyes to make them pop. She tried not to blink as mascara was applied to her eyelashes. A little blush was placed on the apple of her cheek and a mauve lipstick was the finishing touch.

They decided Candy would wear her hair loose. Norri applied a couple of hair clips to keep it out of her face. Candy stood in front of the mirror and was shocked. She could not believe she was the woman who stood before her. Her friends came to stand next to her to admire the end product. Alex was dressed in shades of blue, while Shirl was breathtaking in silver.

"Never in a million years am I going to be able to reproduce this look on my own," Candy commented, still a little stunned at what she saw.

"It is a good thing you are not alone," Alex said. Candy had missed her friend, desperately while she was gone. With Alex marrying Tarsea and Candy being Tolfer's soul mate, they were finally going to be true sisters.

"I cannot believe this is the first time we have gone on a date together," Shirl said.

Candy laughed. "That is probably because Alex and I rarely dated."

"Yes, I guess that's true," Shirl commented. "I certainly went on a lot of first dates. Who would have ever imagined we were from another universe and our soul mates were here waiting for us?"

"Well, actually," Alex said. "Candy and I were born on Earth. You are the only true Troyk woman here. Besides Norri, of course."

"I would have given anything to have been there while you girls were growing up," Norri said. She wiped a tear from her eye. "I am not going to get all emotional like Pattrice. My one consolation is I will be able to see your children grow up." Candy watched as Norri took her pregnant niece into her arms.

"We are going to name my daughter Starta," Alex said, "after my mother, and your sister."

"That would mean so much to me." Norri was obviously struggling to keep her emotions in check. "How do you know it is a girl?"

"The vampire master Yorik told me," Alex answered. "Drake also mentioned I was having a baby girl and she would be compatible with their race. As if she or I would ever end up in the Nightshade universe again."

Candy had never been to the parallel universe these vampires called home. She hoped she never would. A shudder ran through her thinking these creatures had designs on Alex's unborn daughter. "We will protect her," Candy pledged to her friend.

"It's all nonsense," Alex replied. "Won't we all be surprised when I give birth to a baby boy?"

"Well, that is still months away," Shirl added. "We've got three men in the common room, who are probably growing impatient waiting for us."

"Too bad," Alex said. "We never have gone through this female type of bonding before. I kind of like it. Besides, aren't women supposed to keep their men waiting? They do on television."

"Enough," Norri declared. "You girls grab your men and have a wonderful time."

Alex, Shirl, and Norri left the room. Candy looked at herself one more time in the mirror. She looked wonderful in the outfit Leenea had selected for her. But the woman in the mirror was not who Candy really was. What would happen if Tolfer liked her better this way?

Chapter 19

"You look beautiful," Tolfer said as he came and kissed her on the cheek. "I am afraid to mess up your face or your outfit by being more amorous." She loved the mischievous look on his face. "It is a good thing we do not do this every day." Candy released the breath she had been holding, relief washing over her. Her soul mate liked the way she looked, but did not want her to become the creature before him on a regular basis.

"How about we get all messy tonight when we get home?" Candy whispered in his ear.

Tolfer chuckled, "Promises, promises." He threw back the words she had uttered to him on the bridge in the penal colony. It seemed like it had occurred a lifetime ago.

"We should head out," Tarsea said. "They will only hold the reservations so long. You girls always take forever to get ready. Maybe next time you should start earlier." Candy watched in amusement as Tarsea placed a shawl over Alex's shoulders, sheltering most of her upper body from prying eyes. Alex had a half-smile on her face as she looked in Candy's direction and winked. She had shared with her friend how Tarsea always got super possessive of her body when they went out.

Candy imagined he would be perfectly happy never to leave their bedroom. Tolfer seemed more comfortable with Candy's alluring outfit. He was more easy-going compared to Tarsea. Tolfer was nurturing while Tarsea was more controlling. Nature had selected the right mates for both of them. Candy imagined she would have killed Tarsea by now if he had been her soul mate.

They walked through the streets of Aster province. Couples that looked very much like them were out in force. Men dressed as they did during the day, but the women were a different story. Candy felt she was at a runway fashion show. It did not take them long to get to the meeting place. Rather than walking on one of the many paths in the park, they headed directly to the restaurant, since they were late.

One of the men must have telepathically announced who they were since they were led directly to their table upon entering. Walking to where they were seated, Candy felt like she was on display. She was used to men staring at Shirl and ignoring Alex and her. That was not the case tonight. All three women were eyed and admired. Candy could see Tarsea tighten his grip on Alex's waist, while Tolfer chuckled.

She was seated between Tolfer and Starc. Although she had heard that Shirl and Starc's relationship started with issues, tonight they seemed like an old married couple. They were comfortable with each other and what they had together. Like Shirl and Starc, she and Tolfer had had a traumatic experience, which bonded them together earlier beyond just the soul mate link.

Candy looked at the menu, overwhelmed by the selections. "What should I order?" she whispered to Tolfer. To the world they were newly dating and would converse orally in the restaurant. Candy was growing to like the intimacy of their telepathic discussions. Falling back into talking to him, seemed impersonal.

"Do you want to be daring or play it safe?" Tolfer asked. She loved how his breath felt against her ear, as he answered her question with another question.

"Daring," Candy replied, "why take the safe route after everything we've been through? I want something with lots of flavor and spices." Although the food in the penal colony got better when Tolfer started to harvest local herbs, it was still more of a survival exercise than eating for enjoyment.

"I will order for both of us," Tolfer replied. She sat back and listened to Tolfer place their order telepathically. They were having the house special for the evening and two bottles of wine were ordered for the table.

The wine was delivered almost immediately upon being ordered. A small amount was poured into Tarsea's glass, to determine if the wine was suitable. Nothing was worse than wine that was just about to turn. Tarsea nodded his approval of the beverage. Five of the six glasses were filled and the remainder of the second bottle was left in a cooler on the table. Due to her pregnancy, Alex had herbal tea. Candy took a sip from her glass and then sat back, savoring the taste of the wine. She could not pick up the different flavor nuances, she just knew she was enjoying it.

Two bread baskets were delivered to the table. One was placed directly in front of Alex. Her friend and Tarsea had been to this restaurant enough times for the wait staff to be familiar with Alex's voracious appetite. Candy took a roll from the other basket. She did not want the wine going directly to her head after drinking on an empty stomach. The roll was moist and did not need butter. Generally, if something was dry enough that it needed to be slathered with butter, Candy was not interested in eating it.

The discussions around the table were relaxed. Nothing controversial was brought up. Even the communal pathways were full of conversations with nothing noteworthy. Candy sat back and took in her environment. She entertained herself watching the outfits paraded in front of her. Internally, she debated whether she could be daring enough to wear a couple of the concoctions some of the women wore. A number of them were more appropriate for the bedroom.

Shirl must have caught on to what was grabbing her attention. "We should go shopping for more evening wear for you, Candy," Shirl mentioned. "There is a cute place Alex and I discovered on the way to the Aster Province Zoo. Starc bought me this outfit the first time I checked the place out. Alex had tried on an outfit there as well. Unfortunately, Tarsea destroyed it doing God knows what to her in the dressing room." Alex started to giggle. It was a sound she had become accustomed to since coming to the Troyk universe. Her friend never giggled like that on Earth.

Although Candy tolerated shopping, another part of what Shirl had communicated caught her attention. "Aster Province has a zoo?" She had always loved the field trips to the zoo when she was a child. Nothing bad could ever happen in a zoo.

"It is so cool, Candy," Alex replied. "They have animals from other universes. Some are quite frightening. The Giant Larma Beast from Terra Flora is something that could only come out of your nightmares or a novelist's warped mind."

Shirl nodded as she swallowed the piece of bread she was nibbling on. "I saw one of them in the wild. It almost took off my brother's leg. We should go there tomorrow and then go shopping. Between me and Candy we should have Alex properly protected."

Her friend had barely finished talking about protecting Alex when the person they were protecting her from walked into the restaurant. Candy almost dropped her glass when she spotted Raine Narmouth. Tolfer had to steady her hand before she spilled the wine on the table.

Following Candy's gaze, Tolfer saw Raine Narmouth had entered the restaurant. He alerted the people at the table of his presence through both the warrior channel and their familial pathway for Alex's benefit. Their celebratory mood had been changed to once again being on guard. Wine glasses were put down and shoved away.

"Who is he with?" Candy inquired. Raine was with a man who appeared to be a couple of years older than he was. Tolfer had never seen him before. It was not surprising since he did not socialize with Raine Narmouth.

"That is Raine's brother, Chanz," Starc volunteered. *"He is a mind control telepath. The bastard used his powers on Elzbeth to convince her to have sex with his younger brother."* Tolfer knew there had been bad blood between Narmouth and Starc but he never imagined this had been the reason why. He wondered how he would have stood up against such a betrayal. Fortunately, Candy was immune to such suggestions from a mind control telepath.

He turned to look at the expression on his soul mate's face. Tolfer could see the anger building and he took her hand in his to calm her. *"Now is not the time or the place, Canny."*

Candy had not taken her gaze from Narmouth and his brother. Tolfer took his eyes off his soul mate and placed them where Candy was looking. It was clear Narmouth's eyes were glued onto Alex's back. He was relieved both Tarsea and Alex were facing him rather than Narmouth.

"There is nothing we can do about him being here," Tolfer whispered to the table. "This is a public restaurant. We are here to celebrate Candy's and my liberation from the penal colony. Let us not let Raine Narmouth ruin our evening." The people around the table grudgingly agreed.

"Starc, Tolfer, and I will join you girls at the zoo and shopping with you afterward," Tarsea said. "We will make a day of it."

Tolfer could feel Candy's anger further boiling based on Tarsea's words. He knew his soul mate felt she was more than capable of protecting her friend. Tolfer sensed Candy was about to set his brother straight when Alex beat her to it.

"Absolutely not!" Alex exclaimed. "We need to stop letting a certain person influence how we are living our lives. Tarsea, you were going to attend the Prime Council meeting tomorrow to listen to the quarterly state of the province. Besides, you are not a zoo fan and hate clothes shopping."

"If he so much as looks at Alex the wrong way tomorrow, I will open a portal and annihilate him." Shirl shared this sensitive comment through the warrior link. The men around the table with the exception of Starc, kept forgetting how powerful Shirl was. "It is settled then. Candy, Alex, and I are going to have a girls' day tomorrow. The two of us assure Alex's safety."

Tolfer was happy when Candy reached for her wine and sipped. It appeared things around the table had settled and plans for tomorrow were worked out. He needed to get his life back on track in this universe. There were children here who needed him and the work he did.

Tolfer also realized his mother had not totally recovered from her trauma about his decision to follow Candy into the portal. He hated that he caused his mother worry, but he did not have another option except to safeguard his soul mate.

He wanted to take Candy home and make love to her once again. Those thoughts were put on hold when their dinners finally arrived. Candy inspected the dish in front of her and took a tentative bite. To his relief she closed her eyes and a quiet sound of approval came from her throat. He figured he would get some other noises from her tonight when he took her into their bed.

Chapter 20

It seemed like old times. Candy, Alex, and Shirl chatted nonstop about different animals they were seeing at the zoo. She could not remember the last time they had done something together outside of sharing a meal. They were once again the three carefree girls from the orphanage. There were no headaches, loans to be paid, and all the other worries they faced on Earth before coming into the Troyk universe. Once they entered this parallel world, a whole new set of problems were generated. For now, though, they enjoyed each other's company.

Candy stood before the Giant Larma Beast's enclosure. Alex had not been exaggerating when she said this animal would fuel bad dreams for weeks. If she were to have a nightmare, this beast would certainly be a starring character. It had scales down its body and a tongue that continually slithered out of its mouth. "What does that thing eat?"

"When it's not protecting its young, it eats rodents," Alex answered.

"I continually consider my brother Cianan a rat," Shirl commented. "That would explain why the Giant Larma Beast chewed up his leg." Both girls laughed at their friend's comment. Now that he could enter the warrior link, they finally knew her brother could be trusted. That did not mean the siblings had grown any closer. Candy thought of her aunt Darah and what could have been if she had not been insane. Only Alex seemed blessed with her Troyk extended family.

She continued to watch the beast in the natural habitat the zoo had created for it. A flash of color came into her peripheral vision. Candy turned to see Raine Narmouth and his brother approaching them. Without thought, Candy placed herself between the approaching men and Alex. Shirl was quick to follow her lead. The two women created a wall sheltering their friend. What a fool she had been. The first time Raine attacked Alex, it had been at the zoo. It was naïve to imagine her childhood impression that nothing bad could happen at the zoo was true.

"What do you want?" Candy demanded.

"We just came over to say hello," Raine Narmouth answered innocently enough. There was no aggression in his tone or the way he moved. Candy did not sense an attack was immediate. They were in a public place after all. "My brother wanted to meet Alexia. I have told him all about her." Had this slimeball followed them from the Childers's residence?

Candy felt Alex's hand on her shoulder and she shifted her body to allow Alex to move next to her. *"Let's play nice. Maybe they will continue on,"* Alex communicated through their pathway. Candy did not believe that any more than she thought her friend did.

"Alexia," Raine Narmouth stepped closer and grabbed her friend's hand. Candy did not have a premonition of the action so she imagined it was an innocent move. Raine took Alex's hand to his lips and kissed it. "This is my brother Chanz. He works for the government since he is a mind control telepath." The attacker of women said those words with such pride. Candy played the story Starc had shared about the brother's manipulation of Elzbeth over and over in her head.

"It is nice to meet you, Chanz," Alex shared within the communal pathway. *"I wanted to show Candace the Giant Larma Beast before we went clothes shopping. We told her about Cianan's close encounter with one of these animals on Terra Flora."*

"We better head out," Shirl added, *"we are meeting our boyfriends for lunch and this trip to the zoo has really cut into our time to shop."* Both women sharing this information in the communal pathways was brilliant. Everyone around them knew of their plans and would sound an alarm, if anything happened that negatively impacted what had been communicated.

Disappointment was written all over Raine's face. What alarmed Candy was what she saw in Raine Narmouth's eyes. Controlled anger brewed within him. Candy could sense the violence he was capable of inflicting. She did not know if this was the start of a new telepathic gift or all her imagination. Candy just knew she needed to separate Alex from these men.

"Let's go," Candy said. She reached for Alex's hand and removed it from Raine's clutches. "We are going out to dinner tonight and I don't want to wear the same outfit two nights in a row."

"That can wait," Chanz Narmouth stated. "You girls want to have lunch with us."

Candy could feel the pull on her brain. Chanz was using his mind control powers on them. She was not sure what to do. They could not let on they were immune to the telepathic power that ruled this world. Would all three girls be so set on going shopping they did not have a single doubt about going to lunch with these men?

"I am hungry," Alex stated. "*We have to play along with these bastards for now. I am letting Tarsea know what is going on through our familial link. He will use the warrior link to communicate any actions they are going to take. This has got to end today.*"

"I know a great place not far from here," Raine Narmouth said. He grinned from ear to ear. How such a nice looking man had to resort to such measures to get a date was beyond her. When he smiled, it seemed that the heavens sang. It blew her mind how such a lovely exterior could hide such a dark soul.

"I would rather go to the restaurant you took me to on our first date," Alex said. She threw such a dreamy look at Raine, Candy would have thought she was besotted with him. "*I don't want to leave the confines of the zoo until the guys are here. Knowing Tarsea, at least one of them is close by.*"

Candy hoped Tarsea had ignored their wishes and someone was relatively near. In preparing to protect Alex, she had planned for a physical attack, not mind control manipulation.

The choice of restaurants seemed to satisfy both brothers fortunately. Chanz did not use his powers to get them out of the zoo's borders. Alex and Raine led the way. Raine continually tried to hold Alex's hand and she shook it off. Candy knew she needed to distract Chanz, so he would be too busy to convince Alex she really liked Raine.

"What exactly do you do for the government?" Candy asked. "I am new to this world and am still learning how things run around here. Most of my time since leaving Ginkgo Terra has been in the penal colony. You cannot imagine how happy I am to be gone from that place."

"I steer our population by enforcing the choices our government has made regarding the health and well-being of our wondrous community." Candy had not heard such crap in her life. She had to concentrate on not choking on the nonsense the man had just served her. She had always imagined the mind control telepathic government would do their manipulations covertly.

"We are here!" Alex exclaimed. "I am going to have shrimp. It is my favorite thing in the whole world. That crustacean is a delicacy in the Starling Province." Candy was grateful Alex had steered the conversation away from mind control. They needed to talk about harmless, insignificant things until they were ready to take action. Candy was at a loss for what to say to the brothers.

"Alexia," Chanz said, "you are as beautiful as my brother stated. I know you want to have dinner with him tonight and spend the night together."

Candy choked on the water she was drinking. Chance stood and in Candy's mind, she saw him pounding on her back. There was nothing helpful in his manner or motives. She shifted in her seat and caught his arm before he connected. Candy placed a fake smile on her face. "I am fine," she said. "Thank you for your concern."

Chanz looked shocked by Candy's actions. She could see his facial expressions change from surprise to suspicion. They needed to get out of here fast.

"Hi, girls!" Candy looked up and there stood Starc and Koel. "I thought you were going shopping," Starc said, his eyes glued to Raine Narmouth.

"We were," Shirl answered. Shirl made it appear she was now confused. "For some reason we wanted to grab a bite to eat with Raine and his brother. Thanks for the offer, but Candy does need a new outfit. Can we have a rain-check?"

"A what?" Raine said. He looked back and forth between Starc and Alex. No doubt he was trying to figure how he could keep Alex by his side and not alert Starc to what he had planned. Candy really loathed this man. Something was going to happen between Raine and Alex. She could sense it. The problem was, she didn't know what or when. A feeling of helplessness overwhelmed her. What good were her powers if they did not provide specific information?

"We should go," Alex filled in the awkward silence that had followed Raine's words. "Another time, Raine." Alex grabbed Candy's arm and started walking away from the brothers. *Get a move on, Shirl,* Alex continued through their closed link. *I don't want the Narmouth brothers to get any more worked up than they already are. Light a fire underneath your soul mate and Koel. Let's get out of here.*

They walked toward the zoo's exit in silence. She imagined Starc and Koel were upset they could not pound on the Narmouth brothers. Candy could not blame them. Uneasiness surrounding an unspecific event kept brewing in her mind and did not abate. She needed to stay on guard. Candy considered sharing her suspicions with the others. Ultimately, she decided not to. How serious were they going to take a feeling? These new telepathic powers were relatively untried.

Once they left the zoo's property, they walked the streets of Aster Province to the boutique Shirl and Alex kept talking about. One particular outfit in the display window caught Candy's attention. She stood before it gazing at the beautiful tunic. It was pinned to a backdrop and was paired with a short black skirt rather than leggings.

"If ever an outfit was you," Shirl said as she came to stand next to Candy, "that certainly is. Let's go in and have you try it on." Her friend did not have to ask twice. The three women entered the shop with Starc and Koel in tow.

There were three women already looking at the outfits for sale. Candy was momentarily distracted by watching Koel approach each woman and unceremoniously touching each one. What had originally entertained Candy, now made her sad. Of the four friends she had come to think of as brothers, Koel was the only one who had not found his soul mate. Now that she had Tolfer, she understood what having her other half truly meant.

"This should be your size," Shirl started to hand her the tunic she had admired. There was a disturbance in the street that grabbed her attention, before she took possession of the beautiful top.

"We will see what is going on," Starc said before he and Koel ran out of the shop. Shirl looked at Candy, handed her the tunic, and then took off after her soul mate.

Candy sensed Alex was toward the rear of the shop and was busy looking through the racks of tunic and legging sets. Another feeling of apprehension hit Candy as she debated joining the people on the street or staying behind with Alex. The nagging that was preying on her brain did not let up as Candy continued to delay joining the commotion outside.

Movement toward her head caused Candy to step back and pivot around. Her hands were up as she deflected a steel rod that was meant to knock her out. Chanz Narmouth holding the weapon looked startled. He wasn't expecting any resistance from his victim. Candy took the luxury of glancing over to where Alex had been, her friend was gone. She grabbed a display vase to throw at

Chanz, to slow down his attack. She communicated the attack through the warrior channel to alert the others they were needed. Whatever had happened on the street was a diversion. Narmouth dodged the vase. Candy took the opportunity to throw herself forward against Narmouth before he had the chance to go after her again with his weapon. Candy knew Starc and Koel would be there momentarily and they would finish taking care of Chanz Narmouth.

Her knee hit the floor hard as the rest of her body was cushioned by the man she fell onto. Pain rocketed through her leg. As she expected, almost as soon as she was prone, Starc was pulling her up. Koel was holding Narmouth down. Koel snatched a couple of leggings and bound Chanz's hands. People from the street started to enter the shop to see what had happened. The communal pathways started to hum about Chanz Narmouth's attack on the survivor from the penal colony.

All the attention her attack attracted made it impossible to go after Alex. What had happened was too much a topic within the communal pathways for them to leave until the authorities arrived and finished their interviews. Tarsea, Tolfer, and Solfa's team were busy trying to find Alex as Candy was helpless, answering questions. Chanz had stated he had been attacked by her as he asked her out on a date. The lunch date had been communicated within the communal pathways, but chatter found it hard to believe Chanz's story. A mind control telepath could not control what was communicated within the pathways.

Candy and her party were released after about an hour. There had been no communications from Alex. Since Alex was not communicating through any of the channels she still had access to, they imagined she was unconscious or had a head injury inflicted by her abductor. She had failed to protect her friend from a known danger. How would she live with herself if any harm came to Alex or the baby?

Candy paced the common room as half the team searching for Alex returned. She did not know Aster Province like the rest of the group, so she was sequestered at the Childers's.

Norri and Pattrice had both arrived wanting to be near those who loved Alex, as they did. Listening through their familial link had frustrated Norri and she did not want to deal with Pattrice's hysterics alone. For once Pattrice's crying did not disturb Candy. It gave her the necessary distraction she needed from worrying about Alex. She kept telling herself Raine Narmouth loved Alex and would not do anything to permanently harm her.

"I cannot lose her like I lost her mother," Pattrice cried. The traumatized woman was in Norri's arms. "She has to be all right. That baby is going to have to make up for not being able to have a hand in raising Alexia." Candy stopped pacing and watched as Norri continued to hold her cousin. Those two were as close as she was to Alex and Shirl. A bond that would withstand the loss of Alex. Candy had to stop thinking in that manner. Her friend was going to be all right. She had to be.

Listening within the various pathways, Candy hoped for even a smothered cry for help from her friend. If she had been knocked out or drugged, Alex's first communication through the pathways would be almost incoherent. It was imperative Candy jumped on whatever Alex was able to provide. She decided to have some of the herbal beverage to clear away what little static she heard within the telepathic links. Missing the smallest whimper because of static would be too tragic to contemplate.

Leenea was sitting in the kitchen alone. Candy hugged the woman before going to pour herself the herbal tea. She sat next to Tolfer's mother, sipped the beverage, and opened her mind to hear Alex. Never having been into meditation, Candy wished she had the discipline to quiet her mind.

A presence entered her head. At first Candy discounted it. It kept trying to break through whatever barrier that prevented a solid connection. After a few more sips Candy turned off all chatter within her brain and concentrated on whoever was trying to communicate with her.

Whoever was trying to enter her brain was confused and uncomfortable. "Cold," Candy said out loud.

"What is it, dear?" Leenea looked at her concerned. A mother's concern, something that had been elusive in her life. A feeling of belonging washed over Candy. It was an emotion she would have to explore later. For now she had to deal with finding Alex.

"Someone is trying to communicate with me," Candy answered. "It is not like anything I have experienced here or in the penal colony through any of the pathways. I am getting feelings rather than words. This may sound crazy, but I think Alex's baby is trying to reach out to me. Her little girl is cold, which means Alex is somewhere refrigerated." While she was telling Leenea this information she was also sharing it through the warrior channel. Hopefully it would make sense to one of them.

"Chanz Narmouth has a financial interest in an ice factory," Starc shared through the warrior link. *"I do not know why I did not think of that sooner."*

Considering their history, Candy imagined Starc had researched everything there was to know about Raine and Chanz Narmouth after the incident with Elzbeth. That unfortunate episode in Starc's life could be the key point in saving Alex. *"Where is the factory?"* Candy asked, *"I am coming to join you. Make sure that Shirl is there as well. We are going to deal with Raine Narmouth for good this time."* The perfect fate for the predator consumed her mind.

"I was heading home," Tolfer entered the channel, *"Give me two minutes and we will head over together. I know where the ice is manufactured."*

Candy used the two minutes to bring Leenea, Norri and Pattrice up to date. She did not want to give the women false hope, but could not let go of the feeling they were on the right track. The presence in her mind was less frantic knowing help was on the way.

She was outside the house and ready to go when Tolfer arrived. They ran side by side. Tolfer communicated their destination was ten blocks away and everyone would be arriving within minutes of each other. When they reached the factory, her friends were armed with crystal weapons and ready to storm the building. She took one of the guns without hesitation. This time she did not ask if there was a stun setting. If she was going to use it, she was going to go for the kill.

It was late enough in the evening that the factory was closed for the day. If there was a night watchman, he did a great job of not being obvious. Starc had a brick and threw it through the window to allow them to unlock the door. There was a small lobby area they walked through, and then they entered a long hall with what appeared to be freezers on both sides. Fortunately, they were unlocked so they were not going to lose valuable time breaking into them. Dividing into two groups they started entering freezer after freezer, finding nothing. There were only two left to be explored.

Feeling sick to her stomach, fearing she had been wrong, Candy stood before the last freezer. The baby had stopped sending her emotions several minutes ago. Candy grabbed the handle and knew before she had finished the task Alex would be there. Whether the baby was all right was another story. They found her friend wrapped up in blankets shivering. Alex was unconscious and terribly pale. Tarsea lifted her and carried her out into the hall. Leenea had followed them with a tower of blankets that they proceeded to wrap around her friend.

"Take her home and warm her up," Tarsea instructed his brother and mother. "I am staying behind and will wait for Narmouth to arrive. As soon as we have dealt with him, I will head home."

"I am staying, too," Candy said. She was not going to miss out on dealing with her friend's abductor. "Shirl, you need to stay, too. We are going to make your desires come true. Raine Narmouth is going to go through the portal one last time to the darkest hole we can find." Candy had not missed how Shirl or Alex muttered that desire each time the topic of Raine Narmouth came up.

Shirl gave her one of her brightest smiles. "I know just the place to send him." Based on the worlds Candy had been exposed to, she figured they both had the same destination in mind.

They held onto some of the blankets Leenea had brought and entered the freezer where Alex had been held. It was a certainty Raine Narmouth would return shortly. In his own warped way, Raine loved Alex and would not leave her there to die. Candy grabbed the blanket Alex had been wrapped in and took her friend's place on the floor. Although she was quite a bit larger than Alex, she hoped Raine would not notice. The rest of the group was to the left side of the door, in a blind spot. Raine would not notice their presence if he entered and did not turn around before getting to Candy.

She lay on the cold floor, waiting. No wonder the baby had been cold. Candy could not help but shiver from the low temperature. As she lay there, she continually reached out to the baby, hoping to get some kind of sensation from her. It broke her heart when she got no response. After ten minutes of freezing her ass off, the door to the freezer opened. She lay still, as she heard footsteps approach.

A hand gently shook her. "Alexia," Raine Narmouth's voice penetrated Candy's ears. "Wake up, baby. I want to take you somewhere warm where we can be together."

Candy slowly turned over and raised her weapon. "Too late, Romeo. Alex is nice and warm at home. She is safe from you." She looked up and saw the rest of the group circling Raine Narmouth.

"We are ending this now," Starc growled as he bound Narmouth's hands. "Your brother will be facing Troyk justice for assaulting Candy. However, we have a totally different plan for you."

Candy got up and shoved off the blankets. "Shirl, open a portal for the Nightshade universe. We have another payment to render for their part in freeing me and Tolfer." A wicked smile crossed Shirl's face.

Raine started to scream when he realized where they were taking him. It was ironic his obsession had originally spared Raine from meeting his ultimate fate in the vampire world. Nothing would save the lowlife scum now!

Shirl did not say a word. A portal opened before Candy's eyes. Being a mated female crystal telepath, Shirl could open a portal anywhere with very little energy from her amethyst.

Candy did not have a moment's hesitation entering the portal to a world populated by bloodthirsty vampires. She could not think of a more fitting ending for a man who raped women physically after they were mentally manipulated.

Chapter 21

~

The Nightshade Universe

Candy stepped into near darkness. Torches somewhere in the distance provided the only light. Her eyes quickly adjusted. Shirl turned next to her and Candy heard her walking away. She started to follow Shirl and Starc, who was dragging along Raine Narmouth. Shocked by the glowing red eyes before her, she hesitated going forward.

"*They are starving,*" Shirl shared with her. "*The vampires you met in the penal colony were in better shape than these creatures. Do not say or do anything. Let me do all the talking.*" Candy was more than happy to abide by her friend's instructions as she joined Shirl.

A tall vampire rose from his chair and approached them. He was shrouded in a black robe and his head was partially covered by a hood. Candy could not stop staring at his eyes. It was almost hypnotic how the vampire's eyes could bore into hers.

"My lovely crystal telepath and her soul mate are back," the vampire said. "I see you have brought another one of your friends and perhaps a snack for me." Candy hoped she was the friend he was referring to and not the snack. She felt a shiver run down her spine. This was no matinee idol vampire. He certainly did not have the looks of Drake or the blond vampire she had met in the penal colony.

"This piece of scum did harm to our pregnant friend," Shirl shared with the vampire. By now Candy figured this was the master vampire Yorik she had heard so much about.

She knew it was a cliche, but if looks could kill, Raine Narmouth would be dead. It would be a tragedy if Narmouth was given a quick death. Yorik seemed to grow in size before her very eyes. His glowing red eyes transitioned to a browner red, the color of dried blood. "Is the child all right?" the vampire roared.

"The baby is fine," Candy addressed Yorik for the first time. Only someone with a death wish would say anything else. Although Candy knew Alex would be examined by a med-tech when she returned home, they left the Troyk universe before they heard any news. The vampire's anger was directed to the man on the floor being held down by two guards. "I sensed her distress from the womb. That is how we found Alex before Raine Narmouth could do any more harm to her or the baby growing inside her."

The master vampire approached her. Candy knew she had to hold her ground against this creature. He sized her up as she was concentrating on staring directly into his face.

"You are the one they went after," Yorik said. It was a statement rather than a question. "It was worth our people accompanying your friends to rescue you, even if we were not paid with blood. I sense the warrior within you as I would recognize an old friend." She assumed that was a compliment given by a man who rarely gave them.

"We offer his blood to you as thanks for assisting us in bringing Candy back home to the Troyk universe," Shirl once again addressed Yorik.

Yorik approached Raine Narmouth. He waived off his guards and leaned down to bring Raine to his feet. The vampire had a hold on his throat. His captive did not struggle. Candy imagined he was either in shock or so scared he was catatonic. Part of Candy wanted to look away, while another part relished what was about to happen. Yorik bit into his neck, crushing bones in the process. The scream that came out of Raine Narmouth, would haunt her dreams for some time.

After Yorik drank his fill he threw Raine onto the floor. Raine seemed as light as a rag doll when the vampire violently released him. By some miracle, Raine was still alive. He lay on the floor with his hands on the neck wound. Raine was losing his battle at trying to stop from bleeding out.

Yorik snapped his fingers and two vampires knelt next to the dying man and ministered to his wounds. One dressed his neck while the other one gave him an injection.

"What was in the syringe?" Candy asked Shirl.

"It is a serum that accelerates the production of blood," Shirl answered. *"The heart will pump and replace the blood at ten times the normal rate. They use it in the Troyk universe as well."* Candy vaguely remembered getting the same injection after the knife was removed from her shoulder.

"Your telepathic powers are no good here," Yorik informed them. "You might as well ask any question you have directly to me, warrior."

Candy was struck dumb. Her brain shut down with the news that her telepathic gift was worthless here. She wondered if her enhanced ability to fight would also be discovered by these vampires. It was time to take Shirl's recommendation to heart and just stand back and not participate.

"Bring me Drake, Lorenz, and my daughter," Yorik ordered. "They too should benefit from this bounty."

Great, more vampires, Candy thought. They had delivered Raine Narmouth to the Nightshade universe. It was time to leave this horrifying place. The problem was that Shirl did not seem ready to leave. Candy knew there had been a connection between her friend and Drake. She also knew Shirl felt responsible for Yorik's daughter being a captive in this world. With her telepathic powers ineffective in this world she could not covertly communicate to her friend that she wanted to leave.

It was not long before Drake entered the hall. He walked to Yorik and did a half bow. Shirl had told her that Yorik was the master of this hive and Drake was of royal vampire blood. She imagined what Drake did was a sign of respect. Candy saw Drake place a half smile on his handsome face when he spied Shirl's presence. He walked over and kissed her hand.

Shirl was quick to retrieve it back. Little wonder, with Starc standing right next to his soul mate. "You remember Candy," Shirl directed attention back to her. "The two of you only met briefly in the penal colony world, before you left with the prisoners." Candy wondered how many of those men were still alive.

"Yes," Drake replied. He then reached for her hand and brought it to his lips. Her legs got a little wobbly in response to the man's kiss and charm. Where she could only see Yorik as a monster, it was hard to believe the man who stood before her was a vampire. Perhaps just a little anemic.

"They have brought a gift for us," Yorik gestured to the man on the floor. Although the vampires were done tending to Raine, he continued to lie on the ground. "This pariah did harm to Alex and endangered the life of the daughter that grows inside her. I turn him over to you since you had the most to lose from his action."

Candy had no idea what Yorik was talking about. She glanced at Shirl, who shook her head in response to Candy's unasked question. Her friends had told her about the genetic marker Alex's daughter might possess. There had been no mention about Drake's direct claim to her offspring. She was going to have a long talk with Alex about what transpired here.

All attention was diverted to a couple entering the vast room. Candy recognized the blond vampire. He had saved her when he fed on Darah. The girl who walked beside him must be Yorik's daughter Afton. She was as pale as death and looked like she had not eaten solid food in weeks. Candy must have gasped at the sight of the girl, since all eyes were now on her. She looked around, not sure what to do or say.

"My daughter's appearance shocks you, warrior?" Yorik addressed her. "The solution to her health is right in front of her, but she refuses to succumb to what is in her best interest." The girl did not react to her father's words. She just stood next to the vampire she entered with.

"Perhaps if we take Afton with us for a time we can bring some color back into her cheeks," Shirl said. "We will not return her to Ginkgo Terra if you wish. The Troyk universe is very much like the world she left. Perhaps some time with us will bring her back to health and we will return her."

"Do not take me for a fool," Yorik growled at Shirl. Starc stepped between the master vampire and his soul mate. Although Shirl was the more powerful of the two, Starc still felt the biological need to protect his mate. The same was true, where Tolfer and Candy were concerned. "My daughter will stay here and take nourishment as the claiming dictates." Once again, Candy had no idea what he was referring to. If possible, Afton grew pastier.

"It is time for you to leave," Drake said. "I will make sure the man you brought with you suffers in this world. He will not have an easy death. We will keep him alive, as long as we can to assure his punishment is severe enough to offset the degree of his crime. He will finally die when the child takes her first breath."

Candy went to stand next to Shirl as she opened a temporary portal that would take them back to the Troyk universe. They would arrive in the Childers's household rather than through the natural portal on the mountain trail. The fate of the child was still questionable. A special bond was created between them when the baby reached out to her. Candy also wanted to go to Alex immediately to find out what happened when she was in the Nightshade universe. Any claim Drake had to Alex's daughter would have to be nullified.

Chapter 22

~

The Troyk Universe

Candy's senses were assaulted when she re-entered the Troyk universe. She squinted from the light and colors attacking her eyes. The Nightshade world was dark and bleak, while the common room was bright and cheerful. The vampire great hall had been cold and wet, bringing on chills throughout her body. In the Childers' home, she was warm and felt safe. A sigh of relief escaped from her.

Shirl and Starc went to check on Alex. Candy had one more stop before she went to see her friend. Following her nose to where the tantalizing aroma was generated, she knew she'd find Tolfer. Her soul mate must be cooking up a storm for Alex and her unborn child. Only his presence would fortify the strength necessary to deal with the possibility of terrible news about the baby.

Tolfer was stirring a large pot when she entered the kitchen. When he saw her, she was gifted with one of his special smiles. A warmth spread through her body, as it did whenever she was near him. He placed his spoon on a dish and brought her into his arms.

"I was starting to get worried," Tolfer scolded her, "you were in the Nightshade universe longer than I thought you would be." She had communicated to him before they left through the portal. Candy wanted him to know where they were going and for what purpose. Raine Narmouth had to be taken care of so he would no longer jeopardize Alex's health and well-being.

"That is one world I would rather not return to," Candy mumbled into his chest. If it was possible, she would have burrowed further into his body. She hungered for this man, more than her stomach wanted what he cooked. She raised her head and placed her lips on his. Candy fantasized about him lifting her on the counter and taking her right there.

Tolfer did not wait long to deepen the kiss and tighten his embrace. *"Your thoughts are leaking through, Canny,"* Tolfer communicated through their private channel. *"My parents are in the other room. Do not tempt me to do something I would never live down."* Tolfer released her lips and started to lavish kisses on her ear. He took her earlobe and nibbled.

"Hey," Candy giggled, *"I just came from a world populated by vampires. They were nothing like the movies depicted them."* She looked deep into his eyes and moved her hands to his head. Candy loved to move her fingers through his hair. *"You would fit the romantic vampire of my fantasies quite well. Actually, any of my fantasies."*

"You are going to have to tell me about them and I will do my best to make them a reality," Tolfer added. She loved Tolfer's playful manner. Other than the dumb pet names, he had not exhibited this side of his personality in the penal colony. Candy was happy he was back to his old self and was comfortable enough with her to show it.

To her disappointment he released her and started to stir the stew he was making. She stood back in wonder and watched her soul mate. Candy had structured her life to depend on no one. She had even grown to be independent of Shirl and Alex. That was one of the reasons why the other women had grown even closer. Now she found herself totally in love with a man who nurtured everyone around him. She had fought Tolfer's need to take care of her. He had started to do little things for her, without her even knowing he did them. Every day she found herself accepting more and more from this man. She no longer fought it, but longed for his care.

"I love you," Candy said with all her heart.

"I know," he smiled and brought a spoon to her mouth. "Taste this." It did not bother her that Tolfer did not mimic back her words. If there was one certainty in her mind, Tolfer loved her.

Flavor exploded on her tongue. "Wow!" she exclaimed, "That is really good. Alex is going to love it. How is she doing?"

Tolfer turned the flame under the pot off and brought her back into his arms. "She is fine. You got to her just in time. We called a med-tech to check her out as soon as we got home."

Holding her breath, she asked the question she dreaded asking. "What about the baby?"

A wide smile graced his face and Candy knew that everything was all right. "Our little wee niece is just fine. No one was going to let the med-tech leave without her thoroughly checking on the pregnancy.

Relief flooded Candy's being. A moment's repose was necessary for her to gather her relieved, near shattered nerves. There were still a myriad of questions she needed answers to.

"What about Chanz Narmouth?" Candy finally asked. "I cannot imagine he is going to take his brother's disappearance lying down. He was responsible for mind-raping women so Raine could finish the job."

"There had been a witness who saw Raine carrying something into the factory. His finger prints are on the freezer door," Tolfer told her. "He will imagine Raine is hiding and does not want Chanz to know where he is. Their familial pathway would alert others in his family where he could be staying so it would not be suspicious if Raine is not communicating to his brother."

"I guess you are right." Candy wondered if Raine Narmouth was still alive or was still being used as a blood donor for some starving vampires. Drake had been very specific when Raine would finally meet his maker.

"What was it like?" Tolfer asked. Candy knew he was asking about the Nightshade universe.

"Frightening, frigid, and a miserable place, I never want to return to," Candy answered. "We never left the gathering room or whatever they call it. It was like a cold, damp cave. The vampires Drake brought with him were supposedly trustworthy. They were not as bad off as many of the vampires we saw today. Their eyes glow red from the blood lust. They are starving. Yorik and his cronies were more than happy to take Narmouth off our hands."

"Something else is bothering you," Tolfer said. "I can sense there is something you are not telling me." Her soul mate started to examine her neck and other parts of her anatomy. She laughed and batted him away.

"I was not bitten." She lightly kissed his lips. "If they had made a single offensive move, Shirl would have incinerated them. Yorik is not aware of what her power is, he just knows it exists. It was the vampire's protectiveness of

Alex's unborn child that drove their anger toward Narmouth. I don't understand it and it is freaking me out."

Tolfer frowned. "We know they believe she could mate with them."

"When we arrived, they were cordial enough. However, when we mentioned Raine had endangered Alex and the baby they went ballistic. The master vampire believes Drake has a personal interest where Alex and the baby are concerned. I asked Shirl, what was going on, but she would not tell me anything."

"Go check on your friend," Tolfer suggested. "Tell her we will be eating in twenty minutes. This will tide her over in the meantime." Tolfer handed her a small plate holding a roll with some kind of spread on it.

Candy accepted the plate and headed to Tarsea and Alex's room. She was bursting at the seams wanting to know what was going on with Alex and the vampires of the Nightshade Universe.

⁓♦

"Tell me again," Alex said. "How did Narmouth react to the vampires? It is kind of scary, I am eating this all up. I never realized I had such a dark side to my nature."

"Eat this instead." Candy handed Alex the plate Tolfer had given her. "Dinner is in twenty minutes."

Candy examined her friend as she pushed away the layer of blankets she had cocooned around her. "Yummy, salmon spread." Alex bit into the roll and leaned back against the pillows with her eyes closed. The color started to return to Alex's cheeks and she glowed with health.

"Everything all right with you?" Candy asked. "Part of me wanted to stay with you. The part that wanted to see Narmouth pay ultimately won out."

Alex looked up from her snack. "Shirl told me both Yorik and Drake fed from him."

"When we told them what his crime was they became enraged," Candy informed her friend. "They were scary before we told them, but when they found out he had tried to harm you they went postal."

"Postal?" Starc asked behind her. He was standing with his arms wrapped around Shirl's waist.

"It is a slang term for going berserk," Shirl answered. "There were a couple of shooting episodes involving present or past postal workers some time ago. The word started to be used when someone goes crazy. I think it's even in the dictionary."

"Regardless," Candy continued impatiently. "What is up with the Nightshade vampires and your unborn child?"

Candy could see the look that past between Shirl and Alex. It was a look she knew well. They were silently battling over who was going to have to tell Candy. It was information that needed to be shared. Ultimately, it was always Shirl who gave up and responded.

"We told you already that for some reason they believe Alex's unborn daughter carries a gene that will allow them to have children with her."

"Can you believe that?" Alex shrieked. "My baby is the size of a pin head and they think she carries that gene. Regardless, my daughter is never going to the Nightshade universe ever. Did you see Yorik's daughter? That half-human, half-vampire girl looks like death warmed over. I am not going to have my daughter or granddaughter subjected to such an existence."

"Relax," Shirl sat on the bed next to Alex. Shirl wrapped her arm around Alex's shoulder as they did when they were kids. "It takes a crystal telepath to navigate the portal. You and the baby are safe from the vampires of that world. You know Candy and I would never let them get their bloodthirsty hands on you. Not to mention what Tarsea would do to them."

"Why would Drake take such a personal stake in the welfare of the baby?" Candy was frustrated because she was getting the same information that had been shared earlier.

"Candy," Shirl said, "this is not some kind of conspiracy. We do not know why the vampire feels he has a personal stake in the child. I picked up the same sentiment, but did not want to react to it. Maybe because Drake is a product of the oldest bloodline, he has more of an interest in the continuation of their species."

Candy felt stupid that she had overreacted to both Yorik's words and her friends' reactions to her questions.

"I am just happy you found me," Alex said. "How did you manage it, Candy? Shirl said it was you who said I was cold."

"Not you, exactly," Candy answered. "I got a strange sense the baby was cold. It was a type of communication I had never experienced. I would have known if it came from you, Alex."

"The baby has messed up your ability to enter some of the telepathic channels," Shirl continued. "Maybe your body reacted to your ordeal by leveraging one of the communal pathways to warn us you were in danger. I don't think we are ever going to know how it happened. We should just be grateful it did."

Alex let out a loud, long sigh. "We will be eating soon. I better get redressed and use the facilities. How about I meet you in the common room for dinner? Norri and Pattrice should be here any minute."

"They waited this long to see you?" Candy asked.

"Tarsea gave them regular updates," Alex responded. "Norri would have been welcome, but Tarsea did not want to deal with Pattrice while I was recuperating. Solfa will also be joining us and will handle her mother.

Candy watched as her friend got out of bed and made her way to the washroom. Shirl went to the closet and pulled out an outfit for Alex to wear. She knocked on the bathroom door and hung the outfit on the door's hook before closing it.

Shirl came over to Candy and embraced her. "We dodged a bullet this time."

Candy hugged her friend. She was not feeling so optimistic. Something was still gnawing at her. Candy just could not put her finger on what the problem was. Her gift of premonition once again plagued her, because she had insufficient information. Right now it was just causing her stomach to roll and an uneasiness to engulf her being. She merely nodded to her friend and they walked side by side to the common room.

Chapter 23

~

Candy nibbled on a roll. Her system was all tied up in knots and she had no appetite. Tolfer kept glancing in her direction with a concerned look on his face. He gave her distance by not asking her through the soul mate channel what was wrong. Tolfer knew her well enough to know she would reach out to him if she needed him. How could she explain a feeling she could not put a tangible threat behind?

Koel arrived shortly after they were all seated. He looked as harried as she felt. "Chanz Narmouth has opened an inquiry about his missing brother. Alex, Tarsea, and Candy have been listed in the complaint."

"You have got to be kidding me!" Alex exclaimed. "That bastard kidnaps me and I am named in a legal action surrounding his disappearance? You Troyk people have some serious problems in this world." Candy watched as Alex placed her fork on the plate and pushed the dish away from her.

Tarsea reached out and grabbed her hand. He brought it to his lips and gave it a gentle kiss. Candy would have swooned if she was not at a table full of people. She had never seen such a romantic gesture before. Those two fit, like she fit with Tarsea's brother.

"The authorities were called after we left with Raine Narmouth," Candy said. "They would have no idea I was part of the rescue. Wouldn't it look like retribution against me since he was arrested for assaulting me at the dress shop? This is all crazy!" Her insides were doing somersaults. She was so tense it was an effort to move. What she would not give for a good deep tissue massage.

"The Narmouth family is powerful," Tarsea stated. "It is just a last-ditch effort to deal with his missing brother. The med-techs saw the condition Alex was in when they examined her. I do not think we have anything to worry about. Just in case, we need to keep a low profile. Any operations to rescue dissidents will have to be done by another team for the time being.

"Good," Koel looked a little out of sorts. Candy had never seen him look so apprehensive before. "I want Darden to take me to Ginkgo Terra. It is time we bring JoAnna here. She has to be my soul mate. There were five daughters who survived from Benko and his followers. Four of you have found your soul mates in all but one of those girls. JoAnna must be mine."

Candy could not argue with his logic. But what were the odds the little girl she knew as Jo Jo in the orphanage would be Koel's soul mate?

"We do not even know what happened to her after the adoption, Koel," Alex said.

"She lives in Florida with her adopted father," Darden volunteered. "Benko Jarlyn kept track of her after she left the orphanage. Her father runs a five-star hotel in Southwest Florida. She has had a very privileged upbringing. I also believe she is engaged to be married." Darden lowered his voice when he communicated that bomb to his friend.

"It does not matter," Koel said. "He is not right for her, since I am her soul mate." There was so much certainty in his voice. "That emphasizes the need to get her immediately."

Candy knew this latest drama in Koel's search for his soul mate was not causing her anxiety. It would be good to get her mind off of whatever was prickling her nerves. "I will go with you. Jo Jo may be more agreeable if she sees another woman with you. Koel, you have a habit of being a little intense."

Darden shook his head. "With everything going on related to Chanz Narmouth, you should be visible in Aster Province. I think the three of you girls should stick to each other like glue. Who knows what Chanz Narmouth is capable of? He could be as crazy as his brother."

Shirl took a sip of her wine. "That is what you get for being so alluring, Alex."

"I am a f-ing chameleon," Alex cried. "How that man got fixated on me is anyone's guess. But I agree with Darden. We should lay low and be seen in public doing harmless things, like lunch with the girls."

"I am scheduled to go to Gingko Terra the day after tomorrow," Darden continued. "Koel will tag along and we will see if we can find JoAnna."

"What?" Koel growled at Shirl. Candy looked over at her friend to see what caused Koel's dander to go up. There was a huge frown evident on Shirl's face. Her facial expression was like poking a tiger with a stick. Koel seemed to be at the end of his rope.

"I suppose we should tell Jeryl Jarlyn we will be bringing back another possible descendant of one of his son's followers," Shirl said. "He may start to believe Jo Jo is his long-lost granddaughter like he did originally with Candy. I grew up with Alex and Candy. I would risk my life for them and trust them without doubt. Jo Jo is an unknown. We have so many secrets to keep. I am just concerned about bringing her into our inner circle."

Candy could not disagree with Shirl. Jo Jo could present a risk to them all. However, she saw no alternative but to accept that risk. Although she had been adopted, Jo Jo was one of them. They would just have to be careful what they said and did around her until she connected in the warrior channel.

"There is something else I have not told everyone," Darden confessed. "JoAnna is the daughter of Prime Adholm's younger sister."

"She is Chartail's cousin?" Alex asked incredulously, although it was pretty clear that was the case. "They are like night and day. If I remember Jo Jo had hair as black as a raven's wing."

"You should bring the girl here," Leenea said. "She can stay in Tolfer's room until she assimilates to our world. Tolfer and Candy can move into Tarsea's apartment. Alex and Tarsea should stay here because of the baby."

If Candy was not already stressed beyond belief, moving in with Tolfer was the straw that broke the camel's back. She adored the man, but she was not sure if she was ready or capable of setting up a household with him. Their cohabitation in the penal colony was required for safety's sake. This was something totally different.

Tolfer started laughing hysterically. "Candy, the look on your face. You are not being sentenced to die in the Nightshade universe. If it is too soon for us to move in together, I am sure you can stay with Norri and Pattrice."

"Oh, yes!" Pattrice answered enthusiastically clapping her hands. "We would love to have you stay with us." Candy was taken aback by the pure joy in the woman's face. She glanced at Norri, who looked as pleased as her cousin.

"Maybe for a short period," Candy said tentatively. *"I hope you do not mind, Tolfer. I truly love you. I am just not ready to take that big of a step."* Candy shared her feelings with her soul mate as Pattrice and Norri were chatting back and forth about their new roommate and the plans they were putting together. Alex smiled in her direction and nodded her head. Maybe it was time for someone else to care for Candy and these women were clearly happy to do so. They had suffered so much over the years.

"We are having lunch with the girls tomorrow," Shirl said. "It is best we are on guard in case Chanz Narmouth makes a move on us."

They had exchanged the danger posed by Raine Narmouth with his brother. Somehow Candy knew Chanz could be a thousand times more dangerous than his brother Raine. At this point she knew something would happen tomorrow. All three women were in mortal danger. What could possibly happen at lunch?

Chapter 24

～

A beautiful plate of food was placed in front of Candy. Her stomach was still protesting from the uncertainty her telepathic gift was brewing within her. It was such an ordinary thing to do, having lunch with the girls, after everything she had been through. It was hard sitting across from Chartail's friends, Sondra and Jessalyn, unable to tell them their friend was finally all right. She picked at her salad as Alex and Sondra shared stories about the new clothes they had purchased. Alex had set up a double date between her, Tarsea, Sondra, and Sondra's new boyfriend, so they could wear their new outfits. Her friend had never really been interested in boys until she met Tarsea. Their relationship was explosive, while Candy's connection with Tolfer was the comfort she never knew she craved. The sex was not bad either.

Candy could not believe her eyes when she saw Chanz Narmouth enter the restaurant. She alerted Alex and Shirl through their closed link to warn them of Narmouth's presence. Candy did not want Sondra and Jessalyn to know anything was wrong. Alex shifted in her chair, unconsciously scooting her chair closer to Candy.

Her eyes were glued to Chanz. He stopped at several tables and talked to their occupants. There seemed to be some disharmony created with each stop he made. It appeared he was starting an argument between the table's occupants. The restaurant was getting louder and louder as Chanz made his way to their table.

Loud voices rang out, causing attention to focus on the tables Chanz had targeted. Candy in her mind's eye saw Chanz draw a knife and went to plunge it into Alex's back. As he came closer to the table, Candy saw him reach into his jacket pocket. Candy was on her feet and grabbed Chanz Narmouth's wrist before he could execute his plan to harm her friend. In the back of her mind, she thought she heard someone scream "Knife."

While holding back Narmouth's wrist, Candy shoved the bony part of her hand into Chanz's nose with as much force as her new gift could muster. He dropped the knife and momentarily covered his nose as blood squirted from the broken cartilage. Candy had the foresight to kick the knife out of Chanz's reach and prepared for the man to attack. There were people standing around them, but no one intervened to help her. She shifted as Narmouth charged her. Alex had picked up her plate and crashed it over Chanz's head. The plate shattered, but Chanz did not seem negatively impacted by the blow.

He reached out and grabbed Alex. "You ruined my brother's life," he shouted as he went to strike her friend. Once again Candy was able to deflect the blow, since she had seen it within her mind before it happened.

Finally the officials got ahold of Chanz Narmouth. They attempted to bind his hands while Candy went to pick up the knife he had tried to murder her friend with. It would be used as evidence when they tried him. Candy had the blade exposed as Chanz Narmouth shook off his jailers and came at Candy another time. He obviously did not see the knife in her hand as he charged toward her, impaling himself on his own blade. Candy stood in shock as she held the weapon embedded in Narmouth's stomach. He fell on her, his mass bearing down onto her chest. For some reason she managed to stay on her feet, with Narmouth leaning against her. He was dead weight, literally and figuratively.

"Release the knife, Candace," a palace guard she had seen on several occasions spoke to her. "We saw the last part of the shuffle. He ran into his own blade." Candy still held on to the weapon as if her life depended on it.

"Candy," Alex said. Her friend's voice was shaky and she could see her hand trembling as she placed them around her wrist. "It is over. Let go of the knife and let us turn Narmouth's body over to the authorities."

Shirl came up and stood beside her. She too grabbed Candy's arm. Candy did not know why, but she continued to stand her ground. She did not know why she could not give up the weapon. Maybe part of her thought the dead man would come after her again.

"Canny," Tolfer was now beside her. "It is all right, I have you." Alex gave up her position and went into Tarsea's arms. The brothers had been watching over them while they were at lunch. Because of the commotion Chanz had created, they could not get to their soul mates in time.

It was finally hearing Alex crying that brought Candy back to the here and now. She backed away from the weapon and the dead man who had been leaning on her. Once again, she was covered with blood. Shirl had come over and offered her assistance in steadying Candy. Her legs all of a sudden became like Jello. The two backed her into her seat. She reached for the glass of wine she had been nursing and took a huge gulp of the beverage. Candy could barely hold the glass, since her hands were overwhelmed with tremors.

"Breathe, Canny," Tolfer said. "You are holding your breath." She had not been aware she stopped breathing. Candy took a deep cleansing breath, like the ones she took when she was working out with weights.

"Are you in good enough shape to give a statement?" the guard who had talked to her earlier asked.

Candy had heard the question, but could not answer. The buzzing in her head was interrupted by Tolfer answering the guard. "Can you come over to the house later for the statement? She is covered in her attacker's blood. My future sister-in-law is also hysterical. We need to get our girlfriends back to my mom's house and calmed."

The officer looked at Candy and then Alex. "I think you are right. Candace looks like she could use a long hot shower and a stiff drink. We have had several complaints over the years about this one." The officer gestured to the dead man at her feet. "We could never get any evidence of wrongdoing. Well, today we certainly have that and more. A restaurant full of people witnessed what happened and communicated it through the communal pathways. No amount of mind control manipulation is going to change the facts related to how he died."

"Let us go, Canny," Tolfer said as he went to lift Candy's elbow and bring her to her feet. Once again Shirl was there to give him assistance.

"It's over, Candy," Shirl added. "Let's get you home and into a nice hot shower. You can then crawl into bed and sleep or do whatever your little heart desires."

Her heart desired Tolfer. She needed him as badly as she needed to breathe. Without consideration of the blood that covered her tunic, Candy fell into Tolfer's arms. "Let's go home."

Tolfer held his soul mate. Candy seemed in shock. She barely responded to anything, while Alex was still falling apart. They needed to get the girls out of here and safely home. All eyes were on them, as they shuffled to the restaurant's exit. The communal pathways were overloaded with stories of Candy's heroic deeds. She had saved Alex's life today.

As they entered the gathering place park he felt Candy's legs give out. Tolfer knew she could not continue. He brought them both to their knees. Candy brought her arms around Tolfer's neck. She buried her head into his neck and started to cry. A number of CT Guards had come to see if Candy was all right.

They circled them to give their female comrade the privacy she needed. Tolfer knew Candy kept things tightly within her. She never leaned on anyone. It had been a lonely existence, even with Alex and Shirl there for her. Everything that had happened in the penal colony and today had finally caught up with her.

"Let it all out, Canny," Tolfer communicated through their private channel. *"You are safe and loved. Lean on me for a change."* He knew he was the caregiver she needed. She was his strong, almost invisible, warrior woman. *"You do not have to face everything alone anymore. Talk to me. Let me know what you are feeling. Release the anger, the guilt, or whatever is eating away at you."*

She merely nodded against his shoulder. Her grip around his shoulder tightened as her tears subsided. *"I need you to be strong for me, Tolfer,"* she responded. *"I don't have any more to give. I'm ready, take me home."*

Tolfer rose to his feet, taking Candy with him. They started toward his parents' house. The CT Guards continued to be their body shields, running interference in case anyone tried to stop them. He was thankful when they finally reached their home.

"Thank you for your aid this day," Tolfer communicated through the communal pathways to the men who accompanied them home. Various comments were shared before they entered the house. Candy had gained their respect and adoration. They stood by their fellow CT Guard, as the weight of everything she had been through finally brought her down. She had endured more than any of them ever had to go through.

His mother and father were there to welcome them when they arrived. Hugs and kisses were exchanged. His parents did not shy away from the condition Candy was in both mentally and physically. "I need to get her into the shower and clean her up." He spoke rather than using their familial channel so Candy could hear what was being said.

"You do that, son," his father replied. "Norri will be coming over to prepare our evening meal. Tarsea is in his room taking care of Alex. Go and take care of your soul mate."

He nodded to his father and steered Candy to the washroom. Tolfer carefully removed her shoes and clothing. He helped her into the warm shower. Most of the blood had seeped through her tunic. He took a small cloth, rubbed soap on to it, and then carefully washed the dried blood off her body. Tolfer released her long hair from the piece of elastic that had held it tightly at the back of her head. He poured shampoo into his hand and washed her long locks. Candy leaned her head back, clearly enjoying his massaging techniques. After the shampoo and soap had been washed from her body, he exited the shower with her and wrapped Candy in a large cushy towel. He sat her on the side of the bathtub and rubbed conditioner into her scalp, then worked it through her hair.

After wrapping her hair in another towel, Tolfer carried Candy to their bed. "How are you feeling, Canny?"

"Drained," Candy responded in barely a whisper. "I don't understand why that bastard's death has hit me so hard. He would have killed Alex if I hadn't acted. God only knows how many women he had manipulated into having sex with him and his brother."

"I do not know." Tolfer lay next to Candy and took her into his arms. "Maybe because Alex has been your family for so long or it has been one battle after another since you entered this universe. You have barely had time to come up for air. You had all these emotions stored up inside you that needed to be released."

Tolfer was taken by surprise when Candy leaned into him and kissed him as if her life depended on it. "*Take me,*" she ordered through their pathway.

He did not know what stopped him from making love to her. Was he concerned she was once again trying to distract herself from coming to terms with her mental state by exhausting herself physically? She wanted him to be strong for her, but he did not know what that truly meant.

He broke the kiss. "What do you think finally caused you to fall apart?" He tightened his hold on his soul mate. Tolfer knew he needed to get her to come to terms with her emotions. They had a difficult road ahead in preparing for Benko Jarlyn to liberate their world. He needed Candy to be able to release pent-up feelings and energy before it brought her down again. Tolfer knew the future of the Troyk universe was dependent on that. How does a warrior woman balance her strength with her vulnerability?

Candy gazed into his eyes. She appeared to be considering what he said. He was relieved she was not angry that he did not comply with her earlier request. "I guess I take too much on myself. If Utopia had fallen, I would have taken the blame. Had Alex been killed, it would have been my fault for not being strong enough to save her."

"That is a lot to carry on your shoulders, Canny." He pushed back the towel she was wrapped in to give him better access to those beautiful shoulders. Tolfer rubbed them gently. "You are the superior fighter, even though I am probably stronger. Let me and the others carry some of that burden. Every now and then you are going to have to tell me what you are feeling. Do not assume all the responsibility of those around you. The warrior channel is growing every day. Not because a single man will win the day, but a legion of men and women."

Candy gave him a smile that warmed his heart. "I am going to take a short nap. Why don't you help Norri in the kitchen? If you stay here any longer I am going to jump your bones and won't get any rest. Besides, I am starving. I barely ate any lunch. Norri is a wonderful cook, but you are better."

Tolfer laughed. "All right, you can jump my bones tonight. Get some rest."

"Thank you, Tolfer," Candy said. "Part of me knows you are here for me to lean on. I am just in the habit of being on my own. I have always loved Alex and Shirl, but I did not want to rely on them. In the future, I promise to share with you what is bothering me or what is causing me anxiety. The whole premonition thing is driving me insane. A feeling of doom comes over me and I don't know what to do."

"You had that feeling today?" Tolfer asked.

"Yes," Candy admitted, "I knew something was going to happen at lunch. However, it was not clear what would occur. Just prior to Narmouth's attack, I got a clear picture of him attempting to stab Alex."

"Good, we can use those feelings to be better prepared in the future. Do not beat yourself up, but had we known about the feeling you had, we would have had more people guarding you girls. You have a gift. Like Shirl's gifts, we need to learn how to leverage it to the best of our abilities."

Tolfer held his breath. He prayed she would not be too hard on herself for keeping her internal feelings inside. It was something Starc said Shirl struggled with. Now it was his soul mate who was hurting.

"Now that I know these feelings actually result in something bad happening, I will share them with everyone. I understand Koel is a tactical genius. Maybe he can start coming up with contingency plans rather than assaulting every woman that comes up to him."

"Perfect," Tolfer answered. "Hopefully, JoAnna is his soul mate and Koel can start focusing on something else for a change. I understand he and Shirl planned our rescue from the penal colony. They make a great team. With your input going forward, we are going to be in a better position to deal with what life throws at us."

"In the meantime, why don't you get going? My stomach has started to growl."

Tolfer kissed his soul mate and headed to the kitchen. He wondered if she would articulate when she got one of her feelings or if she would continue to hold it inside. Was the soul mate connection strong enough for Candy to change a lifetime habit of being totally self-contained?

Chapter 25

Candy woke alone in bed. Tolfer had awakened her earlier to tell her he was going to work with some of the Troyk children to help them manage their telepathic powers. He did not know it, but he had helped her last night, by asking her to share when her gift became a harbinger that something was about to happen. She rolled onto her back and stared at the ceiling. Candy concentrated on her mental state. All clear, no feeling of impending doom.

She and Tolfer had done a masterful job of jumping each other's bones last night. Or was it in the wee hours of the morning? They had talked for a while when they had finally gone to bed. It cleansed her soul talking to him. When no more words had to be shared, they made love. The first time was a little rough, but they needed to release pent-up energy. However, the second time had been caring and deliberate. Candy actually preferred the less strenuous lovemaking.

She got up, brushed her teeth, and threw on a robe. Candy was not ready to shower and dress just yet. A cup of coffee was calling her name. She could smell the aroma even in the back room of the house.

Candy made her way to the kitchen, where Shirl and Alex were already sipping their morning drinks. Alex continued to drink the herbal teas, regardless of the time of day. She was still having issues managing the pathways, because of all the head injuries she had sustained from Raine Narmouth. At least that chapter of her life was over. Raine was in the Nightshade universe, getting what he deserved.

She poured herself a mug and joined her friends. Alex still looked shaken by yesterday's events. The color had not returned to her cheeks and she was a little green around the gills.

"You look terrible," Candy told her friend. They had been family too long to hold back punches. The three friends were very honest with each other. "Are you still freaked out about yesterday?"

"I would not be feeling anything had it not been for you, Candy," Alex replied. "However, I cannot blame what happened yesterday for my current condition. The presence of my daughter has started to play havoc on my body. Morning sickness has reared its ugly head."

"You poor baby!" Candy knew this was her opportunity to do something she had not done in a long time. Start nurturing her friend during her pregnancy. "Can I make you some toast? I can't screw that up too badly."

Alex smiled and nodded her head. Candy did not know if her friend wanted toast or was just agreeing because she knew Candy needed to do this. Candy pulled out two slices of Troyken bread and placed them in the Troyk version of a toaster. Within a matter of seconds the perfectly browned toast was ready for Alex's consumption.

"I figured you didn't want anything on it," Candy said. Alex accepted the toast and started to nibble on it. Slowly Alex's face started to get a little color back in it. A feeling of warmth and satisfaction started to grow in Candy. She knew she did well for her friend.

"Gee, Candy," Shirl complained, "it would have been nice if you had asked me if I wanted some."

Candy gently slapped Shirl's shoulder. "You have two hands and do not have morning sickness. Why don't you make your own toast?"

"Because I do not want to burn this beautiful house down," Shirl complained. "You know I am ten times worse a cook than you are. Please, make me some toast. I, however, will have some jam on mine."

Candy had missed the interplay between the three of them when they got their own apartments. She got up and pulled out enough bread for both her and Shirl. All of a sudden Candy was starving. Her body was now fully awake and was craving food. She pulled out a pan and started cooking eggs to go with the toast. She had watched Tolfer cook breakfast on several occasions and it did not look too hard.

After the eggs were done, Candy proudly placed two plates before Shirl and her. She had done it. The eggs were delicious. Shirl dug into her breakfast as if it was the best she had ever eaten. Candy felt a sense of accomplishment, she had not felt since the first time she made a base hit playing softball. She figured she was entering a new phase of her life.

"Darden and Koel will be going to Ginkgo Terra tomorrow," Shirl said. "It will be weird seeing Jo Jo after all these years."

"That is assuming she is Koel's soul mate," Alex commented. "Although they are going to have to bring her back because of the headaches, she has probably been suffering. For Koel's sake, I hope they are soul mates."

"She is Prime Adholm's niece," Shirl said between bites. "He is a mind control telepath. Chartail did not inherit that gift, but what if Jo Jo did?"

Candy and her friends stared at each other. They had not seen Jo Jo since she was six years old. What if she had used her mind control gifts to get adopted when the rest of them never managed it? Suddenly Candy started to get a premonition that something was going to happen. It was not too much of a leap to figure it was related to Jo Jo.

Should she confide in Alex and Shirl her suspicions related to Jo Jo? Last night Candy had promised Tolfer she would no longer keep her premonitions to herself. However, she did not want to prejudice her friends against Jo Jo for no good reason.

Taking a deep breath, Candy did what had to be done. "There is something I should tell you both…"

The End

Here is the prologue and part of the first chapter
Nightshade
Book One: Nightshade Saga

Prologue

~

The Nightshade Universe

He was older than dirt, Drake thought after the lovely blonde who stood before him asked his age. How do you explain the unexplainable? Drake's existence defied nature.

This was one of the rare occasions he wished he was something other than what he was. His kind was a blight on any world they inhabited. A mistake, never intended to exist in this or any other universe.

At the beginning of time, as worlds fractured across dimensions, a division went terribly wrong. A sentient energy was forged rather than coming to life organically. The oddity traveled between worlds, leaving holes of negative matter in its wake. These frequency pathways between universes were never intended to exist.

As the energy mass traveled, it drew on the life-force of living particles. When it came across man, it claimed its first victim as a shell to occupy.

After settling into the primitive brain and physiology, it evolved from draining a being's life-force to drinking the fluid carrying the elements needed to regenerate the fragile biological cells, allowing the body to physically continue.

Thus, the first vampire came to be.

Drake had been one of the first men the vampire converted. For eons Drake traveled with this creature, living off the blood of others. Over time they converted worthy victims to join their family. Since women had the ability to reproduce, they only changed the male of the species. As a sense of ennui set in, more of the sacrificed were changed into vampires. The newly made helped to relieve the boredom of immortality.

The vampires grew weary of being intergalactic nomads. Eventually they settled in the Nightshade universe. Satisfied within their own world, the knowledge to manipulate matter to travel between universes was lost. Thus, only the original retained the ability.

There had been so many world divisions since his making, Drake had no idea which world had been his birthplace. It was best not to think along those lines. The ones he left behind had long been in their graves. Their progeny would no longer have known he ever existed. His life was now tied to his creator. The entity seemed content to stay in the Nightshade universe, while Drake had nowhere else to go.

The numerous portals leading to the Nightshade universe provided enough unfortunate beings pulled into their world to offer ample sustenance. Blood was plentiful in those early days. The maker was comfortable living off the unlimited supply of blood, until a woman came through one of the portals and life as they knew it changed.

She had a type of power over his creator Drake had never witnessed before. Her presence seemed to relieve the constant hunger the entity suffered. The master referred to her as his soul mate.

Through their bonding, the master thought he would transform into whatever nature had originally planned. They would venture off together, sometimes disappearing for weeks. Finally, one day the master left through a portal with the woman, never to be seen or heard from again.

After his departure, various legends related to their destined pairing began to be told. Over time, most vampires chose to ignore and ultimately forgot those stories. However, in Drake's darkest times, the thought of one day finding his own soul mate made him persevere.

Over several millennia the numerous portals started to close, until only three were active in the Nightshade universe. The vampire population had become so large, and the blood sources so scarce, most were shadows of what they once were.

Now blood frenzied creatures, they slowly wasted away. No amount of blood could regenerate those beings back into what they once were. Only the vampires who had been created by the master, had been spared the horrible thirst. Their bodies were as they were when they were first transformed. Drake held on to what little humanity he had left, waiting for his soul mate to become reality. Through her, Drake could finally transform from the parasite he was.

The woman in front of him was someone else's soul mate. She had the ability to navigate portals using her telepathic abilities and a crystal. The woman, Shirl, had entered their world and was now being held captive. Drake took the opportunity to offer his protection, capitalizing on the opportunity to spend time with the beauty. He had abused his role as a guest within the Venture Hive, to possess the woman for whatever time he could have with her.

Drake manipulated the telepathic bond that tied Shirl to her soul mate. Until he was forced to give her up, he would hold on to her with every fiber of his being. She was as close as he had ever come to finding his own soul mate.

What little happiness he currently had would be cut short when the daughter of the Venture Hive's master was exchanged for Shirl. Everything would be lost if Afton returned to the Nightshade universe.

Chapter 1

⁓

Ginkgo Terra/Earth

It was all a matter of perspective. The abundance of fall color surrounding her could be taken as natural beauty or a sign of death. Darkness had surrounded Afton Simmons most of her life. She chose the positive view when one of her black moods was not upon her. Today was so beautiful, she figured no one could be depressed. Her eyes basked on yellow, orange, and red leaves still attached to the grove of maple trees before her.

Afton loved the mythical story of Persephone to explain the changing of the seasons. When Persephone returned to Hades in the Underworld, her mother Demeter would mourn her daughter's loss by causing all living plants to go dormant, until her daughter returned to her. It was a lovely story of motherly devotion, something foreign to Afton.

Her mother had taken her own life when Afton was barely three years old. An irreversible reaction to the death of the man she loved and an inability to recover from the circumstances of Afton's conception. No wonder Afton spent most of her existence in a sorrowful mood.

Nana, her grandmother, had spent a fortune taking her to one psychiatrist after another. Years of therapy hardly made a dent in on-going depressions. Even the medications they had given her made no difference. In addition, the side effects the anti-depressants caused were worse than her dark moods.

Her last class was over and she had the weekend to look forward to. Her art class was going to Morton's Arboretum tomorrow to capture the autumn colors on canvas. She was also taking the day off from studying. The freedom of spending a day without keeping her nose to the grindstone put an extra spring into her step. Her first semester at Northwestern University was turning out to be tougher than she had originally thought.

When she reached her dorm, she took two steps at a time as she ran up the back stairs. Afton felt absolutely wonderful. She was going to do her economics homework and then treat herself to an episode of *Sherlock*. Benedict Cumberbatch pushed all the right buttons as far as she was concerned. He was tall, handsome, and she loved his wavy hair. For some reason she thought the long, curly locks made him look vulnerable.

Why couldn't she find someone like him? Men tended to shy away from her pale, delicate looks. The boys had been cruel over the years describing her fragile state. Afton shook her head, driving out the names she had been called. She would not let the past drag her into a dour mood.

Once she reached her dorm room, she unlocked the door. Afton was fortunate to get a single room. Her "medical condition" allowed her the luxury of housing alone, such a privilege was normally not available to freshmen.

She made her way to the fridge. It had been modified with a locking mechanism. If anyone asked about the refrigerator, she told them she was diabetic. Her supposed dependency on insulin made locking it a necessity. Afton even had syringes to add credence to her story.

She unlocked the padlock and opened her fridge to reveal its true contents.
Blood.

Missed how it all began?
Enjoy the 1st Chapter of 'The Chameleon Soul Mate'
Worlds Apart Series: Book One

Chapter 1

~

Arizona

Alexandra Mann, 'Alex' to friends and foes, disconnected from the call center system and let out a long, painful sigh. People never called to comment on how great things were, just to complain.

But she had the ability to stay calm under pressure and deal with any situation. Didn't matter if it was a customer yelling or her two best friends coming to her with their latest crisis. Alex took whatever life threw at her and made lemon drop cocktails.

Finally, Friday was here and Alex was going up to Sedona with three friends. They had been planning this trip for five months, and the countdown was finally over. This weekend was a double celebration: her twenty-first birthday and her best friend Shirl's twenty-third.

She had actually taken a half day of vacation so she and Shirl could get a jump on the traffic that headed north every Friday afternoon. Two of her co-workers were joining them, but had to work all day and would drive up later.

She grabbed her purse and pulled out her phone. The display showed that Shirley Tomlinson called. Shirl, as she liked to be called, had grown up with Alex at a local Phoenix orphanage. Although Alex was younger than Shirl, they were best friends and as close as sisters. Shirl and Candy, who also grew up with them at the orphanage, were Alex's only family. The three were connected, at times it felt like they could read each other's minds.

Alex had given up on the dream of a real family long before the orphanage stopped parading her in front of perspective parents. Years of couples talking and playing with her, only to have them walk away, had taken their toll. The disappointment she felt at the continual rejection caused her to cry herself to sleep on many occasions. She would find herself blending into the shadows in order not to be passed over again.

To this day, she had a tendency to blend into the background. Her best friends were always in the spotlight, where Alex tended to be invisible in their presence. Shirl was tall, blond, and stop traffic gorgeous. Candy, on the other hand, had a self-confidence that made her radiant. When they were together, both men and women would flock to Candy.

Having left her cubical, Alex took the opportunity to listen to Shirl's voice mail message. "Alex, it's Shirl. I've got a killer migraine and I can't make it to Sedona this weekend."

If anyone else had canceled on her, she would have been angry. However, she knew Shirl got terrible migraines that would down a small elephant. It seemed as though the headaches were growing in frequency and she was concerned about her friend. Alex recently started having migraines herself. She and Shirl were so close, she felt they were probably sympathy headaches.

When Alex reached the call center's lobby, she called Shirl before she walked out into the Arizona heat.

"What?" Shirl growled as the call connected.

"How are you feeling? Do you need anything?" Alex asked.

"Can you get me a new brain?"

"Doubtful, but I'll look into it. I am so sorry you won't make it to Sedona with us."

"I know, Alex," Shirl's voice began to fade. "Candy will stop by before she takes her class on this weekend's field trip. Don't worry, I will be fine."

Shirl hung up before Alex could say anything more. Alex placed her phone in her purse and walked toward her car in the stifling Arizona heat. The car was all packed and ready to go for the trip up to Sedona. Since she was not picking up Shirl, she immediately got on I-17 and headed north.

Alex loved Sedona and started thinking about what types of adventures she'd have this weekend. Something unusual always happened when she was there. It was odd, she was never able to put into words what she experienced. Some invisible force always seemed to draw her.

❧

Alex made good time. Leaving Phoenix early afternoon was the trick, beating the hordes of commuters heading home after work. She headed straight to her hotel.

It would be some time before her call center friends would join her. In the meantime, Alex had time to hike in Boynton Canyon. She opened her suitcase, pulled out a T-shirt and shorts.

The Boynton Canyon Vortex was one of the four vortexes that contributed to the energy felt throughout Sedona. Alex generally hiked Boynton Canyon because she felt the best energy there and enjoyed the trails. A lot was written about Sedona's vortexes, including the belief the energy was the result of inter-dimensional gateways. She did not believe all that nonsense, but her friend Shirl certainly did. With that thought, Alex felt the loss of Shirl not being there. She could almost visualize her friend standing next to her, clutching her crystal necklaces.

She walked to her car and made the short trip between the hotel and Boynton Canyon. The parking lot closest to the trail was packed. Fortunately, she had the world's smallest car and found a spot where someone had parked badly, leaving only three quarters of a space. She easily fit into the spot and patted the dashboard of her beloved car. It was fire engine red, with a white racing stripe down the side. She loved zipping around town in it.

Alex changed from her sneakers into her hiking boots, locked the car and made her way to the trail head. She loved the sound her boots made against the gravel trail. Alex had just purchased a new pair of hiking boots as a birthday present to herself. The boots almost came up a quarter of her leg and were kind of clunky. She was not going to take any chances if she came across a snake along the trail.

Although the lot had been full, she didn't see anyone on the trail. A flash of light caught her eye. It was the reflection coming off a bracelet worn by someone suddenly ahead of her. Her eyes left the cuff bracelet to the man who wore it. He was tall with blond hair, and she couldn't help but admire his body. The man was oddly dressed for hiking. It appeared he was wearing a tunic and leggings. He had broad shoulders underneath the blue tunic and the leggings were molded to his powerful legs. She could see the muscle definition of his legs even from this distance. He must have decided to take a little hike before performing in a Shakespearean play. Sedona was known for supporting all art forms.

Alex admired his body, but unfortunately her body was not reacting to his. It never did, regardless how attractive she found the man. Oddly, Shirl and Candy had the same problem. She dated, because girls her age dated. She had not been with a man in over six months. Every relationship was disappointing when it became physical. The guys she dated didn't want to sustain a relationship if they had to deal with an ice queen in bed.

As she continued on the path, she kept an eye on the man, closing the gap between them. He was carrying a number of sacks that seemed to slow him down. Another oddity about the man. Who carried sacks on a day hike, rather than a backpack?

He was in her sight one minute and the next he vanished. Where did he go? Alex ran forward, thinking the man had fallen and needed help. She arrived at the spot where she had last seen him and there was no sign of him.

An invisible force pulled her forward off her feet. She screamed, as the motion continued and her vision went black. Her lungs seized and she fell into what she could only think was an endless void.

Missed Shirl's Story?
Savior the 1st Chapter of 'The Crystal Telepath'
Worlds Apart Series: Book Two

Chapter 1

~

Sedona, Arizona

She exited the car, so weak she could barely close the door. The remnants of the second migraine this week had left her feeling lethargic. Shirl Tomlinson knew she had to power through, regardless of how dreadful she was feeling. Her best friend, Alexandra Mann, had been missing for almost a week. As she walked to the front of the Sedona Police Department headquarters, she was oblivious to the beauty of the surrounding area. Several people exiting the building made way for Shirl as she entered. She barely noticed their presence or the way the men perused her body. She was too sick to care.

For a relatively small town, the place was extremely busy. Barely able to stand, she staggered toward the front desk. She had to dodge a number of officers; otherwise, she would have ended up flat on her face on the marble floor. The man who stood behind the counter saw her distress and made his way around the restricted area to aid her. The artificial light was so bright, she had to squint her eyes as she watched him approach.

"Miss Tomlinson, are you all right?" the concerned officer asked. Shirl wished she could remember the young officer's name. He was wearing a name badge, but her vision was blurry and she could not make out the letters. She just wanted to crawl into the corner and fall into a deep, painless sleep.

"I am recovering from a migraine and I am not feeling quite right," she said. One severe headache after another had tapped her strength. She did not know how much more she was going to be able to take. Having only minimal health insurance coverage, her options were limited in her quest to find what was wrong with her. Every doctor she saw scratched their heads, baffled by the escalation at the severity and frequency of the headaches she had been suffering the past two years.

"I'll get Commander Lewis. He will give you an update on our efforts to find your friend." The officer took a couple of steps and then asked over his shoulder, "Can I get you any water?"

Shirl shook her head. She had taken medication before she left the hotel room. Everyone in the Sedona Police Department knew her by now. She arrived on Monday, as soon as she was able to drive. Alex had been missing since last Friday. For three full days, the police station had been her home away from home.

She sat on the bench, clasping the crystals that hung around her neck. As each day ended with no sign of Alex, Shirl got more frantic, fearing she would never see her friend again. What would she do without Alex in her life? They had grown up together in a Phoenix orphanage. Whenever anything went wrong, she always ran to Alex for help. Although Alex was two years younger, Alex was always the responsible one.

Commander Lewis appeared and sat next to Shirl. He was a good looking man, probably in his late thirties. The man was also tall. Generally she had to look up at him when they talked, she liked that. For some odd reason, she did not trust men she had to look down upon. She knew that was stupid, but that was how she felt.

Lewis was the second highest ranking police officer in the department, under the chief of police. Shirl could see from the expression on his face, he did not have good news to share. At least they hadn't found a body. The last two nights Shirl had woken in a cold sweat, dreaming she'd been taken to the morgue to identify Alex's corpse.

"I don't know what to tell you, Miss Tomlinson. There have been no sightings of your friend. We know she checked into her hotel Friday afternoon and was not seen again. Her car was found in a parking lot near Boynton Canyon. We believe she went hiking, but there are no signs of foul play. We have had men up and down that canyon looking for Alexandra. There was a part of the trail that looked like someone was dragged for ten feet or so, but there is no evidence she fell. Why don't you head home? I'll call you if we discover anything."

Shirl felt tears falling down her cheeks and reached into her purse for a tissue. "I can't leave here without Alex or knowing what happened to her." People did not just disappear off the face of the Earth. Sedona seemed an unlikely place for human trafficking. A new age cult, perhaps, but Alex wasn't the type.

"Can I at least take you to dinner? You look terrible." Shirl had to smile at Commander Lewis's comment. Men usually fawned over her. It was nice to have a man be honest with her about her appearance. He was a no nonsense guy, saying what was on his mind.

She didn't feel threatened by him. Commander Lewis was the type of man to drag his wife along, eliminating any type of impropriety. It would be nice to get her mind off Alex, even for one meal. "That would be nice. I can't remember the last time I ate." She had a couple of power bars in her car, but hadn't been able to stomach the idea of eating them.

"Why don't I pick you up tonight in your hotel lobby after I get off, around seven." The seasoned police officer knew this meet-up location would be nonthreatening compared to meeting her at her hotel room. "My wife Carol will meet us at the restaurant." Yup, she called that one right!

"I guess at this point, I should at least ask your first name," Shirl said. "It would be weird calling your wife Carol while calling you Commander Lewis."

"Frank, my first name is Frank."

Commander Lewis patted her hand and returned to work. She watched as he crossed into the restricted area behind the front desk. A large clock displayed three o'clock. She had four hours to kill before he would pick her up. There was no sense staying on the hard bench. She could get an update at dinner tonight. Besides, they had her cell phone number if they found Alex in the meantime.

Shirl walked to her car and sat behind the wheel for a while, not sure where she wanted to go. The medication had kicked in and she felt a little better.

She started toward Boynton Canyon. Shirl rarely went hiking with Alex. She didn't like the dust that covered her on the few occasions she went. Alex didn't make a big deal out of having to go alone.

Generally their friend Candy was along and she would hike with Alex. Candy had grown up in the orphanage with them. It was hard not calling her to join Shirl in Sedona while she waited for news of Alex. Candy was a high school coach and her team had just returned from a tournament. She hadn't even told

Candy that Alex was missing. Shirl didn't want to worry her friend in case Alex reappeared. That possibility continued to slip away.

When she arrived, the parking lot was relatively empty. Alex's disappearance had been all over the local newspapers. People were shying away from this particular trail, afraid a wild animal had attacked her friend. There was no evidence to support the claim, but that did not stop the rumor mill from spreading that story.

Boynton Canyon was beautiful with its deep red rocks. Shirl had always been fascinated by this place. It was one of the four vortexes Sedona was famous for. The energy emitted by the vortexes always renewed her.

These sites were believed to be multiple dimensional pathways emitting spiraling spiritual energy. Shirl soaked up any article on the subject as well as anything dealing with mystical powers.

One of the few items she had from her birth mother was an amethyst crystal that started her fascination with crystals and healing stones. She wore four to five crystals a day, depending on her mood. Her mother's amethyst was the only crystal she wore constantly. It seemed to balance her in some odd way. Shirl felt less alone, like having family close by. She knew it was stupid, but maybe one day it would lead her to some discovery of who she was meant to be.

Curiosity about the section of the trail with the drag mark Commander Lewis mentioned got the better of Shirl. Grabbing a power bar, she started toward the trailhead. She'd walk the path Alex had taken when she disappeared. If she got too dusty, she'd take a shower before Frank picked her up for dinner.

She walked slowly, conserving what strength she had. Between nibbling on the nutrition bar, the medication, and the vortex's energy, she felt vitality coursing through her body. As she walked the trail, she held onto her crystals, trying to channel Alex. She was not expecting anything to happen, then her mother's amethyst started to glow.

Shirl held the crystal in front of her and stared at it in wonder. As much as she knew about crystals, she had never read anything about them glowing. She felt a slight pull and stopped.

The air ahead shimmered and she felt the continued emission of energy. Slowly, she approached the anomaly. She could see the trail on the other side of the air displacement.

Shirl looked down and noticed the dirt and foliage along the path looked as if something had been dragged along it. It ended right in front of what she could only think was an event horizon. Alex must have been pulled through the point of no return. The gravitational pull would have been so great, Alex would not have been able to escape from it.

Taking a deep breath, Shirl walked into the unknown.

❧

Inside a black void, she felt as if falling. Twisting and turning, she had no control. Deafening, high-pitched sound pierced her ears. Her crystal glowed brighter.

Terror taking hold, she attempted to grab her crystal necklace. After her second attempt at regaining use of her flailing arms, she secured the amethyst in her hand.

Just short of all-out panic, she started to think about home. It worked for Dorothy in Oz, allowing her and Toto to return to Kansas.

She crashed against the ground, out of the portal's grasp. Shirl slowly climbed to her feet and realized she was no longer in Sedona. It must have been a portal to another dimension. That could be the only explanation why she was no longer on the trail surrounded by red rocks and dirt.

She stood on a mountain path, overlooking a city built of pale stone. The community was abloom with purple flowering trees and plants. The violet sky must be a result of the colored pollen emitted.

Shirl was surprised her mind was reacting rationally, although she was still a little dazed. Her normal reaction would have been to panic. Instead, she took in her surroundings and making scientific assumptions. She could not remember the last time she had thought so clearly. There was no pain or pressure impacting her brain.

Alexandra was somewhere in this city, she was certain of it. Shirl was not sure how she was going to find her or what type of people she would encounter. But she had to start looking.

She started down the mountain pass, paying close attention to her steps. The trail was steeper than the one in Boynton Canyon. Her sandals were comfortable, but not equipped to traverse the rocky path. She was also a little wobbly from the rough ride within the portal and had eaten no food to speak of for days.

Sweat trickled down her neck. She brushed at the liquid and her hand came back covered in blood. Shirl felt the same trickle on the other side of her neck. She was bleeding from both ears.

Another step. Bright red streamed from her nose. Her shirt collar was soaked with blood. A strong wave of nausea washed over her. She grabbed a tree branch along the trail.

Leaning on the tree did not abate the nausea. She fell to her knees and retched along the side of the trail. With little food and nothing to drink, it was closer to dry heaves.

Voices and footsteps were coming closer. Eyes popping open, she glanced through a red haze. Not only was she bleeding from her ears and nose, blood vessels must have broken in her eyes.

Shirl could hear the two men address her, but could not comprehend what they said. Her ears were buzzing and she could barely concentrate through the nausea that still overwhelmed her. One of the men knelt next to her as she felt herself fall into unconsciousness.

Coming Soon: Book Four of the Worlds Apart Series
'The Mind Control Telepath'

About the Author

When Evelyn Lederman retired from her career as an insurance executive, she cheerfully anticipated the freedom to finally spend as much time reading as she'd always wanted. The twist in her story came when as-yet unwritten characters started cropping up in her thoughts, asking her to tell their stories. Now, she spends her days in Florida on the beach... with her laptop.

'The Chameleon Soul Mate', 'The Crystal Telepath', and 'The Warrior Woman' are the first three books in her paranormal sci-fi romance series, Worlds Apart. The Nightshade Saga is her second series, with 'Nightshade', as the first book in that series.

Keep up to date with her at EvelynLederman.com or on Facebook. Contact her at evelynlauthor@gmail.com.